BOOKS BY BRIAN MCNATT

Estranged

The "Legends of Heraldale" series
Legends of Heraldale
Legends of Heraldale II: Past Sins
Legends of Heraldale III: Warborn

The "Life Out There" series
A Life Out There
Le Fay
The Wolf-Lords

Also available on Audible
Legends of Heraldale

THE WOLF-LORDS

Cover image by KY Dalley

Table of Contents

THE WOLF-LORDS

By Brian McNatt

Dedicated to precious people lost in dark times.

Always loved, always remembered.

CHAPTER ONE

Princess Candida, 10 years old and already burdened with the reputation for idiocy which would haunt her all her life, sat atop a stack of hay and watched her siblings playing at archery with an aching want to join in. The sun shone high and blindly off the late fall snows lingering upon the palace roofs and outer walls. Clouds north and west promised more snow before the day was out, but even Candida knew this would not be for hours yet.

"Not bad, for a little runt," said Caelestis, almost the oldest of Queen Celeste's children. The feminine, black-furred Wolf-Lord stood in the north courtyard and eyed the arrow embedded off-center in the distant target, grinned and ruffled the white-furred Regina's head. "Not bad at all. Now step aside and let a real killer show you how it's done."

Regina ducked out from under their older sibling's clawed hand and backed away, glancing over at

Candida in the nearby hay stacks with a wide, toothy grin. Candida, hardly thinking about the whys of it, mirrored her twin grin for grin. Regina's smile quickly faltered and they looked away. Candida kept her smile on for a few seconds more, then dropped it. She kicked her legs idly in the hay and pondered why people might show their teeth and when.

Caelestis breathed deeply in, held the breath for several long seconds, breathed it back out. Breathed it in again as they nocked an arrow and lifted their bow. Arms straight, eyes narrowed and trained on the distant target, arrow drawn back. A second passed. Another. Then Caelestis' attention flicked away from the target to somewhere behind Candida and Regina. Their eyes widened and their bow grew slack, a hand shooting up to point at something unseen. "WHAT IN BLAZES IS THAT!?"

Candida blinked and looked in the direction her older sibling had pointed she looked for 10 seconds but saw nothing more extraordinary than Queen Celeste in the distant sky, taking the youngest among them, Gosse, through his wyvern-riding lessons.

Turning back around, she caught sight of Caelestis running back to them from the target, the arrow embedded dead-center.

"Hey!" shouted Regina, the smile back on their muzzle. "You cheater!" they bellowed, laughter escaping them as they gave the older Wolf-Lord a shove. Then the both of them were laughing, leaning against each other for support as they did so.

Candida sat in the hay, looking from her siblings to the target and back again, utterly confused. Her legs bounced harder in the hay, her hands tightening into hay-crunching fists at her sides. "I do not get it."

Shoulders sagged. Laughter died out. Caelestis wiped their eyes and turned to Candida, muzzle twisting into the far opposite of a smile. "It's just a joke, you idiot. Can't you even understand a Goddamn joke? You too stupid even for that?"

Candida swallowed and looked down, ears pinned back. She didn't like the way Caelestis was talking to her, had been talking to her more and more often the last few weeks. It was the same way their parent, Queen Celeste, talked to Candida all the time.

"It's alright," said Regina, somewhere nearby. "I'll explain it to you later. Right now, you wanna come try some archery? I betcha bored just sitting there on the sidelines."

"I am not bored!" said Candida in a shout, making Regina and Caelestis startle beside her and drawing the eye of a few passing palace workers. Candida put on the same smile Regina had given her before. "I like watching you two do bow and arrows! You are both really good at it! And I have had a story in my head, too, repeating over and over. It is a new story, fresh from Miss Hollinger in the palace library, about real history, yes!"

Caelestis groaned. More loudly, Regina said "Oh wow! You really know a lot of stories by now, huh? Can you tell me this one?" As they said this, they set their bow aside and sat before Candida among the hay bales.

"I sure can!" shouted Candida, the smile feeling better on her muzzle now as she looked up at Caelestis. "You wanna hear the story too? It's a good one, Miss Hollinger told me! Real history, like we're gonna be someday!"

"You're not gonna be history," snarled the older Wolf-Lord, looking more like their shared parent than ever. "They're going to write brand-new history books just to leave you out of them." But even so, they sat cross-legged beside Regina.

"It is a story about Queen Morgause, who the unicorns and gryphons call General Nero," began Candida, once everyone seemed settled. "And her evil twin sister, Morgana le Fay!"

Caelestis began to say something. Regina elbowed them quiet, gaze remaining focused on Candida.

"Once upon a time, there were two sisters who loved each other more than anyone else in the whole wide world. One was named Morgause, queen of all Wolf-Lords, and the other was named Morgana, the most powerful sorceress of all time. Everybody loved them! But there was something wrong with Morgana. She was deaf active!"

"You mean defective," said Regina.

"Like you," said Caelestis.

"Sure," said Candida, legs bouncing in the hay. "Morgana got old! Her hair went grey and her bones got frail and she got wrinkles everywhere! She got scars! Wolf-Lords aren't supposed to do any of that! She got old, and Morgause remained young and healthy, and this made Morgana angry, bitter! The bitterness turned into jealousy, and the jealousy turned into hate, until finally Morgana wanted to kill her own family!"

Caelestis began to say something again. Regina elbowed them in the side again.

"On a moonless night, when Wolf-Lords are at our weakest, Morgana visited Morgause's castle with claims of family love, and then took a knife, and then carved out her sister's heart to put inside herself!"

Candida loosed a scream, an all-too-real scream, arms flailing as she mimed the gouts of blood gushing and spurting from her chest. Caelestis was grinning.

Regina had gone pale. A peculiar silence fell over the courtyard.

Grinning and laughing, Candida looked back to her siblings. "And then Morgana put her twin's heart inside herself to grow young and strong again! What a story, yes? What a story!"

"Y-yeah," said Regina, standing up. "What a story. Thanks for telling it. I should go. Time for lessons."

"Lessons?" Candida dropped her smile and stood. She could not remember there being any lessons scheduled for the day, not for Regina. "What lessons? What?"

But Regina turned away without answer. Turned and walked away stiff-backed, away from Candida without another word and without another look.

"Caelestis, what," Candida began, but the older Wolf-Lord was gone. All the other Wolf-Lords were gone. Gone from the yard, gone from the surrounding walls, gone from the blue skies high overhead. Candida stood alone, increasingly afraid. And Regina walked away, nearly to the main door out of the courtyard now, nothing beyond the door but utter blackness.

"Regina!" shouted Candida, reaching out for her twin. But Candida's arm was red, the white fur soaked through with blood. In her claws was grasped the large and still-beating heart of a Wolf-Lord.

Candida—

—No, my name is Holly now, my name has been Holly for 16 months—

—stared at the organ a moment, shocked dumb, and then she looked up again to her twin. Regina stood a step away from the door, no longer the child of Holly's memories but the towering adult they had grown up to be. As Holly stared, the other Wolf-Lord turned back to her. Their eyes were dull and dead. Their muzzle was twisted with agony. Their chest had been carved open, the blood pouring out, gushing out, staining everything red.

Holly looked away, looked down at herself, beheld the beating heart in one hand and the bloodied knife in the other and screamed.

***

Holly woke up. For several terrifying seconds the past and the present blurred beneath the lingering dread of memories turned into nightmares and she did not know who, what, or where she was. But then, she did remember. She was a grown wolf now, no longer the child in desperate need of love and care. She lay in bed with her kitsune wife, Shun. She lived in the frigid north, the pains of her family and her childhood far behind her.

Holly sat up in bed, breathed the cold air with relish as she eyed the not-quite-dawn light coming in through the window to her left. To her right, Shun broke into a harsh coughing fit, rolled over in her sleep, and settled back down with a limp wag of two of her three tails. Holly remained with her blankets gathered in her lap and watched her wife sleep with a warmth which felt as fresh and surprising then as it had the first night in their first shared bed. She wanted to lean down and kiss her wife on the cheek, but too many nights lately were plagued by coughing fits and insomnia for the kitsune. Every moment of sleep was a blessing.

Instead, Holly stood and dressed. Downstairs, breakfast was half-warm oatmeal and a dried apple. Holly ate quickly, ears perking near the end of the meal at the beginnings of movement somewhere overhead. A yawn, a creak of the bed, a thud and not-quite-whispered curse as Shun tripped over the previous day's clothes she always left scattered where they fell. Holly grinned and added their last scrap of bacon from the enchanted ice box to the simmering oatmeal for Shun to find when she came down. Today was a special day, and it called for a special meat.

The clop of hooves on wood heralded Nessa joining Holly in the kitchen. The pinto unicorn filly whinnied a bright "Mom!", trotted over to press the side of her head against Holly's right thigh. Holly smiled wide and held out a bowl of mixed oats, sliced carrots, and raisins. The unicorn took it in the sunflower glow of her magic, pressed her head against Holly's side again, then trotted off to eat in front of the hearth in the den. She passed Shun stumbling into the kitchen, the kitsune bleary-eyed and yawning as she wrapped her usual scarf around her neck. "Morning, mother!"

"Morning . . ."

Holly held out her wife's bowl of oatmeal and bacon. Shun took it with a wandering smile, slumped into a chair at the main table, began to eat. Holly rubbed her wife's left shoulder, worried and unsure what to do. "How doing?"

Shun waited to finish chewing a bite before answering. "It's just a cold, you know. I'm not going to fall to pieces the moment you look away from me."

"Cold for whole week," said Holly, moving her ministrations to her wife's other shoulder.

"It's just a bad cold, then," said Shun. With bacon in her gut, her smile was firmer as she looked up at Holly. "Really, it'll be gone tomorrow, mark my words."

"You will need to write them down, first," said Holly. She plastered on a smile of her own as Shun laughed, did her best to ignore how the laugh tremored on the edge of turning into a coughing fit. For her wife's safe, no matter how it made her heart quake.

"Are you going out with Nessa and her friends for story time again?" asked Shun after a moment, returning the main of her attention to her breakfast.

"Yes."

"Anything special on the agenda?"

Holly parted her lips, but hesitated to answer. Glancing up at Holly, this seemed answer enough for Shun. "The madwolf? Again? Someone might think you're more doing it for yourself at this rate."

"Nessa enjoys the stories," insisted Holly, though her hand fell to her side as the remark struck too close to home. "They are context. To make my . . . to make Morgana seem less . . . trust me."

"I always do," said Shun, and this, Holly thought, was as fine an end to the conversation as any. "I always do."

***

"Time for a final story. Once upon a time, long before the great war that drove the Wolf-Lords and our siblings, the kitsune and Jackals, from distant Heraldale, our kinds were ruled in peace and prosperity by twin Wolf-Lord siblings. They were Queen Morgause, known better nowadays as General Nero for her feats against the barbarous humans, and Morgana le Fay, who was not evil at the start of things. It was a time of magic. A time when even Wolf-Lords, with patience and practice, or the direst of need, could use magic like our unicorn creators. Once discovered, the practice of magic became a lifelong commitment. These Wolf-Lords became known as the Fay, the faeries. The most powerful of them was Morgana le Fay herself."

"How powerful was she?"

"Is this a true story?"

"Morgana is evil!"

"Ahem."

The three children tucked away in the snow burrow with her, Nessa and a pair of young owl-gryphon friends, mumbled apologies for their interruptions and settled back down.

"That is better. Now, Morgana le Fay. She was the most powerful sorceress anyone had ever seen. Still is, to this day. Powerful enough, some said, to challenge the three Primes of unicorns, gryphons, and dragons, if she wanted to, but life was kind in that regard, and there was never any reason to find out.

"The twins, Morgana and Morgause, led their peoples well for a long, long time, countless centuries, though many would say from the start that Morgause bore the brunt of that labor. Morgana was a sorceress! A scholar! She wanted to learn, to know how things worked, and why. Always, she was pushing this and testing that.

"One night, as she was enjoying herself as the guest of honor of the king of Gryphonbough, there passed overhead a brilliant Elemental migration."

"Like what we are seeing tonight!"

"Exactly, Nessa. Morgana's fascination was captured at once by the brilliant display of living magic flying overhead! As many Elementals as there were stars in the sky. Stone Elementals, Fire Elementals, Water, Wind, Gem, Silver, Plant Elementals! Morgana was entranced, and a question was born in her heart. Where did the Elementals go after the migration? What did the living embodiments of magic call home?

"As quickly as Morgana asked this question, she acted upon it. With barely a farewell to her hosts and a thanks for their hospitality, she transformed herself by magic into a gryphon and took off after the departing Elemental host. For five days and five nights she flew at their tails, out of Gryphonbough, out of Heraldale, across the great width of the Zakarian Confederacy, which in those days was not quite united yet. Never stopping, never resting. No mere gryphon could have made the journey, no dragon, no wyvern. Morgana sustained herself on her own magic, but even so, the days went on and farther, farther from home and all she had known the Elementals led her, over verdant fields and massive forests where no Wolf-Lord had ever walked before. Through terrible, blizzard-scoured tundra, where the immortal, heartless ice giants swatted Elementals out of the sky by the dozens. Past mountains tall and black, and beyond oceans wracked with the white foam of storm-tossed waves. Onward and onward the Elemental migration flew, farther and farther, and before much longer even Morgana's heedless hope began to waver. The sun—"

"Holly!"

The call of her name snapped Holly's muzzle shut. Ears perked, she glanced at the thinly-veiled exit to the snow burrow, a finger brought to her lips to shush the children as they began to giggle.

"Holly!" Shun called again from somewhere outside the burrow, closer than before, her tone suggesting her own amusement. "Come on out, Holly! I know you're around here somewhere. I can smell you!"

Holly counted on her kitsune wife smelling her out. She kept quiet and motioned for her audience to do the same. Her ears remained perked, tail wagging helplessly behind her as overhead, light footsteps crunched through the snow. They passed by once, twice, soon circling the snow burrow in tighter curls.

Then, everything went quiet. Holly waited with baited breath, her small audience waiting with her, guessing at her plan and eager to see how it played out.

"Is Shun gonna—" Nessa began to ask, suddenly interrupted as a figure burst through the roof of the burrow.

Well, half a figure. Shun, the three-tailed kitsune's orange fur fat and fluffy in the winter environs, hung upside-down in the snow burrow Holly had dug for her little storytelling session with Nessa and her friends. Shun wriggled helplessly as she tried to size up the situation, and Holly could easily imagine her wife's rear half sticking up into the air outside, three tails snapping about, legs kicking feebly. The thought made her laugh.

"Alright," growled Shun, looking away from Holly to mock-glare at the trio of kids across from her. "Whose bright idea was this, eh? Who's the ringleader in this operation?"

The two gryphons quickly pointed talons at Nessa between them. The unicorn filly looked left and right in alarm for a moment, whinnied, and pointed a hoof forward, past Shun and at Holly.

"Ahah!" crowed Shun in triumph, the kitsune twisting around to look behind her, this happening to put her muzzle right-side up as she grinned at Holly. "It was you all alo-mmph!"

As much as Holly liked to listen to her wife talk, she leaned forward and quieted the kitsune with a deep, loving kiss. Shun, surprised at first, quickly and eagerly returned it, a hand reaching back to curl through Holly's long red hair, a shiver racing down the Wolf-Lord's spine to get her white fur standing on end.

"Eugh," groaned one of the gryphon kids. "Grown-up stuff. Come on, girls, let's go make a snow-gryph."

"A snowmare!" shouted Nessa, jumping to her hooves. "It is a mare . . . made of snow!"

"Your head's made of snow!" said the other gryphon child, but she smiled kindly as she began to lead the way past the make-out session for the snow burrow's exit tunnel. "But, a snowmare it is. THEN a snow-gryph."

"Hold it right there," huffed Shun, finally pulling out of Holly's surprise kiss to snag hold of Nessa's scarf. The kitsune flittered through a brief coughing fit before she continued. "You'll have to put a raincheck on that, I'm afraid. We're all three of us going to meet Laura at the train station. You like Aunt Laura, don't you, Ness?"

The unicorn filly, briefly shrinking down at having to say farewell for now at her friends, perked back up immediately at the news of her favorite minotaur in the world coming back home to Eishaven. "It will be nice having someone else with hooves around! Miss Nimue, over by the ocean, does not count. She is old and mean."

Holly heard the gryphon girls giggling at this as they left up the tunnel to the snowed-over field outside of town they'd made their little hidey hole in. The sound made her frown. It reminded her of life before meeting Shun, trapped home with family who thought of her as a mere dumb servant. "Nessa, it is not polite to say such things about people. Especially when they are not around to defend themselves."

"The girl's not wrong, though," said Shun, earning her a look of vindication from the unicorn filly. Holly gave the kitsune a warning look and she quickly amended, after another bout of coughing, "but that's neither here nor there, so listen to your wolfy mother, kid. Right now, we've got to get going if we want to greet Laura off the train, so you both get me right-side up before I pass out from all the blood in my head!"

***

Once they all stood free beneath the cloud-tinged sky, Holly wrapped her black cloak more tightly around herself and breathed deep of the early winter air. Hardly thinking about it, she walked a short distance across the snow field, skirting the holly trees lining it to the northeast and up a ridge, wife and adopted daughter trailing close behind.

From the ridge, Eishaven sprawled outward before them. It was a sight Holly had yet to grow weary of the three years and change she and her friends and family had called the place home. The port town, the icy Northern Seas, the surrounding forests of holly, pine, and aspen, as familiar to her now as her own wife's body. At that time of day, gryphons flew the skies on business, preparing the town for the night's festivities when the annual Elemental migration made its way overhead. More gryphons, alongside a scattering of minotaurs, sphinxes, and Wolf-Lords, worked boats in the harbor, the soft echo of their work songs carrying on the wind even up to where the small family stood.

The whistle of a nearing train sounded, sharp as shattering ice. Shun coughed, spitting something into the snow. "Hun, as lovely as the view is . . ."

"Right, right, sorry," said Holly, resisting now with practiced ease the urge to apologize another five or six times as she started down the ridge toward town. "On we go!"

***

The train station along the southern border of Eishaven was the largest building in the refugee town, three stories tall and built of stone, its conical roof the only undeniable sign of zakarian influence. It had been funded and built primarily by the ruling council of Zun

K'hor, the zakarian state including the region Eishaven occupied, a sign both of acceptance into the greater whole and, as Shun had cynically pointed out, a way to keep the profit flowing in if Eishaven ever became something worthwhile.

Holly didn't wholeheartedly agree with her wife's assessment, but she did think the station was more than the village would ever need for a long while. Few others stood around on the platforms with her and her family as the train wheezed to a final stop, mostly non-gryphons waiting to welcome friends and family come north to see the Elemental migration as well. Greetings were sent Holly's way as she, Shun, and Nessa took their place on the platform, mumbles of "Good afternoon, ma'am" and "Fair weather, aye, sheriff?", greetings she could grin and nod to without further commitment. The few gryphons who were there, always a few, glared heedless of Holly and Shun, glared at Nessa guarded between them. Holly always noticed the aggression, understanding it only reluctantly. Nessa was one of two unicorns in the entire village. And with the wars consuming Heraldale . . .

Someone coughed in the scattered crowd behind Holly, a dry cough which rattled in the chest. Echoed a half-dozen times through the crowd as the train doors opened and the passengers disembarked. Unlike the villagers, the newcomers were mostly reptilian zakarians, of similar height to Holly, slim-built, their shark-like skin ranging in colors from mustard-yellow to the same holly green as Holly's vest. They wore heavy coats and pants to help ward away the cold, thick scarves and long cloaks giving sense of one broad, vague mass moving forward.

Among the crowds, it was easy to pick out the lone minotaur. The horns gave her away. Holly grinned and began to wave, calling out "Laura! Over here!"

The minotaur, already heading their way out of the train, broke into a trot at Holly's call, her wide muzzle splitting into a grin once she got close enough to safely drop her multitude of bags and open her arms. "Holly!"

"Laura!" Holly danced forward to meet the hug with one of her own. "I missed you, friend! It has been so long, but now you are back and free of that dumb old sphinx! What was it like working for him, by the way?"

"More boring than you would expect," Laura remarked with a laugh, pulling out of the hug to look Holly over. "You've put on some weight. Looks good on you. Oh, girl, is that grey in your hair?"

Holly winced, a hand reaching up reflexively to brush through her hair. The grey strands, a stark contrast to her vibrant red, had been noticeable the past month. She had done her best not to think about the grey.

Laura patted Holly's shoulder in what Holly guessed with some confidence as sympathy, then turned to the rest of the small family. "Well then! Little Nessa, I see your horn's sharpness is finally coming in, careful not to poke anyone's eye out when going in for a hug. Shun! Get in here, you scammer and scoundrel!"

"I believe the phrase you're looking for is 'beloved entertainment illusionist', friend." But the kitsune strolled forward for a hug all the same, coughing once on the way.

Holly watched the two old friends catch up for a moment, then turned and gathered up Laura's bags. She felt warm deep inside, a warmth which had nothing to do with the magic she had been learning to control and use in the year since her battle with Morgana le Fay. It was the warmth of friends long-missed and returned at last, and all the happy days such reunions promised.

"Come on, girls. We should have a few hours still for dinner and settling in before the Elementals get here."

As they walked through town for home, Shun keeping Nessa entertained behind them with little illusions of fiery figures dancing, Laura caught Holly up on all the news she had gathered in her travels alongside the Painter. News it was best not to burden children with.

"It's all no more than you can expect from this sad world. Nothing but war and misery every direction you look. The Avalon Empire is beginning to make fresh attacks upon Gryphonbough. Many are dying there and the forests are burning. A terrible storm struck Wedjet, in defiance of all sphinx predictions. The Dragonback Mountains are waking, the air over the Midlands heavy with their smoke and ash. A governor down south in Zun K'dan attempted to lead his whole region in secession two months ago, and the UZC army is still rounding up and executing his followers. Slave traders setting up ports on the desert continent, famine, wildfires—"

"And to the east?" asked Holly. She kept her gaze ahead, acting the story of a relaxed sheriff as they strode the main Eishaven thoroughfare, trading waves and greetings with her fellow villagers. There were more businesses and homes closed that day, the owners locked away, sick. She told herself not to worry.

"I'm not sure you want to know."

"But I still ask."

The low crunch of snow filled the silence between them for almost a minute before Laura spoke again. "When we fled Romulus, we revealed to the Confederacy and to the other Wolf-Lord nations that Romulus was using prisoners as slaves. The volcanic fallout from that continues to build to what I might call . . . cataclysmic. Economic, political, military sanctions from almost all corners. Blockades across Romulan waters. Rebellions across the countryside, all met with ever more vicious military force—"

"Military?" asked Holly. Her heart, already low, found ever-deeper fathoms to explore. If her parent, Queen Celeste, was putting down rebellions with the military, then . . . it would be Regina leading them. Regina, Holly's twin, waging war upon their own people.

As Regina lay catching their breath on the ground, Candida kicked the sword from her sibling's slackened grip, giving her own a playful twirl before bringing its tip to the other Wolf-Lord's exposed throat. "I win."

"So you did."

"You went easy on me."

Panting, Regina still somehow managed a grin. "You've been working hard all day and I've been standing around doing nothing more strenuous than glaring at guests asking too many questions. You'd be surprised how uneasy I took it on you."

The news should not have struck such a blinding blow. Holly knew her twin, as kind as they had always been to her, had also been as involved in the slavery as the rest of their family. But even so, there'd been the hope of remembering her twin fondly . . .

"Your homeland of Romulus is dying," said Laura, drawing Holly from her thoughts. "Dying like a rabid beast that KNOWS it's dying. Would be a mercy, I think, if it were put down rather than forced into this slow, pitiable death spiral. Thank God and anyone else listening you got out of there when you could."

"Yeah." Holly tightened her cloak about her, thought of Shun behind them, Shun who held Holly's heart in her hands. "Thank God I got out."

They left the main body of Eishaven behind and strode toward the crow-gryphon compound. Kurt was still out working, but the rest of the gryphons made sure the second half of Laura's homecoming was easily as warm as the first. Holly watched from a safe distance as the minotaur disappeared beneath a rush of laughter and flapping wings, quickly turning and carrying the luggage to Laura's personal quarters while Shun took Nessa to hers.

Evening and dinner rolled around. The sky cleared and the first of the Elementals began passing overhead. They were the first and highest-flying, the vanguard, discernable to the ground-bound as only bright streaks of colored light. Holly watched them go from the blanket she had draped over the top of a short hill near the compound, Shun beside her on the blanket, a small platter of fruits and grilled sunderfish between them. At the moment it was only the two of them there, Nessa down at the compound with Laura and the rest, enjoying dinner with playmates her own age.

"Life is good, yeah?" asked Holly.

It took a moment for Shun to clear her throat enough to answer. "Yeah. Life is good."

The air was cold, growing colder as the sun sank below the horizon. Villagers lit bonfires along the outskirts of Eishaven to keep the watchers safe and warm. A deep expectancy settled across the land, breaths held and eyes trained to the west and to the skies.

The sun finished its descent. The last edges of its light slowly faded and night came to life. The stars twinkled jewel-bright overhead. To the north, thick ribbons of Aurora glimmered. From the woods at their backs came the cries of birds and hunting things. More distantly, the steady rush and crash of the ocean, the icy tide battering the black-rocked shore. Holly pulled her cloak closer around herself and leaned against Shun.

Suddenly, in the dark of the night they could see it. Miles to the west and approaching fast as a gryphon could fly, a vast wave of light, blazing with more colors than the most esoteric rainbow, flowed toward Eishaven and the surrounding lands. At its approach, Holly felt a sense of wonder and exhilaration she could neither understand nor resist.

"Here it comes!" someone among the gathered watchers shouted, and in a blink, the Elemental migration was upon the town, arcing over it, continuing on. Elemental spirits, thousands of them. The living embodiments of nature magic dancing, tumbling, swirling through the sky to the gasps and cheers of the mere material beings below. Fire Elementals, living tongues of flame leaping unpredictably about. Lightning Elementals, branching bolts of raw energy. Gem Elementals, glittering shadows of garnet and emerald and purest diamond. Plant Elementals, green lights which twined through the air like vines across a wall. More Elementals, more than Holly could have counted if she'd had all night, vibrant and alive like an orchestra of light.

As the minutes passed and the migration continued, here and there one streak of light would break off from the rest and rush down to the gathered crowds, eliciting wild cheers from all around. Holly always tried to cheer the loudest of all. Most people, whether Wolf-Lord or gryphon or unicorn or dragon, went all their lives without being graced by the favor of an Elemental. To have one leave its migration to join with you was as much an omen of good luck as it was a bestowment of magical power. Holly dreamed—

This train of thought was broken as a streak of light larger than most broke off from the wave and flew down to Holly and Shun on their short hill. Holly eeped and stood at attention, silly as it might have been, felt her heart leap into her throat as she found herself the focus of a Metal Elemental. "Oh gosh."

"Calm," said Shun beside her, looking like she meant to say more before a sudden coughing fit overtook her.

Holly remained calm, focusing on her breathing as the Elemental, a rough orb of liquid silver-like metal, circled her once, stopped at a hover in front of her. To Holly's surprise and confusion, the mirror-like surface of the Metal Elemental did not reflect her or her surroundings. It showed instead the upper half of a cardinal-gryphon, the vibrant red feathers of a male . . . no, Holly realized after another moment of examination. A cardinal-hippogryph, the horn white and slender. "Why . . ."

The Metal Elemental rejoined the migration.

Holly stood as ice upon the hill, her eyes remaining caught on the waves of light high above for a moment more before slowly sinking down to the dark world around her. Her chest and throat ached with the pain of crying, though no tears came to her, not even when a few scattered barks of laughter rose from the nearby crowds who must surely have seen her be so dismissed. She heard the laughs, and the rush of waves, and nearby, nearby—

Shun was still coughing. Worse than coughing, gagging, a hand clutching desperately at her chest. Holly's self-concern died at once and she reached out, thinking at first her wife was choking on a bite of dinner. Then she took hold of Shun's arms and felt the kitsune was cold as the surrounding snow, which shouldn't have been possible. Shun possessed a Fire Elemental. She didn't get cold, ever.

Overhead, the Elemental migration passed on toward the east, all light fled from the darkness. "I-I can't—" Shun began, before another coughing fit struck her. She was still coughing as she collapsed into Holly's arms, Holly holding the smaller woman easily. Gone was all joy or excitement, gone even were hurt and sadness, replaced by panic verging on terror as Holly held her wife gone now silent and limp in her arms.

Across Eishaven, fires guttered out.

28

CHAPTER TWO

Three weeks later.

58 dead.

Holly stood on the black-rock shore, the sky a scalloped grey.

Crow cloak drawn tight around her, watching the tumultuous northern sea.

Waves churned white by storm winds crashed against the shore.

Filled the air with tang of frost and salt.

Holly beheld, barely felt, lost in thoughts and memories.

"It's Spell Rot, for sure," said Laura, the minotaur carefully stoking the hearth Shun had been laid next to.

Holly felt her legs tremble beneath her, fell into a chair before she had the chance to fall to the floor. "You're sure?"

Laura sighed, turned, sat by Shun's head, dragged a hand through her red hair. "I am. I saw it before, years ago, when it struck the Wolf-Lord household that had . . . bought me for a new daughter. We all fell sick, but minotaurs deal with disease better than most. I got better first, and I ran with all the schooling they'd given me. No gold, though. They would have come after me for the gold."

She glanced down, adjusted the blankets her oldest friend had almost disappeared under. "The symptoms here are undeniable. It's Spell Rot. And I'll bet money Shun won't be alone like this for too long. It's quite contagious."

Laura hadn't been wrong. Every passing day brought more sick villagers. The more there were sick, the more there were who died, the deaths striking randomly, blindly. Shun held on as the days mounted to weeks.

"It's her Fire Elemental, I reckon," said Laura, falling into a chair in the kitchen one late afternoon. The chair nearly buckled beneath her weight, her force, her sheer exhaustion from tending to the sick with whatever aid her alchemical expertise could provide. "Elementals can become real attached to their hosts after a while, and Shun's Elemental is a powerful one. It's fighting the disease with her. It might even win, eventually, but if this were the casinos of Cairn Fenris, I wouldn't put much money on it. God, if there were a cure . . ."

"But there is no cure," said Holly from the far end of the table, almost as tired as the minotaur, physically and emotionally. She barely remembered, but when she was six years old, Spell Rot struck Cairn Romulus. All Queen Celeste's children but Gosse, the youngest, fell sick with it. Gosse would get it later. Many servants died, but the royal children survived. Spell Rot had no known cure, but it could be survived if the ill were tended to well enough, and whoever caught it once would never catch it again, which was how Holly and Laura went among the Eishaven sick without fear. But properly tending to a victim sick with Spell Rot until they grew better was a long and expensive undertaking, and Eishaven, a town of refugees and migrants, was not rich.

From somewhere upstairs in the plain log cabin, both women heard Nessa fall into a dry coughing fit.

Holly closed her eyes against the spray of crashing waves. The cold salt served for her tears. She had not felt so powerless since the worst years of her life trapped in Cairn Romulus, with family which wasn't family. She could hear again the words of Queen Celeste, growling her hateful truth.

"You just can't help it. Born so wrong and weak. Candida, look at me when I'm talking to you . . . You will never get better, Candida! Never! You're broken and useless, and you will never be more than a waste, a problem, an EMBARRASSMENT!"

"I'm sorry," said Holly. She couldn't help it. Not quite cured yet of the old way of coping. "I'm sorry. I'm sorry, I'm sorry, I'm . . ."

Someone watched Holly. She opened her eyes, scrubbed at them with the heel of a hand, looked about. The storm overhead had grown worse, and soon there would be snow, or perhaps a hard, sleeting rain. The last ship on the sea was hurriedly making its way to the relative safety of Eishaven's port. And half a dozen yards away to the left, down the beach, stood the unicorn mare Nimue, the sole unicorn in Eishaven other than Nessa. In the stormy morning gloom, the unicorn looked a white phantom, old and wizened, mane long and wispy.

Holly kept quiet, wary regarding the mare. Nimue was an old, reclusive figure in the town history, living there many years before Holly had come, disliked widely by the community and for good reason. Nimue's people, the unicorns of the Avalon Empire, were why so many gryphons called Eishaven home in the first place.

Eventually, Nimue broke the silence hanging over the scene. "Princess, I am under your protection as much as anyone else here, and I want to talk. Come with me, please."

Holly startled. She had not been expecting any words as respectful as "please" from the mare.

Before an answer could be given, the unicorn turned and began to trudge along the beach to the short outcrop of cliff in the distance, and the weather-worn lighthouse the unicorn called home atop it. Unable to be knowingly rude, even to a unicorn, Holly hurried to follow.

A long, sick walk followed, and after it, an open door and a warm, surprisingly warm, welcome. Holly had never been inside of the lighthouse before, or inside of any unicorn home, for that matter. From the surprising roominess of everything once she'd stepped past the threshold, she suspected unicorn magic at work. A ramp running along the left-hand wall rose to the lighthouse's second floor, where the main work of maintenance was done. Downstairs, without walls or doors to separate them, there was a hearth and a broad, water-filled bowl. An enchanted icebox. A long table, covered with a messy mix of plates, scrolls, and half-empty inkwells. A flat, blanket-shrouded pillow, large enough for the unicorn to lay on without any part of her hanging off. Well-filled bookshelves lined the walls, and alongside them paintings of unicorns in armor standing proud before dazzling castles. Propped against the wall beside the hearth stood a tall spear of a solid, silver-white metal, its blade a narrow teardrop.

"It is a lovely place. You must have worked—"

Holly stopped walking when her eyes fell on the armor. Old and weathered unicorn barding draped over a rickety mannequin, old but well-tended, hardly remarkable but for the infamous ocean-blue colors, the white rose emblazoned upon the sides. A short sword lay on a table next to it, alongside its black scabbard, the blade glittering like stars in the night sky and similarly adorned with the symbol of the white rose.

The symbol of the Knights le Fay, the unicorn devotees of Morgana le Fay, established by her long before her original banishment. Murderers, traitors, and thieves in the downfall of Wolf-Lords in Heraldale. Holly was alone and unarmed with an enemy of her people.

"Do you drink?" asked Nimue, heading for the icebox.

"When I am thirsty, sure," said Holly, tearing her gaze away from the arms and armor to continue following her host. Seeing the unicorn's raised eyebrow, she thought back over what she had said and what she had missed, and groaned. A true sign of how harried and tired the ongoing crisis had made her. "Sorry, sorry. Shun told me when people ask that, they mean to ask if

I drink alcohol. And I do not. Alcohol does not . . . agree with me."

Nimue nodded, turned to cabinets set in the wall, with the yellow glow of her magic levitating out bowls and small packets. "Tea, then. It will only be a moment. Warm yourself by the fire."

Though hesitant to turn her back to the unicorn, Holly did as told, quietly relishing the extra warmth. Soon after, Nimue walked over, levitating a large kettle over the flames before settling with a grunt. A harsh, dry cough followed the grunt, and something must have shown on Holly's face, for next Nimue scoffed. "It is not the Spell Rot, wolf, though it might as well be. A mere cold. I get them every year, at this time. This year, though . . . I do not see many winters left ahead of me."

Holly didn't know what to make of this admission of mortality. She hooked her fingers together in her lap, as she had sometimes seen Shun do while meditating, and said nothing.

Silence. Then the kettle whistled. Nimue levitated it from the fire, poured the deep brown drink into two bowls set between herself and Holly. Job done, the unicorn leaned forward into the steam rising from her bowl, breathing deep of the sweet, tangy scents there before speaking again. "I am not a good person."

Holly looked again at the Knight le Fay artifacts, not sure if she needed to say anything to this.

"Yes, you're right," continued Nimue. "I was . . . one of them. The blood of the innocent and the evil stains my blade. More innocent than evil, I suspect, devoted to maintaining the powers that be more than I ever was to crusading for peace, or truth, or justice. And then, just desserts as the unicorn empire I paid no mind to declared me and my own traitors to be hunted down and executed. Quite thoroughly, I should say. Am I the last of the Knights le Fay? Probably. Unless you count that thrice-damned Lord Mordred, and I wouldn't. Wasting away here, poor and forgotten, I wouldn't."

Holly lifted her bowl with both hands and sipped her tea. It was delicious, warming her through from her core. "If I went to the southeast and told the Queen of Romulus who you were and where you are, they would send armies to kill you, and every crime of mine would be forgiven. I would return home a hero, my family finally loving me even despite my autism."

"But would you?" asked Nimue, sipping from her own bowl. "I am old enough to be called ancient. I don't think that is the sort of person you are, whatever 'deficiencies' you or your society might claim you to have."

"Then what kind of person do you think I am?" asked Holly, tired. She didn't know what she was doing there, talking and drinking tea. People needed her, family and friends. There was work to do. "Why bother talking with so much work to do?"

"You are a storyteller," said Nimue, sipping again. "You have a story to tell, before the end. I have a story too, if you are willing to listen. You'll like this one, I think."

Holly couldn't imagine liking anything at the moment, not when her wife lay in her death bed back home and their adopted daughter was galloping swiftly after. "Ma'am, I should be going, if—"

"There is hope for them, wolf," said Nimue.

Holly snapped her muzzle shut. Pain flared in her chest, twisting through her at these wanted, unwanted words, this impossible promise.

Nimue nodded. "I can't promise you unicorn magic. I can't promise you some Imperial advancement or cure. I can only point the way to something better. The Knights le Fay and our priestly attendants, as you may know from your stories, if you have not restricted yourself to Wolf-Lord matters, were the traditional guardians of the most holy of unicorn relics, the Waters of Life. The unicorn counterpart to the dragons' Eternal Flames and the gryphons' Aetherial Chalice. The

Waters, if you know your stories well, could undue any hurt, even at the brink of death. In the presence of love, the Waters could make possible miracles."

Holly's fingers tightened their locked grip. She knew already the stories, the histories. She knew what Kurt and other gryphons told her, how the Waters of Life were lost with the destruction of the Knights le Fay. She knew, but the words would not come to her, as so often occurred in moments of lonely stress.

Nimue continued. "It was the last months of the war. The northern gryphon realm was hurtling headlong toward collapse, but I and a few others of my knights had a final duty. A brother of mine, Sir Lancelot, had fallen in love with a gryphon queen. With the magic of the Waters of Life, there was a child. A hippogryph girl."

Holly leaned back where she sat, mouthing the words. A secret hippogryph. A secret ROYAL hippogryph. Her thoughts whirled with the revelation and its accompanying implications. There had not been a true hippogryph in a thousand years. If true, if the unicorn was not lying . . .

Nimue tossed her mane in what Laura had taught Holly was a dismissive gesture. "None of that matters. More likely than not the child died with her parents, or was stolen away as a secret weapon of the Avalon Empire. What matters are the Waters of Life. I was their final guardian. As Avalon victory neared, I fled east, pursued by Imperial agents. I could not trust myself, in my age, to protect the Waters forever. I could not trust them to the Confederacy, who remains a steadfast trading partner with the Empire. I could not trust them to you Wolf-Lords once I learned the sordid tale of how General Nero fell from grace. No offense."

Holly found her words enough to say "None taken." She remembered well the cruelties and evils of her parents, Queen Celeste and Morgana le Fay. "But then, where . . ."

"I offered the Waters to the only group in all this world that I knew holds no enmity, no alliance, no inherent inclination but for the development of life. The Elementals."

"The—" Holly reeled, caught beneath her onslaught of thoughts. She forced herself to breathe, hands gripping tightly together. Slowly, the rush calmed and she could focus on what mattered. "You gave the Waters of Life to the Elementals?"

Nimue nodded. She looked suddenly tired, weighed down by a weariness of centuries and drained by the conversation. She lowered her head for another slurp of tea, gone cold now with the telling of the story. Her voice ached as she began again. "I assume they guard the Waters to this day. Find your way to the House of

Incarnation. If the key to saving Eishaven, to saving your loved ones, is anywhere, it is in the home of the Elementals. Find the House of Incarnation . . ."

Nimue's head fell to the floor beside her mostly-finished bowl of tea, eyelids slowly fluttering closed. For a moment Holly sat there and watched the unicorn, uncertain if she now shared the lighthouse with a dead person. She leaned forward, ears perked, barely caught the sound of faint breathing. She placed a hand on the unicorn's side and felt it rise and fall. Holly sighed and pulled away. Only sleeping, not dead. Good, she decided. Old folks deserved their sleep.

Holly gathered up the bowls and stood. She poured them out and set them in the sink, saw to the fire in the hearth to be sure it would keep, and then, after a moment's hesitation where she tried to decide what Laura or Kurt would do, she scrounged around for a blanket to cover the slumbering unicorn, remembering from days spent helping care for elderly gryphons how easily the elderly could catch cold.

Satisfied with her work, Holly stepped outside. The cold wind hit her with renewed savagery after the lighthouse's warmth, rolling across the long stretch of snow-bound rock between her and town with a low, haunting wail, cold fingers pulling at her, whipping her hair into her eyes. Holly pulled her black gryphon-feather cloak more tightly about herself and looked around. The cloud cover had grown heavier. A light snow fell, a strange occurrence for the time of year. It was the sort of weather which made it terribly hard for her to believe in hopeful tales of hippogryphs and Waters of Life, and Holly knew she would have to decide what she dared to believe, and quickly.

"Holly!"

At her name, Holly looked around again. At first, she saw nothing but white and grey and the faded browns of withering Eishaven. But then a black figure emerged from the haze of falling snow, swiftly resolving itself into a sleek raven-gryphon with a bright red scarf and the brighter yellow eyes of a Wolf-Lord. Holly's heart rose at the sight, buoyed by what she might have called love. "Kanti!"

The raven-gryphon swept down for a landing, transforming as she did. Black feathers melted away into black fur. Talons shrank, split into hands. Body shortened and limbs lengthened, shifting into a bipedal form. Beak softened and flattened into a muzzle, grew teeth, became a face full of fear. Where a raven-gryphon had been, a black Wolf-Lord ran the last distance toward Holly; Lady Kanti, known better to the world as the infamous pirate and smuggler Captain Blackbird.

And for the last many glorious months, the shared lover of Holly and Shun.

"Permission?" asked Kanti, skidding to a stop before Holly, her eyes wide with the question.

"Granted," answered Holly, opening her arms. The word was barely free from her muzzle before Kanti pulled her into the fiercest embrace, one Holly hadn't known she'd needed until she had it, one she returned with a hitch in her breath and a tremor in her shoulders.

"I came as soon as I got your message," the shorter Wolf-Lord said, continuing to press close. "Laura told me everything, and I came looking for you. I'm bringing supplies in, food and supplies and whatever else I could think you'd need, but I had to fly ahead after I heard . . . heard . . . God, Shun, Nessa, th-they . . ."

"I know," said Holly. She closed her eyes and hugged her lover more tightly, and while they embraced at least, the cold seemed not to touch them.

CHAPTER THREE

In the family den, the wood walls draped with the flickering lights and shadows of the fire in the hearth, Holly told Laura and Kanti everything. Nimue's past as a Knight le Fay, the chance of a hippogryph out in the world, and most importantly in Holly's eyes, the location of the Waters of Life and their best hope to save Shun, Nessa, and everyone else.

"I don't believe her," said Laura. The minotaur paced the length of the room, from the door to the kitchen to where Kanti lurked near the stairs up to the second floor, newly dressed in her spare clothes and ears perked for the slightest sound of distress from Shun or Nessa. "I just don't believe her."

From where she sat on the stairs, near Kanti and across the room from the fireplace, Holly watched her old friend with confusion. "But why would she lie about this? For as long as we have called Eishaven home, she has always been a grumpy recluse, but never openly antagonistic to anyone. Why would she start now? Why kick us when we are down?" She hoped she used the phrase correctly. Shun would tell her if she did, but . . .

"She's a unicorn, Holly," said Laura, stopping her pacing to glare into the fire. "She's a unicorn."

"And you are a minotaur," said Holly. "And Kurt two houses down is a gryphon. And Kanti and I are Wolf-Lords. If we are comparing hurts, we are going to win that argument."

Laura winced. One of Kanti's hands found Holly's and squeezed. Holly, for her part, felt wretched. It was the only time she could remember bringing up the attempted genocide of her people by gryphons, minotaurs, unicorns, and dragons over one thousand years ago. She had never before felt the need. Only dragons, unicorns, and the most powerful of Wolf-Lords and kitsune lived long enough to have lived through the atrocities. Choosing not to hang onto the sins of the past was how she'd been able to befriend Laura and the gryphons in the first place.

"And besides," Holly continued, before the silence could grow too uncomfortable. "She is not just a unicorn. She is a Knight le Fay. A refugee like anyone else here."

Nobody said anything to this, not at first. Laura knelt and stoked the fire. Kanti rolled Holly's hand palm-up, gently caressing the pads of her fingers and staring away at seemingly nothing. Holly watched them with breath held, gripping the banister tightly with her free hand. She wished she was on a stage. When she was on a stage, with a story to tell, words came easy for her, easy and strong.

"The House of Incarnation," said Kanti, voice soft. "Where is it? What is it? I've never heard of such a place."

Holly had. She smiled despite everything. "It's an old, old Wolf-Lord story. From before we left Heraldale. Morgana le Fay went on a journey to discover where Elementals came from and where they went. She flew after their migration for days, for weeks, far beyond the farthest explorations of unicorn- or gryphonkind. The land they eventually led her to was cold and barren, wracked by lightning and fierce windstorms. There, she found a cave, and beyond the cave—"

From upstairs there came an eruption of coughs, young, dry, and pained. A second round of coughing followed hot on its heels, older and more breathless.

Holly shot to her feet and ran for the stairs, Kanti close beside her. On the second floor, as Kanti peeled away for Holly and Shun's shared bedroom, Holly followed the first coughing voice to the Nessa's room at the far end of the hall. She found it dark and cold, the window blown open and the small fire blown out. Nessa lay shivering on her blanket, the unicorn filly's coughing fit already calmed into wheezy, scratchy gasps.

Swallowing a lump in her throat, Holly crossed the room to close and latch the window, then brought the fire roaring back to life with a clench of her left fist and a flex of her magic. As the bedroom warmed, she knelt beside Nessa. The unicorn, young and small, hadn't awoken, and as the minutes passed and Holly combed a hand down her neck to her shoulders, the unicorn's breathing softened to something almost normal. Until the next fit, when she would grow colder yet, and harder yet to wake up, and the stench of rot would start to seep out . . .

Holly did not cry, but she wished she would. For the wife and daughter she had chosen. For the life she had chosen, slipping away from her with each rattling cough, each drip of blood in their spit. She loved them both, Shun and Nessa, loved them wholeheartedly, in ways her own parent had never loved her. And now they were slipping away. Slipping away toward death.

"M-Mother?"

Holly blinked, found Nessa looking up at her with bleary eyes, confusion and fear in her young, trembling voice. "Are we going to die?"

The pain at these words drove a silver stake through Holly's heart. Biting her lip, she brushed the mane from Nessa's eyes. "No, sweetheart. You are just very sick. But you are going to get better, I promise. When you came to us, I promised your mother I would keep you safe, and I will. I promise."

The filly nodded, yawned, sank back into sleep. Holly watched her for a moment more, to be sure her sleep would be untroubled for at least a little while, and then left the bedroom. She met Laura out in the hall, looking on with her own concern. "Is she sleeping again?" asked the minotaur

Holly nodded. She was tired.

Laura sighed. "She's a unicorn, but she's young. She's not . . . strong."

"How long?" asked Holly

"All else holding steady?" asked Laura in return. "Two weeks . . . no, 16 days. I could keep her stable for 16 days. That's with the promised supplies Kanti is sending our way. Even her resources will be strained, taking care of a whole town. I can't give you any better news than that."

Holly nodded, her mouth dry as wyvern skin. She slid past the minotaur to her and Shun's bedroom down the hall, closing the door behind her.

The room was dark. The little light allowed came from the heavily-curtained windows, grey and cold as the stormy skies outside. Still though, Holly saw well enough to join Kanti beside the wood bed against the far corner, the other Wolf-Lord almost invisible in the dark aside from her yellow eyes shining with tears. Shun lay asleep in the bed, buried beneath a mountain of blankets, as small and frail as Holly had ever seen the kitsune. Her breathing came weak and raspy, like Nessa's, and she did not stir when Holly brushed the back of a hand across her cheek. Cold, and too cold.

"She woke up a little bit from her coughing fit," whispered Kanti, words coming slow and halting. "Enough to notice me, at least. She, uh, she smiled and . . . and tried to blow me a kiss, heh."

Holly nodded. It sounded like a Shun thing to do.

Another moment, then Holly carefully sat herself down on the edge of the bed, brushing again her wife's cheek. "I am going to go away for a while," she said, voice low even though the chance of waking the kitsune was minimal. "I am going to get what we all need. I will be back as quick as I can. You will barely even notice I was gone."

"That either of us were gone," added Kanti.

No answer came. None was expected. Holly kissed her wife on the brow, and then turned to begin gathering her things. Wherever she went in search of the Waters of Life, it was a long journey ahead of her.

For the first time in over a year, she took her black Lunar Steel sword from its place of honor over the bed. The last, most precious gift from her twin, Regina.

***

In the White Marsh of Denning Island, off the southern coast of Romulus, General Regina and their sword danced. Screams tore through the dense battlefield, explosions from rockets and charged spell blasts sending rock and muck scattering through the air as the fort town of Denning made its last, desperate stand.

Wolf-Lords fell all around, their blood and ashes staining the surrounding marsh in red and black. Regina pushed the advance, golden armor dented and stained, white cape worn grey, muzzle a snarl. Their white sword sang, batting away spells and bullets slung their way. Black blood arced, splattered the trees, a Denning-Wolf screaming dead to the marsh ground. Another's ax split in twain, then their head a moment later. Onward Regina marched.

The wooden gates of the fort town fell. Regina strode over them, caught a bolt in the chest, spun with the force to swing and slice the Wolf-Lord soldier in half at the waist before they could get another shot off.

Soldiers swarmed into the breach past Regina, Wolf-Lords and Jackals and Kitsune, slaughtering foes, once-citizens of their own nation. Regina stood in the middle of the courtyard and let their soldiers pass them by, breathing, merely breathing. They watched as their foe turned to flee, all fight driven from them, engulfed swiftly in flames from kitsunes. The cannons on the walls were thrown down and the flags declaring the proud sovereignty of the Denning Islands were torn from their poles, swiftly replaced by the gold and red of Romulus.

Victory.

Untouched by the bloodthirsty thrill of their troops pillaging whatever treasures the fort or its last surviving inhabitants could provide, Regina strode up the steps to stand upon the shattered walls and look out over the marshes. The air stank with blood and gunpowder, stained with smoke which cast the sky in angry greys and blacks. Fires burned unchecked near to the marsh town and far. Disregarded for much longer, Regina figured, everything they had wasted two gruesome months in battle over would be destroyed, a desolate wasteland where once had been the shining jewel in Romulus's crown. It would not be the first such wasteland left in Regina's wake as the fires of rebellion rose and fell in the country. Not even the third.

Lost with such thoughts, Regina stood on the wall and did nothing, even as the celebrations behind them turned to deeper, bloodier debaucheries. The ringing of weapons thrown down and pleas for mercy turned to screams of horror which were in turn nearly drowned out by the murderous, lusting howls of Regina's troops, barely hiding the sounds of breaking bones and smacking flesh.

There would be survivors. Regina could already see a few slipping away in the distance, lost in the chaos. Some of them would surely reach the mainland and spread word of the Desolation of Denning to all who'd hear it. And there would be another town—or five—raising arms in protest, and Celeste would send Regina to quell them, Another place of ash, another piece of the homeland dead. Even they could see where it was all going.

Anything to keep the peace. Anything to keep Romulus strong against the slander of the other Wolf-Lord nations. Anything to put the Embarrassment of Candida behind them.

"General!" shouted a voice behind and below Regina. Lieutenant Talbot, the Wolf-Lord still strong and chipper despite the months of hardship, as if the death and cruelty had been a joy instead of a tragedy. "General

Regina, come down! There is wine! There is food! There is good, willing flesh—"

"Send for the kitsune," said Regina, ignoring the troublesome soldier. "Have them quench those fires immediately before the whole island goes up in flames."

"Oh, let the land burn!" laughed Talbot, joined by a number of other nearby soldiers. "It's not our land!"

Regina supposed it wasn't, not anymore. The fighting was over and the land was dead, necrotic. Whatever scattered remnant of Wolf-Lords remained would keep hiding in their ash-choked burrows until the soldiers were gone, and whoever came next to try making a living would—

Something small, cold, and wet touched upon Regina's muzzle. They jerked their head back at once, blinked, brought the hand not clutching their sword up, palm raised and fingers spread. They watched, mystified, as the falling ash from the spreading fires turned before their eyes into light pinpricks of snow.

"Talbot," they tried to say as they turned, stopping as no voice came out. All sounds had died out, replaced by the howls of a harsh, ice-choked wind. Their surroundings disappeared beneath the vision of a cold and desolate wasteland of ice and snow. They knew at once it was not a kitsune illusion placed upon them, nor an Elk illusion. They could feel the cold of the snow beneath their feet and blowing against them, could feel the sting of the wind in their eyes. They could smell nothing, no life anywhere around them to lend the air an odor.

No, there was a smell, Regina realized in the next moment. The air sang with the sharp tang of salt. And beneath the rush of the wind, rising over it, the roar of waves crashing upon a beach. The ocean was near.

The next stage of the vision slammed down into place with such startling force, Regina almost toppled backward. A black beach stretched east to west before her, and beyond the beach a grey ocean topped by wild and foaming waves. Regina knew the land, or its like. There was beach like it along the northern borders of Romulus, stark, unforgiving land which continued on past the border into the United Zakarian Confederacy.

As Regina stood, mesmerized, the black rocks of the beach heaved upward, forming a raven-gryphon. And riding upon the raven-gryphon, a Wolf-Lord garbed in a sweeping cloak of black feathers. White-furred, the same white fur as Regina. But where Regina's hair was cut short and was the same color as their fur, the other Wolf-Lord's hair streamed behind her, long and fiery, and she held her black sword overhead as she and the raven-gryphon faced to the east.

Regina's empty hand balled into a fist at the sight of the other Wolf-Lord. Their heart dropped, leaden with a sickening rush of love, anger, relief, disgust, joy. They knew the other Wolf-Lord. Would have known her were it decades since their last meeting instead of a mere three years.

"Candida," Regina bit out, settling on what seemed the most useful emotion for the moment. Anger. "Twin sister . . ."

There came a final image before the vision ended, a glimpse of a port city, its bay filled with black sails and the air heavy with the scents of exotic Heraldale spices. Then Regina stood once more on the blasted wall and watched the burning white marshes of Denning, heard once more the sick revelry of their soldiers, felt once more the smoke and grime of battle upon them.

"My general," called out Lieutenant Talbot, and by their tone Regina knew they had been privy to none of the vision. "Is all well up there? Is the view really so good?"

Regina withdrew a whistle from the inner lining of their cape. It was a short, thin whistle, carved from jade and tipped at the end with topaz. Regina blew a high, almost soundless note on it, returned it to its pouch, and at last turned to look down at Talbot. "I have had a vision concerning the very future of Romulus. Inform my second that they are in command now. I must go."

"Go?" Talbot frowned, the tawny Wolf-Lord ascending halfway up the steps between them. "This is the day of your greatest victory, my general! Where could you possibly need to go so soon?"

A shriek pierced the smoke-laden air, answering Regina's call. They turned from Talbot to watch a slim, well-muscled wyvern drop from the skies to hover before the fort's wall, its chest scales peppered with a scattershot of crimson marks. Regina sheathed their sword, grabbed the beast's dangling reins, and swung over onto its saddled back. Practiced hands strapped them in as they spared a final look to Lieutenant Talbot and the few other Wolf-Lord soldiers drawn to watch by curiosity. "North. Home. A family reunion I never dared hope for is awaiting me."

CHAPTER FOUR

"If you're really going to try this, I'll help however I can. You know, I know, we all know, that nobody knows where to find the home of the Elementals. Or if they do know, they sure as Sheol aren't shouting it from the rooftops. Your best hope is going to the University of the Starpoint, in Akela. I am acquaintances with an alchemist there, Guru Veda. Her specialty is Elementals and their lore. If anyone, anywhere, can point you in the direction of this House of Incarnation . . ."

In her raven-gryphon form, Kanti wore neither saddle nor reins, and Holly did not need them. She rode clutching tight to her lover's back, muzzle wide in a grin despite the deathly seriousness of the journey. She might even have laughed, if not for fear of catching something in her mouth.

The land and the ocean passed below them, the beach winding away behind them as they flew east along the coast to the port town of Quicken Bay. Holly paid it no heed. Her focus kept to the far horizon, to the wind of flight streaming her hair behind her, the world opening, spreading all around them with each beat of Kanti's wings.

God above them, to have wings. Holly rode upon Kanti's back as she flew and marveled at the speed and power with which the other's wings worked to carry them flying through the cold northern skies. If Holly could have chosen her form, as other Wolf-Lords with proper shapeshifting abilities could, she would give herself wings. Broad red wings, like her hair. She remembered Wolf-Lords in Brillant with wings, back in the day. Enjoying the winds of spring as freely as the wyverns more commonly ridden.

Not having wings, and not having the ability to give herself wings, Holly rejoiced in the next best thing. "Thank you for this!"

"Don't mention it!" Kanti called back at her, head twisting to give a smile Holly returned. The raven-gryphon looked forward again, put on a fresh burst of speed as she pointed ahead. "There! We're almost there! Quicken Bay!"

Holly focused ahead, tucking Kanti's red scarf out of her way. Through the thinly falling snow, she saw a port town past many leagues still of high hills. In the late evening light, the sun rapidly disappearing behind the pair, it was an impressive enough sight. Not half the size of distant Brillant. Not even a quarter the size. But larger than Eishaven, and so large enough. Ships of wide diversity filled the port, from the Confederacy to the far away kitsune nations of Inari and Okami, many bearing the black hulls or black sails proclaiming allegiance to Kanti, or as the world better knew her, Captain Blackbird. The streets of the town were strung up with lanterns of red and gold, and the air as Kanti flew them closer to the ground in preparation for a landing was filled with scents reminding Holly of life in Undertown years ago, strange smells of cooking which refugees and immigrants had brought from the world over. It was a good smell, however it might have clashed from one breeze to the next. Holly liked it.

They landed beside a large frosted-over fountain in a public square, Kanti taking care not to disturb any lanterns as she came in. Holly hopped off, gave the raven-gryphon a playful pat on the rear—earning her a squawk and a blushing hiss of "Such shenanigans for the bedroom!"—and looked around. The ground was cobblestone, grey slick with the white of snow, made warmer in patches by the orange light shining from the windows of surrounding buildings. The buildings themselves seemed unaccountably strange to Holly for a moment, until she took stock of the crowds milling to and fro all about them and found herself, for the first time in many years, surrounded primarily by fellow Wolf-Lords rather than gryphons, and the buildings which seemed so strange to her, too tall, too closed, too narrow, were Wolf-Lord buildings.

"This feels weird," she said, looking at last to Kanti as the black-furred Wolf-Lord finished her transformation out of her gryphon form and hastily adjusted the red scarf around her neck. "Are you, uh . . . going to be okay, wearing only that? You have nice fur, but even so . . ."

In answer, Kanti grinned and snapped her fingers. The red scarf grew with a spreading glimmer of magic, swept down Kanti's body, split and changed and thickened until she was wearing deep red pants, shirt, and coat which all looked sensible enough in such climes of ice and snow.

"Oh," said Holly. "Quite fantastic."

"Indeed." Kanti looked around them, seeming to gauge the crowds as Holly had earlier, and then nodded toward a southward road. "Come on, then."

They walked, becoming no more than another pair in the crowds. As they walked, Kanti explained their purpose in Quicken Bay. "It's one thing to sail ships discretely from the Wolf-Lord nations to your little town to keep it supplied. It'd be quite another to try sailing anything from Romulus to any of the other nations, with the blockades and the embargos and all the rest going on."

"Blockades?" asked Holly. "Embargos?"

"Economic punishments," said Kanti, stopping them in front of a store whose front was all frosted glass, blasting the street with the bright warmth of the lights within. "For Romulus' use of prisoners as slave labor. It's supposed to cause internal pressure to force Queen Celeste to capitulate, but Celeste's been too stubborn— and happy to use her army to stomp out that internal pressure—for it to really work. But still, the point remains it makes us getting to Akela in a ship or normal air-yacht damn hard, and I wouldn't be able to fly all the way there in gryphon form even without a passenger weighing me down. No offense, my love. Your curves are sexy."

"No offense taken." Holly looked away to the store they stood before, saw the words emblazoned across the glass and felt an eyebrow rise. "But where does Quicken Bay come into all this? Where does a booze joint come into all this?"

"Quicken Bay's home to our best chance at getting under those blockades." Kanti looked to the store as well, grinning. "And in there's our best chance at getting that help."

***

They bought three large, green bottles, each more expensive than Holly by herself could have afforded after a year's worth of work. With the bottles in hand, they continued on, the crowds gradually dispersing as the sun finished its eastward fall into night. The streets grew darker as the open and operating businesses thinned, Holly beginning to notice boarded-up storefronts, houses with windows shattered and snow building up inside. Overhead, the lanterns were left behind, leaving only the scattered street lamps to light their way into the seedier side of town. The snowfall faltered, stopped, but the clouds remained, the air dark and cold and still.

Holly had barely noticed the ghost of light spread across the snowy road before they turned left. The new street was shorter, taken up mostly by empty lots enclosed in barbed-wire fences. At the far end stood a large warehouse of red brick and brown glass, the lights shining in a scattered few of its windows, smoke of various colors rising from various chimneys.

"Oh, thank God," said Kanti, taking one of Holly's hands in her own and picking up the pace of their stride. "They're still awake. And working, too! That means they'll be in a good mood."

"Who?" asked Holly.

"A good business associate of mine, the Mechanist."

With Shun not there to do so, Holly sighed and rolled her eyes. "Why are so many of the people I meet through you people who use jobs as names?"

"Lack of imagination, I suppose." Kanti let go of Holly's hand as she marched up to a broad set of wood doors tall enough for a full-grown wyvern to drag itself through. She grabbed one of the handles and gave it a tug. The doors swung open with little resistance, forcing Kanti to hurriedly back away so as not to be knocked off her feet. She shot a grin Holly's way before leading the way inside.

In sharp contrast to the bitter cold outside, the insides of the warehouse were warm. Hot, even, Holly decided as she shut the doors with a bang of wood on metal behind them. She had to shrug off her black feather cloak as she looked about. The warehouse rose three stories tall, the upper floors composed mostly of wood beams and metal gangways beneath a metal-ribbed glass roof.

Hanging among these gangways were a trio of airships in various states of deconstruction, spell-channeling beams removed, whole sides split apart to reveal the inner workings of metal and crystal. One hung lower, its spilled insides reaching all the way to the crowded warehouse floor to mingle with the many tables covered in tools and technical equipment Holly couldn't begin to recognize, though the clang and roar of metal forges nearer the far wall were recognizable enough.

"Hey, Mechanist!" shouted Kanti, stepping farther from the main doors and holding one of the bottles of wine aloft. "It's Kanti! I've got something for you!"

The sounds of clanging from the unseen forges ceased. A voice called back in answer, distant but growing nearer, "Blackbird!? What in Sheol are you doing, kicking about here? What kind of—ah, booze!"

The creature accompanying this thick voice as it scuttled into view from behind the mess of smoke and sparks and hanging air-yacht parts froze Holly where she stood, the barest gasp of utter horror slipping from her pressed-tight lips. It was a spider, of a sort, but a mantis-armed spider the size of a swan-gryphon, large enough for Holly to comfortably ride on, if she ever felt so inclined. Crackly red hairs did little to hide its thick, black carapace, like a tarantula going bald. From its back grew several stubby spires of red crystal, each glowing with their own low light.

A crafting spider, some dim, barely-heard piece of Holly's frazzled mind supplied. Hardly seen out of the south of the Zakarian Confederacy. Hardly something for her to be losing her mind over.

"The finest Old Willow vintage," said Kanti, popping the cork for the wine bottle as she stepped forward to meet the monstrosity. "All for you, old friend."

"Your young friend there looks like she might need some of it herself, haha!" remarked the crafting spider, though it—he, Holly tried to remind herself—did not hesitate to snatch the wine bottle from Kanti's hands in one of its nimble claws. It reared back until its abdomen butted against the greasy floor, the head of the bottle disappearing beneath a horde of raking, grasping—

Holly looked away before her stomach could get away from her, pretending to examine the work benches covered in tools and disassembled mechanical contraptions lining the walls of the warehouse workshop, trying not to hear the roiling sounds of gluttonous drinking over the tempered fires of the forges.

"You alright?" asked Kanti, voice a hushed whisper.

"Just, uh, spiders," was all Holly could manage.

"You're being a little bit rude," said Kanti.

"I know," said Holly. "But spiders."

The sounds of drinking ceased. Holly dared look forward again at their host, in time to watch the gryphon-sized spider toss the empty wine bottle away. The glass shattered against the bricks of a nearby pillar and the spider laughed, pounding his gripping claws down on the floor as he did. "So, what can I do for you? Coming to my workshop so late, hefting drink so rich, it must be a big ask. I am still hard at work on your last request, you can see, yes, hard at work. Not easy, refitting an Imperial troop carrier for such pressures upon its hull. Harder still, to be sure it's waterproof and airtight. Hah! Drink will help."

"I hope so," said Kanti, already unbagging the next bottle. "Things changed. I need that blockade runner sooner rather than later."

The Mechanist, to Holly's quiet horror, did not have the black, blank eyes of his smaller, non-sapient kin, but eyes like her own, pupils and irises and all, scattered irregularly across the stretch of his body which served as his face. She noticed this as he narrowed these eyes at Kanti in suspicion. "How much sooner?"

"Two days," said Kanti, before hastily adding "from now."

"TWO DAYS FROM—" The Mechanist reared back on his rear-most two pairs of legs, towering over the pair of Wolf-Lords and loosing a stream of crackling yowls and garbles. Holly scrambled backward a step, two steps, finally regained control of herself and half-drew her black sword from its scabbard. Ahead, Kanti made no move but to hold aloft the second bottle of wine. "Morning, two days from now!"

"Late evening, four days from now!" the Mechanist bellowed, green spit flying from its mandibles, the green spit hissing and sending up thin billows of smoke where it struck the workshop floor, filling Holly's nose with the tang of scorched metal.

"Lives are on the line and I'm appealing to your better nature!" Kanti tossed the second bottle of wine toward the giant spider. "Late morning, two days from now! That's my final offer!"

The Mechanist caught the bottle from the air with nimble claws, uncorking and throwing his body back to drink. Holly turned away, unable to bring herself to watch the act. Her heart seemed to roll in her chest, a feeling of utter sick horror building up inside. Her grip on her half-sheathed sword remained. "Kanti—"

"It's alright. I have this, my darling."

The sounds of drinking ceased. Glass shattered again on the floor, the Mechanist's chuckle crawling lowly after it as the giant spider backed away. He balanced on his frontmost legs, a horrible, unbalanced mass of carapace and fur hooking the pincered tips of his rear legs onto the lowest-hanging of the metal gangways overhead, hauling himself up to clamber overhead to the cacophony of creaking metal and straining ropes. "You forget yourself, little wolf. Your final offer is nothing when set against my final demand!"

Kanti's shoulders relaxed. The black Wolf-Lord's tail gave a brief wag behind her. "Okay, then. Let's hear it."

"Mid-afternoon, two days from now! No earlier, genuinely not possible! Double my pay! A meeting with the Painter to get myself a prophecy!"

Kanti looked behind her at Holly, the look on her face as if seeking permission whether to accept the deal or keep trying to negotiate. Holly looked to the dark night waiting outside the windows, thought of the 16 days Laura had given them, and looked back to Kanti and nodded. The other Wolf-Lord nodded in return and looked to the Mechanist still clambering with turgid menace overhead. "Alright. We—"

"One more thing." The Mechanist chuckled again as he moved to crouch high above Holly, let go, caught himself on the gangway by his rear legs to dangle over her, close enough she could have reached a hand up and shook one of his grasping claws. She startled from the sudden proximity, her heart giving another lurch. She went to stand beside Kanti again, narrowly avoiding another dribble of spit which got the floor hissing as it burned. The Mechanist laughed, all eyes rolling until they focused on Holly. "One last demand, this one from you. The cause of all this sudden rushing, if I had to guess. You see, wolf, it is so rare when I get the chance to work with precious Lunar steel."

Holly said nothing at first. With the slowness of one expecting to find a terrible sign of the end, she looked first from the Mechanist to his burning spit on the floor, and then to the sword still gripped half-sheathed at her side. She drew the sword fully from its scabbard, her grip on its hilt steady as she held it before her, watching the hazy lights of the workshop gleam along the length of the black blade.

Candida frowned, raising her sword and stepping back to allow Regina room to stand. As her twin recovered, Candida looked closer at the sword gifted her, recognizing at once it was of far higher quality than those used by the Cairn Romulus royal guard or standing army. And for a moment, staring at her dim reflection in the black blade, Candida allowed herself to see a future of her in the same knightly armor Regina wore on duty, standing watch over peace signings and royal galas, or leading a charge against some unseen, unknown mass of enemies, or . . . or . . .

"It's right there in your hand," spoke Regina, their own sword retrieved and sheathed, their voice soft and pleading.

"I have to object to this," said Kanti, a hand strong on Holly's shoulder. "This sword is of EXTREME sentimental value to my lover. You have no right to—"

"It's alright," said Holly, though her heart ached as she said the words, a feeling of betrayal striking her at right angles to all she wanted. Yet she managed to keep her hand steady as she returned the weapon to its scabbard, undid the straps of the belt, held it up and out to the Mechanist waiting above, leaving her only her untrained magic and her parrying dagger on her hip to defend herself. "I have this, my darling." And when she spoke the words, she thought not only of Kanti beside her, but of Shun as well, already too far behind her.

"Yes!" The Mechanist cackled with a haggler's glee as he snatched the sword from Holly's hand, almost as quickly tossing it aside to the many other piles of metals and ore collected around them. "Haha, yes! Pass that last wine and let's get to work! We have a blockade to run!"

CHAPTER FIVE

The next day, as the Mechanist and his crew set to renewed work on fulfilling Kanti's order for a blockade runner, Holly donned a hood to hide her telltale red hair and set about exploring Quicken Bay. She tried to stay in the warehouse at first, to help however she could, but after an hour of stress, singed fur from the flying sparks, and barked reprimands from all corners, Kanti pulled her aside to one of the side doors, as apologetic as Holly had ever seen her. "Hey, maybe you ought to see what there is to see around here. I think we've got things handled as well as we can here."

"I used to work the morning shift at an ironworks in Brillant," said Holly in return, trying with little success to rub the soot out of the fur along her arms as she did. "The more hands at work, the better. And besides, they are letting you work with them without complaint."

"I'm not being left clumsy and slow by a mortal terror of the person I'm working for," said Kanti, an unexpected bite in her town. At Holly's flinch, she sighed and rubbed the bridge of her nose. "I'm sorry, I'm sure it's nothing you mean to be feeling. But just get out there in the fresh air for a while for me, won't you? It will give you stories to tell Shun and Nessa when we get back home."

"Eishaven's not home for you," said Holly. She wished she had her sword at her side to grasp for support. "You live elsewhere, in riches and luxury. Eishaven is just where you vacation."

"But it IS your home, at least for now," said Kanti, smiling as she took Holly's shoulders in her hands. "And you and Shun are NOT mere vacation flings."

***

Alone, Holly walked the cold, meandering streets of Quicken Bay and found the experience like entering the coastal town for the first time again. In the early day, there were more people out on the street than the night before, more businesses were open, and Holly saw both people and business more clearly. She did not like what she saw, past the obscuring flakes of falling snow and billowing breath, not one bit.

It had been years, but Holly still remembered Brillant well, still considered that shining city, at least in part, home. She remembered the gleaming, polished wood and stone of storefronts, the rich dress and ready laughter of the Wolf-Lords going about their days and living their lives. She remembered the parks, well-tended and beloved, how trees rose in careful groves and flowers lent their scents to the day's symphony of experience. She remembered a sense of thriving, of life marching on even in the leanest, meanest days down in Undertown, of which there had been plenty.

Quicken Bay was not a living town. Holly felt as if she walked among dead wolves who had not yet realized they could stop moving. Storefronts were ill-kept or closed up all together. No smiles reached out to her, and on every street corner there were town guards as well-armed and heavily armored as the most vicious and extreme of Brillant's soldiers.

The dark-armored soldiers, armed with a various array of steam rifles, shields, and heavy clubs, numbered 16. Between two of them near the rear of the marching procession was dragged the bloodied, beaten form of a crow-gryphon, barely believed to still be alive in the underground dusk.

"STOP! PLEASE, STOP!"

Ears turned in her direction, but the soldiers all marched on. All but two, stopping, turning back her way as Candida hurried toward them. One of them, idly swinging a club at their side, bore the gold bars of a captain on their pauldron, perhaps the leader of the group. Candida ran faster. "Sir, Sir please, there's a misunderstanding, you have to stop, I didn't know—"

KA-CRUNCH.

Candida slammed to the ground on her back, muzzle erupting into fireworks of agony. Blood splattered out a broken-jawed cry.

Holly's left hand moved to where the hilt of her sword should have been and closed on empty air. She stopped walking in the middle of the street, ignorant of the mumbles and sneers of the people forced to shuffle past her, stood a long moment looking at her empty left hand. She clenched it into a fist again, the sharp, sudden pain of her forfeiture making her inner magic flare until the glass of a nearby storefront cracked. She felt them, the magic and the cracking glass both, hurriedly opened her hand in a fear she dared not voice. Without conscious command, her legs began moving again.

She found her way to what must have served as the town park, once upon a time. It stood empty, the trees all sick and bare of leaves, the flowerbeds barren, the pond choked with a thick green scum. The closest approximation to life was a large sign near the entrance Holly stopped briefly at, a wooden sign longer than she was tall, painted white and demanding in thick red letters for passersby to "JOIN THE ARMY!"

She found her way to the docks. Most of the ships she saw the night before were gone. Those which remained were sail-less, bearing the thick armor and heavy cannons of the Romulan navy. Jackals and gryphons sat near the piers in rags, huddled shivering near signs begging for spare coins, cowering away whenever any of the many patrolling soldiers wandered past. The water beneath the piers shimmered with shifting, hazy rainbows, like the fat backs of iridescent beetles.

The bells of the clocktower near the center of town rang their heavy peals. Holly found her way to the open square she and Kanti first landed in, her belly grumbling. After a bit of looking around, she found a food wagon serving all the favorite foods Shun had gotten her into, a touch of warm familiarity she desperately needed in the moment. She bought herself two plates of savory Takoyaki, the kitsune vendor eyeing her warily as she paid with zakarian coins. She ignored this with practiced ease and went to sit at the fountain at the center of the square. She ate quickly, while the fried balls of batter and octopus were still almost hot enough to burn her tongue, and tried not to think of how much better her wife's take on the dish was. This warmed her belly and shut it up, which was enough.

A musical note, high and steady, cut across the town square as Holly was finishing off the second plate, silencing several conversations. She joined the many others in the square turning their attention to a stage suddenly rolled onto the scene, a flutter of surprise and recognition standing the fur on the back of her neck on end. A kitsune paced the stage, short and sandy-furred, three tails waving anxiously behind him. The poor nerves could only be seen in the tails, though, the rest of the fennec-kitsune the perfect picture of confidence as he smiled and waved to the slowly gathering crowds.

"Welcome, welcome, one and all! You there, girl, cute as a doll! Come hear a story to thrill and join, and perhaps at the end you'll share your coin!"

"Rookie mistake," said Holly to herself with a smirk. "NEVER remind your audience they are expected to pay you for their time."

"Nobody asked you," growled another Wolf-Lord in the crowd.

The fennec-kitsune continued, practically dancing from one side of the stage to the next as whip-cracks of his tails conjured illusions of dirty barn walls, a wyvern, and two white-furred Wolf-Lords in royal regalia, one of them sporting long hair a startling, familiar red. "Come hear the story that will make you roar, of Princess Candida, the traitor!"

Holly's smirk died choking on the street. She slowly sat again on the edge of the fountain. She sat and watched the stage, watched and listened for an hour or longer as her life, HER life, the events and adventures which had led her to Brillant, to Shun and the gryphons, and to freedom, were twisted and befouled into something vicious and hideous for the crowd's jeers and laughter.

"At last, I shall ruin my beloved parent's grand party! The embarrassment shall last for all time!"

"Ah, Brillant! Just the place for a schemer like me to rule the roost, hehehehe!"

"Gryphons rule, Romulus drools!"

"Now, Gosse, you shall die!"

Holly didn't want to watch, but she couldn't look away, couldn't stop hearing. She learned how as far as her home country of Romulus knew, there was no kitsune thief, and Holly—or Candida, as the makers of the play still knew her as—had conned her way into trusting twin Regina's place to steal all the valuables herself.

She learned how as far as Romulus knew, her months living in Brillant were a reign of terror, spent associating with terrorists and criminals, culminating in the destruction of the governor's fortress and the cold-blooded murder of beloved Prince Gosse; not the bully and braggart Holly had known, but a brave, virtuous wolf of the people.

She learned how as far as Romulus knew, Candida was the villain of the story, and nothing more.

Holly returned to the small room she and Kanti rented a few streets down from the Mechanist's workshop warehouse, the food heavy as lead in her belly. She undressed and fell onto the bed, staring alone at the ceiling for a long while and remembering the words Morgana le Fay had spoken to her, once upon a time.

"No, no, you're right!" said Morgana, following after Candida, tenderly cupping her muzzle in her hands. "You're right. You never had a choice, in those days. Neither did I. We all get to make so few real choices throughout our lives, you see. We are all beholden to the whims and choices of the world around us, how the world perceives us! It doesn't matter our choices or our actions, you and I will always be the traitors, the murderers, the fools, the monsters! The only freedom, the only true choice, is to embrace this! Come with me!"

Eventually, when the light coming in through the frosted window was nearly gone and the room sat in twilight, the door opened and Kanti slipped in, pausing startled at the sight of Holly on the bed. "Holls, what," the black Wolf-Lord began, stopping quickly as she seemed to notice something in the gaze Holly turned her way. She closed the door behind her, then undressed, body dark and beautiful in the twilight, the sharpest of contrasts to white-furred Holly.

Holly closed her eyes as the bed creaked, a soft hitch in her breath as warm hands massaged through the thick fur and crooked scars of belly and shoulders and sides, warm hands, practiced hands. Kanti smelled of fur and hard work, a strange and enticing scent all its own. "G-God," Holly managed.

"What happened?" asked Kanti.

Holly bit her bottom lip. Her claws dug into the sheets of the bed as Kanti's massage found muscle kinks Holly hadn't even noticed. "I . . . I sssaw the play. Abo-o-out m-me. About my e-e-evil—"

"Propaganda nonsense," said Kanti. She leaned in upon Holly, kissing and nipping across Holly's lips and along her throat. Her last words before the kiss grew deeper, became MORE, were "Don't think about it, my darling. That's an order."

Hands twining through Kanti's mess of hair, Holly readily gave herself to the command.

***

Strange dreams came to Holly as she slept, substantial as the waking flesh. There was a broad valley, and she lived in the valley. A forest, its trees and their leaves as brilliant red as her hair. The forest spread, turned into fire. A Wolf-Lord stepped out of the flames, black-furred top to bottom, a unicorn horn sprouting from their head like bone. Their maw opened wide, wider, swallowing everything. A crash of thunder—

Holly jerked awake, almost shouted her alarm, strangled it for the sake of the morning's peace. She closed her eyes again, not for long, breathed deep as she clutched the bedding beneath her and grounded herself. Somewhere nearby, a gryphon sang low, almost mournful. Farther away, Holly caught the vague tones of workers sliding up awnings and readying their shops for the break of day. By the light coming in through the window, and by the particular chill in the air, she guessed it to be early, but not so early as to fall back asleep. The bed was cold and empty except for her.

A messily scrawled note waited on Holly's clothes beside the bed. In the light of the window, she recognized Kanti's handwriting.

"Gone early to help the Mechanist. With luck, will be ready to leave by noon. Ordered breakfast to be brought to you at the seventh bell. You might keep to the room for safety.

"We will save Shun & Nessa. We will save Eishaven. You are a hero. Love, Kanti."

"Love, Kanti," Holly repeated aloud. The words made her feel like smiling, despite everything else. Against such words, the thoughts of her country-wolves mattered little.

**

The air was frigid and the sky white-grey with clouds when noon came and Holly stepped out of the tavern. All around was quiet. Other Wolf-Lords kept their heads down and hurried on their way wherever Holly glanced. Doors slammed shut and shutters rolled down.

Holly moved one intersection in the opposite direction of her brief walk back to the Mechanist's workshop, found the streets there as deserted as those behind her. Nothing moved but the creaky swing of a few lanterns strung over the street and a dusting of snow caught in the whispering wind. For a moment, Holly felt transported back home to the growing desolation of Eishaven.

"CANDIDA!"

Something passed through Holly at the sound of her old name spoken in her own voice, a frightened and frightening energy which straightened her back and set her heart racing. She turned the way she had come, saw an achingly familiar Wolf-Lord coming to a stop a few yards down the street, gold armor gleaming, white cape billowing like a hero out of legend. "Regina."

The twins stood opposed in silence for a long stretch of seconds, looking each other over and sizing each other up. A paltry pinch of time to encompass the years which had come to separate those who had once been inseparable, impossible to take in all the triumphs and heartbreaks, the scars born and the vistas reached. Holly noticed how Regina's gaze lingered where Holly's sword should have hung and spoke before anything could be said about it. "It is good to see you again, Regina. Despite everything. I missed you."

For a moment, Regina's gaze softened. Only for a moment, a glimpse of sunlight past drifting, sky-encompassing storm clouds. "Do you expect me to have missed you? Three years you've been gone, and all our family can see when they look at me is YOU! Three years of Gosse's blood on my hands for having your face! Gosse! Our baby sibling! Dead because of you!"

Holly flinched away. She looked down at the snowflakes gathering on the pitted stone street, her own hands balling at her sides as she thought about Gosse, horrid, brutal, villainous Gosse for the first time in years.

Gosse grabbed her by her shoulders, bruise-hard, their smile turning soft as poison-drenched silk. Candida froze at the touch, fur standing on end, whimpered as their hands slid down her arms, her sides, her belly, appraising as they might a choice wyvern for sale. "All the scars I remember, still there no matter what you dress over them. I wonder if someone pays the fox there to ignore them. You've put on weight, too. Before long you'll be fat and ugly. Sad."

. . .

Gosse, grinning, twirled their sword almost lazily, struck once to leave a bloody cut up Candida's right cheek, her grunt of pain drawing another giggle from them. They swiped again, Candida yelping at the white-hot agony of her left ear's top half-inch getting cut away, her cry dying in her throat as Gosse next held the tip of their sword beneath Candida's chin, forcing her head up to look them in the eyes. It hurt, horribly, Candida's mind screaming for her to look away to anywhere else, Gosse seeming to know this as they stared down at her with a moonlit sickle smile, the smile of a scythe mid-swing for the barley.

. . .

"I HATE YOU!"

Gosse . . . charged and leapt at Candida, sword raised high, eyes ablaze. "HATE HATE HATE—"

"I think you and I remember two very different Wolf-Lords," said Holly. Her left hand came up, found her left ear, a half-inch shorter than it had been when last the twins met. "They were out of control. They were going to kill me and people I loved. People I still love."

"People you still love?" asked Regina, drawing their sword but leaving it hanging at their side for the moment. "Am I still counted among that prestigious number, or is it the domain now of foreigners and criminals like those gryphons you fled with?"

Holly eyed her twin's white sword warily. She reached for the hilt of her own sword, remembered again it was gone, and turned her thoughts instead to flight. But Regina stood between her and the way she needed to go. "They never had a hope beneath laws looking to make them slaves. I had to do something."

Regina's gaze turned down, head shaking, bouncing the flat of their blade against the palm of their hand. They looked back up at Holly, their shoulders settling. "As do I. You have one chance. Wherever it is you've been hiding these past three years, go back. Now. While you still can."

"But I cannot," said Holly. She swallowed, drew the parrying dagger she kept on her left hip instead, held it straight and ready between them. "I will not go back. I will not stop. You cannot make me."

"Yes I can!" snapped Regina, their full anger finally bursting to the surface. They lunged, stabbing for Holly's throat.

Holly skipped back, slashed up, knocked the attack away.

Regina pressed on, turned her knocked-aside stab into a spin and swing.

Holly stepped into the arc of the swing, angling her dagger down not to block, but to graze her twin's right bicep as their slash went harmlessly past.

Regina hissed, darted back and out of reach. They glanced down and watched the red cloth darken, snapped back to Holly. "First blood," they noted, nodding in recognition.

"The last blood, please!" begged Holly. "I do not want—"

Regina lunged again. Holly reflexively raised her dagger to knock the attack aside, realized the first strike was a feint a moment too late to block or dodge away from the long slice to her right thigh. "Gah!"

Regina kept onward, marching forward with a stab, a stab, a narrow slice. Holly backpedaled, blocked the first, took the second in a shallow groove through her left shoulder, knocked aside the narrow slice with a backhand. Regina, overextended, lost their grip, their sword tumbling away into the snow.

Holly swung her dagger wide, a blind, clumsy slash which Regina allowed to clatter harmlessly against the side of their cuirass. Before Holly could draw away,

Regina then pinned the blade to their side with their arm, yanked Holly forward, and latched their jaws over her throat.

"ACK! Grlk!" Holly choked in her panic, felt her twin's fangs piercing through her flesh, deeper, into the muscle, sending the blood gushing down her throat and chest. She fell backward, her back hitting hard against a wall, one hand clawing at Regina's eyes and muzzle to make them let go, the other desperately pulling at her pinned weapon.

A moment passed. The edges of Holly's vision crisped black. Out of breath, every gasp accompanied by the taste of blood gurgling up her torn throat and out past her lips, she fell from the wall to the ground. The movement allowed, for the briefest of moments, a leg to wedge between her and Regina, foot planted in the other Wolf-Lord's gut.

Holly pushed. Regina, snarling, slowly drew back to the thick sound of tearing flesh, their teeth and muzzle bloodied and foaming. The cold air was torment against Candida's ruined throat. She fought past the pain and breathed deep, used the extra space to free her dagger and press the blade to Regina's throat.

The next moment lasted for hours. Both twins close, Regina's eyes fountains of rage and loathing, Holly's eyes hot with tears, hurting worse than her chewed-raw throat. She pressed her blade harder, a moment's lapse in her temper all which stood between life and death—

A shadow fell over the scene, a torrent of heated air scattering the surrounding snow. Regina, startled, jerked away from the blade and looked up at the blocky troop carrier hovering over the scene, allowing Holly enough lull to shove them the rest of the way off.

The rear of the air-yacht lowered into a ramp, Kanti hurrying out onto it to look down at the pair. "Holly!"

Escape loomed within reach. Coughing as her throat began the slow, clumsy process of healing itself, Holly lurched over and up onto her feet, felt her personal magic pulsing inside, rushing and rolling like the vicious edges of a vast whirlpool. She watched her twin clamber back up, heard the sudden thunder as a dozen Wolf-Lord soldiers bearing the colors of Romulus stormed onto the scene, a few taking potshots at Kanti and the hovering troop carrier with their steam rifles, most moving to surround Holly and block all avenues of escape.

"Take her alive!" screamed Regina.

Holly bit down her panic and seized at her magic, pulling the sizzling, burning power up, up, up, and then out and away from her with a clenched fist and a furious wave of her arm. "BACK OFF!"

The attack was crude, not even worthy to be called a spell, child's play in the shadow of great sorceresses like Morgana le Fay, but nonetheless effective. The power burst from Holly like a tidal shock, sending the soldiers toppling and their weapons scattering, throwing Regina through the storefront behind them, shattering the wood and stone and glass of the surrounding buildings. The frozen earth itself cracked at Holly's feet, and overhead the troop carrier wobbled, threatening to crash.

Kanti screamed, then disappeared back into the airship. After a moment it first steadied, then lowered closer to the ground, wedging itself between the buildings. Kanti appeared again at the rear ramp, on her knees with an arm held out for Holly. "Hurry!"

Far from hurrying, Holly felt moments away from collapsing after the sudden drain of power. She staggered, caught herself against a lamppost, looked to the greying darkness of the store her twin had disappeared into. She saw no signs of movement, coughed, pushed herself off the cold metal to stand free. She had to jump to reach Kanti's hand, and even when she had it, she nearly slipped free with the slickness of her bloodied hands until the other Wolf-Lord grabbed at Holly's elbow with her other hand and pulled.

A moment where it seemed Holly's weight might drag Kanti off the ramp. Then Holly lay on her back on the troop carrier's metal floor. The boarding ramp lifted back up into the air-yacht's rear, forcing her to roll deeper inside and cutting off Regina's shouts for the soldiers to "Get the wyverns!" The floor of the air-yacht lurched, carrying a strange sensation of unseen but incredible speed to Holly's mind, a tingle in the air and a difficulty to get back to her feet.

"Oh God," said Kanti. She stood staring aghast at Holly, gaze roaming across the various injuries Regina had left her with, returning again and again to her bloodied and raw throat.

"Be fine," Holly said, wincing as each word brought another wave of pain, her voice itself barely a whisper. Sheathing her dagger, she leaned against the ship's inner hull, coughed again, reached up to feel her throat. The stab to her shoulder and slice to her thigh were made with Lunar Steel and needed to be bandaged, would need to be allowed to heal at their own pace. Her torn throat, untouched by Lunar Steel, could be left to her meager Wolf-Lord healing factor . . . meager, impotent, unreliable. Holly felt the bleeding stop. Beneath the blood, scar tissue, messy sprawls of it, inside and out. It didn't seem to be hampering her ability to breathe, not yet, but . . .

"That was Regina?" asked Kanti, still staring at Holly with wide eyes, her voice fearful. "Your twin? That was 'the nice one' who just bit your throat out?"

"Not . . . bitten out," Holly defended, though each word spoken was a battle

Before either could say more, the sound of bullets pinging off the armored hull of the troop carrier caught their ears. Kanti swore and hurried away to the other end of the craft, falling into a leather-backed chair to begin working a number of levers and pedals. Past her, the whole front of the craft seemed made of paneled glass extending two or three feet into ceiling and floor, allowing a limited glimpse at what was above and below them. At present, they were speeding over Quicken Bay toward the waterfront.

With Kanti busy saving their lives, Holly took the brief moment of respite to take in her surroundings. The ship, which she was beginning to suspect was no mere Avalon troop carrier, was wide, long, and barren. Grated metal floors and ceiling, behind which were nestled brightly glowing crystals for lighting. The walls were marked in unfamiliar lettering, but scrawled alongside them were translations for what cargo or equipment went where. Weapons, too, were mounted along the walls, steam rifles and crystal lancers, and beneath them stacks of spell charge packs bound tightly together in nets.

"Up front," darling," Kanti called back to her. "You'll want something to hang onto for what's coming next."

Holly hurried up to the front of the craft, staggering toward the end to slump against the metal wall to Kanti's right. To her confusion, the ship was angled to send them plowing into the ocean still some distance below. "What?"

"It'll be alright in a moment, darling, just hold on." Kanti pulled a ceiling-mounted lever, filling the craft with the hiss of seals and clank of armor plating folding in. Her hand then found Holly's, who was for once grateful of the unasked-for touch as the craft dove downward.

The craft shook as they hit the water and plunged beneath. Metal groaned, somewhere, and the crystal lights flickered alarmingly for a moment. Holly thought against her will of being trapped in a dark metal box in the middle of the ocean, living only as long as the air held out. But seconds passed, and then a minute, and nothing went catastrophically wrong. Holly slowly relaxed. She managed a smile and a whispered "Brilliant."

"Worth every coin," Kanti agreed. They remained holding hands as the craft levelled off in the water. They looked out to the dim, swirling world beyond the troop carrier's glass, lit only barely by the ship's own lights. As tired as she was, and as much as her wounds from fighting Regina were truly starting to hurt, the eeriness of the scene was undeniable to Holly. "Creepy. How . . . find way?"

"A sophisticated, unbearably complicated, array of tracking, compass, and sonar spells," said Kanti. The black Wolf-Lord tapped three glowing crystals in the board before her, locked a control spar into place, and then stood and turned to cup Holly's cheeks, eyes on the new mess of scars and patchwork fur consuming the whole front of her neck. "Ohhh . . . Holly . . ."

"Not . . . so bad," croaked Holly, the loudest she could manage. She took her lover's hands in her own and moved them down to the long cut in her thigh, only now beginning to clot. "Here, though . . ."

"Crap, yeah. Come on, there's a medical kit over here. Laura taught me a thing or two, let's get you bandaged up. The blockade runner will keep itself for a little while . . ."

CHAPTER SIX

Astride their wyvern, Regina watched the last ripples from the troop carrier's unexpected dive smooth away to nothing. They frowned, clenched the reins in their hands as they scanned the horizon, Seconds passed into minutes and no more disturbances wrought the waters, no sign of their sister fleeing the oceans the way she had fled the skies. No mere desperation tactic, then. She could be a mile away already, well beyond Regina's grasp.

"Captain," said Regina, looking to one of the surrounding soldiers. "Take your wolves and search the town. Find out what the fugitive was doing there, how long she'd been there, who she spoke to. Everything. You will be well-compensated for sending this information straight to me first, you understand."

"At your command, my general," said the grey-furred Wolf-Lord. They signaled for their wyvern-riders to form back up, and then looked back at Regina. "Where will you be heading in the meantime?"

"Cairn Romulus," said Regina. The thought sickened them. They wished there was a way, any way at all, they could have dealt with this Candida situation on their own, apprehend her and throw her back out to wherever she had been hiding the past three years, to be forgotten all over again. But events were already out of control. They had gone in hot, emotional, reckless, and now it was all out in the open.

Not sparing another word for their soldiers, Regina turned their wyvern to the south, and flew.

Time passed, an hour slipping away unnoticed. Trusting the wyvern, Scattershot, to know the way home, Regina sat tall and straight in their saddle and thought. With the heat of the moment behind them, they found themselves remembering . . . they hesitated to call them better days. Early days of growing up together, winter childhoods in the castle library, reading books or scouring old maps of all the amazing places they could travel and see when they were older, free of Celeste's iron grip. Summer nights sleeping out on one castle tower or another, watching the stars, mapping constellations and wondering how different they might be in ancestral Heraldale.

Then the years passed and Candida— a cruel name—was treated by the rest less and less a sister, a daughter, more and more a servant. Help feed the wyverns. Help distribute the laundry. Go tend the garden, go clean the stalls, go stand against that wall, hold that shield, don't dare move, Gosse needs to practice their aim. And Regina, too happy to not be in their sister's place, had said nothing about any of it, not to Celeste, not where it could have done any good.

And then, the events of three years before. The day Regina decided to help their sister, to insist they and Candida covertly switch places to show her and everyone else how capable she could be.

Disaster.

Tragedy.

Consequences.

Regina believed what Candida had said about Gosse. Aside from Celeste, Gosse had always been Candida's most vicious and consistent tormentor, their death almost certainly self-defense. Justified, however much it hurt. And if Regina had been there in Brillant, those fateful days of doom, to act as always a shield and bulwark against the worst . . .

Oh Toqeph, thought Regina, still tasting Candida's blood on their muzzle, dried and sickening. How had they reached this point?

A low screech from Scattershot tore Regina from their thoughts. They looked around and found they now flew through the black mountains of southern Romulus, where Cairn Romulus, the seat of the nation's royal power, sat content. Ahead, Regina saw the old castle nestled against its mountain, black stone and white snow, long banners of red and gold breeze-battered atop its many towers.

A trio of wyverns flew from the mountain castle to meet them. On two of them Regina caught the glint of armor and steam rifles. The third, in the lead, bore no armor or weapons, only a feminine Wolf-Lord of black fur, dressed in a vicious crimson suit of the old military fashion, sharp angles and high collars.

Without word from either party, Caelestis left their guards and flew beside Regina. They landed their wyverns in the central courtyard a fair distance apart, dismounted. Gazes met. Hackles were raised as they drew near, then began to circle and size each other up. One full rotation brought them back to their starting positions. A low growl from each—

Then Caelestis smiled and strode forward, a hand taking Regina's shoulder as foreheads pressed together in wordless familiar affection. Much of the tension fled Regina and they allowed themself to at least marginally relax for the first time since the campaigns to quell the civil unrest began.

"You are back," said Caelestis, almost a whisper. They parted, hands remaining on shoulders as the elder sibling pinned Regina down with a stare. "Is it true? You were here and gone so quickly, returning from Denning, I didn't even get the chance to see you. Does Celeste speak truly?"

Regina nodded, a storm in their breast. Caelestis swallowed, gestured to their own muzzle. "The blood . . ."

"It's Candida's," said Regina, and then, seeing the look on Caelestis's face, added "she got away. It was a close call."

"It won't be next time, though," said Caelestis. They looked away, to the grand doors into the grand castle, muzzle twisting as their smile turned small and mean. "Next time you'll get the traitor. Drag her ragged and pleading back here. Then we can start avenging Gosse, for as long and as thoroughly as we want."

The storm in Regina's chest birthed lightning at such talk. She asked "Where's Celeste?"

"In the throne room," answered Caelestis, dropping their hand as their guards rejoined them at last and backing away, nodding to the doors. "With guests."

***

In Cairn Romulus, in accord with ancient Wolf-Lord traditions, there were two throne rooms. In the public, surface-side of the castle, the throne room was light and airy, all stained-glass windows and polished marble walls with filigree of gold and pearl. Visitors went there. Acquaintances. The brave, kindly face.

Guests, however, went to the second throne room, buried deep beneath the castle and accessible only via a pair of secret tunnels and certain properly configured enchanted teleport pads. It was high-ceilinged and dark but for braziers placed near to the tall-backed throne, the shadows enveloping the outer edges of the room hiding always the exact number and arrangement of guards. It was here Queen Celeste, and the ruling monarch of Romulus for generations past, kept their most secret and deadly councils. It was here where fates were decided.

Regina teleported into the throne room via a spell pad, blinked and waited for several seconds as their eyes adjusted to the sudden change in lighting. Once adjusted, Regina blinked again, still unsure of what they saw.

Across the room from them, Queen Celeste sat tall and regal on their throne. Feminine as per their habit, a lush crimson dress to contrast their snow-white fur and waist-length hair, sleeveless, matching fingerless gloves reaching up past their elbows. Over it all a deep gold cloak, metallic in texture, glimmering with the ever-ready presence of Celeste's Lightning Elemental.

To Regina's passing shock, they sat in easy audience with a unicorn mare. Tall, inarguably a giant among unicorns, but slender, unnaturally so, her rigid stance and raised horn giving Regina the impression of a blade, a long blade of ivory made to slip between armor plates and pierce lungs or hearts. And the mare was white, unyieldingly so, with a stormy grey mane and tail and hooves which looked forged from silver.

Regina began to stride forward, a hand moving to grip their sword hilt, ready to draw, a call of greeting—or warning—on their muzzle. Then the mare turned to look their way, head tilted at an inquisitive angle, and Regina's stride faltered, their grip on their sword grew slack, and the words died in their muzzle. The strange unicorn's eyes were not unicorn eyes. They were gems, the most startling, exquisite star sapphires. They were unlike any eyes Regina had ever seen.

"The deliveries will be made as planned," said Celeste, perched upon their throne like a hungering carrion bird. "Including the choicest of fresh bodies for your needs. Your payment is considered acceptable . . . le Fay."

The strange unicorn mare looked away from Regina and back to Celeste. She bowed her head once, the tap of her horn tip ringing through the throne room like a clear crystal bell. As she rose, her horn shimmered, and her body dissolved into a mist of miniscule crystals, diamonds, each swiftly popping like bubbles until nothing remained to show the unicorn mare had ever been there.

Celeste huffed. "She's always been such a showoff."

Several seconds passed. Regina shook away their daze and strode forward again, stopping when they were even with where the unicorn had stood and well within their parent's range of attention. Regina looked from the empty space up to Celeste, frowned with confusion. "That was—"

"For the purposes of that specific body," said Celeste, relaxing back in their throne, "that was Lord Beauty. A Lord of the Avalon Empire. Our main window into the goings-on of old Heraldale.

"But that is all irrelevant," the queen continued, leaning forward again. "You are injured. Your vision, then, it was true?"

"It was, my queen," said Regina, swallowing their countless other questions for another day and kneeling to show proper respect. "My fugitive twin, Candida, has returned to the lands of the Wolf-Lords. I fought her in Quicken Bay."

"And is the foul wolf dead? Is our national pride restored?"

Regina hesitated for a moment before shaking their head. "No. She escaped, my queen."

A long silence, kept from totality by the crackle of the flames in the braziers and the light patter of someone pacing in the surrounding shadows, and then "How."

"I almost had her," said Regina, struggling to keep any defensiveness out of their voice. "But she has begun to harness magic. I was caught by surprise. Before I could recover, she escaped in an Imperial troop carrier with, I believe, Captain Blackbird." Regina debated whether or not to bring up the troop carrier disappearing into the ocean like a fish, decided not. They couldn't explain why.

Celeste's frown grew. They glanced once to the nearby darkness. Stood. Strode down the steps leading up to their throne and began to circle Regina, their long claws sparkling now with lightning dancing among them. "Escaped. Can you tell me where the . . . rotten piece of irritant mold is going? Can you tell me where she's been hiding these three years? Can you tell me anything I couldn't learn from any random soldier grabbed off the streets of Quicken Bay!?"

Regina felt the charge in the air, remembered the helpless pain of being struck by their parent's lightning in a moment of rage. It had happened before, only twice. When Regina's deception the night Candida first fled the castle had been found out, and months later, when the news came of Gosse's death and Candida's second escape. "I, I didn't give her much chance to talk, my parent. I didn't want to risk being swayed by her. But she did seem desperate, as if whatever drove her was a matter of life and death."

"Good," said Celeste. They stopped their circling at the steps to their throne again, gaze locked away from Regina and into the shadows. "I want her desperate. I want her in pain. I want her here in chains, beaten and broken, and whatever hopes she had for the future in utter ruin."

"And she shall be," said Regina, the words burning poison in their mouth. "I will leave at once, put out an alert to all the major cities and overseen routes, pursue every lead I find—"

"Not alone."

Regina looked up, frowned. Celeste ascended the steps to their throne, sat, beckoned with one hand to the darkness. Regina startled as a kitsune stepped into view, his coat a dull red, his left eye hidden beneath a black patch, his clothes the somber grey samue work robes of the Nameless Order. Five tails swished through the air behind him, and at his belt hung a katana of absurd length.

"Some remain friends of Romulus, despite the slander Candida caused to be heaped upon us." Celeste's voice took on the official tones of their role as head of state. "Allow me to introduce you to the Butcher of the Nameless Order. Considering the fugitive Candida's suspected involvement with the murder of a monk of the Nameless Order in Brillant three years ago, and her continued involvement with a deserter of the Nameless Order, he has generously offered to assist in bringing her to justice today."

Muzzle splitting wide in a hideous grin, Butcher drew the first several inches of his katana from its sheath, the blade the unmistakable color of polished silver. "I'm going to find yer dirty twin, and I'm gonna behead her, and then I'm gonna kick her wee stupid head down the highest hill I can find! And then I'll do it again from atop an even higher hill! AND SHE WILL RUE THE DAY SHE EVER MET THE INCREDIBLE BUTCHER! KAHAHAHAHAHA!"

Regina stared. Raised an eyebrow their parent's way. Turned and stared at the strange kitsune a moment more. "Why are you talking like that?"

Butcher blinked, sheathed his sword before stepping closer. "Talking like what, ye wee ninny wolf?"

"Like that," said Regina, standing up from her respectful kneel. "That accent. You're talking with a unicorn accent. Why."

"Bah!" went the kitsune, rolling his one visible eye. "I don't know what yer going on about, and I haven't the time to decipher through yer weird wolfy wiles. Come on, come on, lean down and give me a bit o' that muzzle!"

Regina's hand found their sword hilt again, gripping it tight as she stepped toward the clearly insane kitsune with every ounce of her size and authority. "You want WHAT, you crazy little—"

The kitsune, Butcher, reached out and dragged a cloth across Regina's muzzle. It came back dirty with red, reminding Regina again of how close they had come already to snuffing their twin's life out.

"Blood has history," said Butcher, his strange accent growing subdued as he held the bloodied cloth up in the palm of one hand. The other reached out, fire curling over the fingers as they danced over the cloth. As Regina watched, reluctantly fascinated, magic-laden smoke rose from the remnants of blood, swirling in the air in sync with the fingers. "Blood has memory. When trying to find where yer prey is going, a good place to start is where they've been."

The blood smoke coalesced, flattened, solidified into a thin, flat surface, like rust-colored ice upon a frozen pond. Within, they saw a sprawling, yet cluttered port town, with gryphons in the skies and trees to the east and west. Regina, though they had never seen the town in person, recognized it from descriptions in official reports. "Eishaven."

"And the hunt is on," growled Butcher, and he laughed again.

CHAPTER SEVEN

The submersible troop carrier carried little distraction. Once the spell systems were functioning and their course set, Kanti didn't even need to remain at the controls, instead retreating to the rear of the craft, where she proceeded, with the ease of long practice, to set up a hammock hanging from the ceiling in which to read a book.

Holly remained slumped against the wall near the front of the troop carrier, her wounds to her shoulder and leg cleaned and expertly bandaged, her eyes remaining out the forward glass to the watery world beyond, watching the dark ocean depths with an almost slack-jawed fascination. Near the start of the journey, as a full sense of safety settled in and Holly could fully appreciate whole new experience the pair of them were sharing, a song came to her, one taught to her by Kurt and other members of his family, an old and haunting melody made more-so b by the whispering rasp her voice had become.

"The ocean calls, oh child,
Its waves crowned with white.
Large as the sky and twice as wild,
Mysterious as the night.
"Listen close as the waves break,
Listen well, oh child of mine.
Much good does the ocean make
In the sunlight when it shines.
"Every river to the ocean goes
And every winding stream.
It takes the world's fears and woes
Like an ever-living dream.
"Heed not the ocean, oh child,
Despite its waves so bright.
Many a soul has surface beguiled
To depths filled with Wights."

Out in the inky waters, barely lit by the lights of the troop carrier, Holly didn't see any wights, unless they appeared only in the form of sea creatures. She caught glimpses of fish darting past quick as a flash. Eels, bone-white and languid. Once, an hour and a half into the journey, the currents beyond the ship shifted and they found themselves spearing through a vast field of jellyfish, ghostly pinks and translucent blues emerging from and disappearing back into the darkness for as far as the eye could see. It had been like magic.

Soon after, they heard the singing. Holly knew it from weeks spent whale-watching on boats, the great creatures perhaps mistaking the troop carrier briefly for one of their own. But though she had heard whales sing before, the song took on strange new tones beneath the waves, heard echoing through the metal hull. She didn't like it.

"My darling," said Kanti, snapping Holly from her thoughts as the other Wolf-Lord loudly turned a page in her book, "do you think you could cease that infernal tapping, that ever-ceaseless gentle rapping, rapping on my airship floor? I ask you this, and nothing more."

Holly looked down, jerking her left hand from the grated metal surface. Her cheeks flushed as she looked back to Kanti, saw her looking Holly's way with one eyebrow raised. Before she could remember Shun's teachings "I'm sorry. Sorry. I didn't mean to. Sorry."

Kanti winced, set her book aside, rolled up and off her hammock. She rejoined Holly before the glass, sitting cross-legged and reaching out to the culprit hand. "May I?"

Holly considered for a moment. "Yes," she whispered, in her new, husky croak.

Kanti took the hand in her own, did little things which brought a quirk of a smile to Holly's muzzle, stroking the back of the hand, turning it over to stroke along the palm and each finger, as if to take stock of all the scars. "I'll need to get you a new sword when we reach the university. Or perhaps a full suit of armor. A good, long staff, long and light, plenty of reach. Big, Lunar Steel gauntlets for punching and catching swords. Tell me about Regina. Please."

"Regina?"

"I picked up a few things secondhand from Laura, those many months she was working for me in Carcosa. A few more things from our dearly beloved Shun. It's not hard to make guesses when you care enough, darling. She was the only one in your family to treat you decently, right? Like family should?"

"They," corrected Holly, struggling to get her voice over a whisper, to ignore the rising tang of blood somewhere deep in her throat. "Yes. Thought world of them. Could only. Be . . . marred reflection. But fled castle. Saw real world. Shun. Laura. Kurt. Family . . . cruelties. Country cruelties. Regina complicit. Wholly complicit."

"Well, you're not wrong," said Kanti, shrugging. "But that doesn't mean their love for you was always a lie, you know. They could have come right up behind you and stabbed you in the back before you ever knew they were there, but they didn't. They called out to you. That has to count for something."

"Yes," whispered Holly. She sat up straighter, pulled her hand free. "She good wolf. I'm—"

"No, no, you're right!" said Morgana, following after Candida, tenderly cupping her muzzle in her hands. "You're right. You never had a choice, in those days. Neither did I. We all get to make so few real choices throughout our lives, you see. We are all beholden to the whims and choices of the world around us, how the world perceives us! It doesn't matter our choices or our actions, you and I will always be the traitors, the murderers, the fools, the monsters! The only freedom, the only true choice, is to embrace this! Come with me!"

She stopped, but even she could see the damage had been done. Kanti, frowning, cupped Holly's cheek. "I knew it. It's that play, then, the one you saw the kitsune putting on."

"Old thought," whispered Holly, the best defense she could muster. It was even true. An old ghost of how she had once wholeheartedly thought of herself, dead but still rattling its chains somewhere in the back of her head. Kept there, perhaps, by the words of Morgana, the Wolf-Lord who had fathered her and Regina in secret. No more, but no less either.

***

Much more time passed before either spoke again. Kanti, returned to the control chair and gaze forward, asked without looking "What do you know about Akela?"

Holly, half-asleep, blinked, yawned, pulled herself up to give her stiffening body a stretch. "Akela," she whispered. "Largest realm after Romulus. Most populous. Romulus, abs—kack—absolute monarchy. Fenris, republic. Tabaqui, sisssssster nation, con . . . constitutional monarchy. Akela ruled council of 12, 12 richest. Most powerful. Mostly Wolf-Lords and Jackals. Proud, fierce, not war-like. A renowned university. Maurus attended. Students, craftsmen, scholars. Cult of Burning King strong foothold."

Kanti sighed, sounding like she had perhaps already known this last piece of information. "Those loons are the last thing we need right now."

Holly waved a hand in vague distress, unable to speak aloud the vast words she held on the subject. The Wolf-Lords and kin shared a complicated relationship to the Burning King. They sided with the gryphons, unicorns, and dragons at the discovery of his crimes and his resultant exile, but many through the following millennia thought this a mistake, thought this left them open to the war which drove them from Heraldale. "Of all wolves, only Akela supported Queen Morgause's want join Burning King. Revenge Heraldale."

"Where do you stand on that?"

"Burning King stole magic," whispered Holly, swallowing the thick blood back down. "Try imagine? No magic, remembering only in stories . . ."

Kanti frowned. "Most Wolf-Lords can't do magic."

"Morgana le Fay," whispered Holly. She raised a hand, palm up, clenched it into a fist as she felt her personal magic, sparked to greater strength by the brush with the Eternal Flames at Morgana's castle, rise briefly again to the surface, sharp with the smell of ozone. She remembered the little magics she had cast in the year since, small acts of levitating objects, of starting fires in the hearth or at the stove. She remembered the bone-breaking burst of magic she had cast from herself to escape from Regina and their soldiers. "Certain others . . ."

A small off-white crystal orb, easy to overlook where it floated untouched near the ceiling of the troop carrier, loosed a soft tolling and began to glow a light blue. Kanti went "Aha!" and disabled the guidance spells. The black-furred Wolf-Lord grinned with old excitement, manipulating the control spires with a deftness Holly quickly found dizzying. "Going up now, darling. The waters ahead are too shallow for this ugly tug. Hold on to your stomach, regret every bite of food you've ever taken, and get ready for a view to die for!"

"But I'm not ready to die!" whispered Holly as the troop carrier rose. They burst from the waters and suddenly light, blinding light, warm and welcoming in ways the crystal lights of the troop carrier weren't. After hours in the ocean gloom, Holly winced from the light, blinked until her sight adjusted. Looking ahead through the glass, she gasped.

In the ancient days, when building above-ground rather than deep into the earth, Wolf-Lords had preferred the grand solidity of pyramids. It seemed to Holly a remnant of this had survived near to the modern era. The land she saw before her as the troop carrier flew a leisurely approach, a large peninsular outcropping from the main of the island, was dominated by a vast city rolling with the dip and curve of the land. Smaller, block buildings of white stone were predominant, sweeping down toward the ports and beaches. Scattered through them were taller structures, almost barrels, flat-roofed and decorated with columns of a red stone. At the farthest tip of the peninsula sat the greatest of these temples, a pair of them, surrounded by tall walls and connected by many bridges. Within the walls were also other, smaller buildings, long halls and steepled towers of grey stone, adorned with statues of Jackals and Wolf-Lords in billowing robes.

"Behold," said Kanti, the troop carrier flying over the shoreline and its clustered buildings, heading toward the grand buildings at the city's peak. "Nagagram. And before us, the University of the Starpoint. If we can't find the help we need here . . . well, I can't imagine not being able to find the help we need here."

"Hope so," whispered Holly. She clasped her hands before her heart, thought of what Shun might have said, seeing all she was seeing.

"Finally, a place not covered year-round in snow!"

The thought made Holly smile.

Down below, the crowds walking the streets were Jackals and Wolf-Lords for the most part, though kitsune were not unseen. Many watched their coming from the walls of the University, causing a stir of nervousness in Holly. "Will Romulus troubles follow us here?"

"Hard to imagine," answered Kanti, the black Wolf-Lord's voice the perfect mask of joviality. But then, less certainly, "at least, not until we're done and gone. Akela has been one of the most vocal against the crimes of Romulus. If they find out you're here, I might worry more about getting flooded with invites to dinners among the ruling families, rather than threats from

Romulus. They would try to use you to further their own political ambitions, and failing that, probably push to have you thrown from the country as a citizen of Romulus."

"You are not calming my nerves."

"Sorry. Worst comes to worst, I'm friends with the leader of the university, which traditionally enjoys vast independence from the Akela government. You will be safe here, darling."

Holly wanted to believe this.

Soon, Kanti landed the troop carrier in a small clearing ringed with bright red royal poincianas, near the base of the northernmost of the two grand temples. She powered everything down, then led the way down the ramp and out onto the grassy field with an easy, relaxed stride.

A tall, creamy-furred Jackal stood waiting for them, arms folded behind her and well-groomed tail batting the ground, stirring the folds of her maroon sari. Two Wolf-Lords flanked her, unremarkable but for the Fenris-style short, blunt crystal lancers slung over a shoulder each.

"Guru Rathna!" said Kanti, arms raised as if to make certain their greeting party actually saw them. "Exactly the Jackal I was hoping to see! Haha, the years have been truly kind to you!"

"A bold fool, aren't you?" spoke Guru Rathna, accent so similar to Kanti's, but clipped, her tone cold.

Kanti stopped walking, cheerfulness faltering, replaced with confusion as she pointed at herself. "Who, me?"

"Slimy scoundrel," continued the Jackal, stalking forward when Kanti wouldn't. "Cheater, swindler, as fallen from the paths of learning and righteousness as any dirty soul I've ever met. You've got a lot of guts showing your gorgeous face around here again, after that night by the lake."

Kanti flinched at each insult flung her way, but her ears perked at the end, head tilting with curiosity. "Gorgeous?"

Guru Rathna stopped bare inches from the black Wolf-Lord, hands reaching up to rest on her shoulders. Then she lunged forward, muzzle clamping over Kanti's, and for the next several seconds the pair was engaged in a fierce, breathless wrestling match of a kiss, bodies pressed close and hands . . . wandering.

Holly stared, her face burning with her blush as she watched. Seeing this, and comparing it to the similar ferocity with which Kanti and Shun always enjoyed their embraces, she wondered if this was how she and Kanti looked while kissing. The pattern would fit.

The pair eventually parted, both needed a moment to catch their breath. Grinning, Guru Rathna licked her muzzle before glancing past Kanti at Holly. "And who is your new friend, you incorrigible pirate?"

Standing straight again, Kanti turned and gestured Holly forward. "More than a mere friend, I'm afraid. This tall drink of water here is one of two lovers of mine, Holly. She's wanting to talk with one of your staff here."

"Veda, ma'am," whispered Holly, hobbling forward and giving the Jackal a stiff bow. "If it is no trouble. We are in a terrible hurry."

"My goodness," said Rathna, the Jackal smiling and returning the bow. "Someone finally won this scoundrel's heart. My metaphorical hat is off to you and your third. But that is neither here nor there right now. The universe says that we all always receive what we give, and so I shall help you, and perhaps one day you or someone else will help me. Come along, then, follow me."

Easier said than done, Holly soon found. Rathna's stride was long, and the wound Regina inflicted on Holly's leg slowed her. By the time they had crossed the field and ascended the shallow stairs to the north tower's open entrance, Holly had fallen to the rear of the group, breathing hard and clamping a hand against her leg bandages. She almost called for the group to pause and give her a moment, but Kanti beat her to it, disrobing as she did so.

Before Holly could begin to process what was happening, the black Wolf-Lord transformed into her raven-gryphon form and used one grand wing to half-push, half-scoop Holly off her feet and force her onto Kanti's back. "Wh-whoa! Hey, no, you should not have to—"

"Nonsense," said Kanti, quickening her pace to rejoin Rathna at the group's head. "It's the least I can do for anyone who 'won my heart', hehe."

Holly didn't know how to argue against this, and so she didn't try. It was, after all, a comfy ride.

The halls they walked were mostly empty, a rare Wolf-Lord or Jackal walking by, glancing their way, and then hurrying along with an extra-tight grasp on whatever book or pack of scrolls they were carrying. Looking around, there were more statues of fearsome Jackals lining the deep red walls than there were actual, living people.

"You came during the winter months, said Guru Rantha as explanation, arms folded behind her as she led them up one broad flight of stairs, and then another. "Many of our students and disciples return home to friends and family this time of year, allowing the university to, for a little while at least, revert back to its traditional function as a temple of worship, meditation, and contemplation. With the growing tensions with Romulus, though, I worry that many of those who left will not be able to return, and some who stayed will not be allowed to for much longer. How horrid, for such tragedies to be the way of this world."

Three flights of the broad stairs and a long, shadowed hall brought them to a room of unexpected light. Guru Rathna's guards threw open a heavy pair of carved wood doors, and before them spread library enough to steal Holly's breath away. Long wooden aisles of books and scrolls ran parallel to the doors, half again as tall as her, able to see clear to the other side of the room some many dozens of yards away. More book-laden shelves lined the surrounding walls. On tables sat yet more books, spread scrolls, mounted orbs dark as obsidian or filled with coiling lights. Overhead, the ceiling was all glass, looking out on a perfect blue sky and a merry sun, which alerted Holly to the presence of enchantments at once. She had seen the height of the temple. They were nowhere near the top floor.

"Just wait here a moment," said Guru Rathna.

Before Holly could ask what for, she caught the hurried patter of feet on the gleaming wood floor. A red-furred Wolf-Lord in messy black shirt and pants slid out from the end of a nearby aisle, feet skidding before they managed to catch traction again and turn. The newcomer, who Holly suspected of meeting before despite her general face blindness, nearly dropped the stack of books in their arms, slammed it down on the nearest table, and hurried to stand before the group, gaze catching for a moment before the Wolf-Lord dipped into a bow. "Guru Rantha! I'm so sorry, I didn't know you were coming! Everything must seem a mess here—"

"Everything here looks fine," said Guru Rantha, smiling and motioning the newcomer to rise. "Whatever mess you see is not worth the stress you assign to it, Seraphina. You must learn to see things at their proper size, and no smaller or larger."

"Yes, Guru Rathna," said the Wolf-Lord, Seraphina. Holly watched as they rose from their bow, hardly able to believe her eyes or ears. She remembered a humble farm surrounded by fields of gold, a welcoming family of four happy to give her food, lodging, and clothes as she struggled to find her path. She remembered a beautiful Wolf-Lord her age, desperate to go to university, seeing Holly—still Candida then—off at the train to Brillant with a smile and instructions.

"There you go. Give your ticket to the uniformed wolf at the front there, then take whatever seat suits you. Whatever UNOCCUPIED seat suits you. Enjoy the ride, listen to whatever advice my dads gave you, and assume anything that sounds too good to be true actually IS too good to be true."

Candida blinked. "But you and your family were too good to be true."

Seraphina blinked, blushing as they dragged a hand over their muzzle and eyes. "You are too cute. Just . . . get on the train."

"Seraphina," said Guru Rathna, heedless of Holly's unspoken thoughts as they gestured toward her and Kant. "These are two esteemed guests, and friends. They have come on a matter most urgent in search of Guru Veda. If you would be so kind as to take them to her, I don't think she should be overly busy this time of day."

"Not at all, my teacher," said Seraphina as they bowed again.

Guru Rantha smiled and nodded, turned to look up at Holly. "There you go. You are in good hands now. If you need anything, merely send young Sera here along and I'll see what I can do. Now, unless there is anything else . . ."

"Thank you," said Holly, putting on the smile Shun had shown her. "For everything."

The Jackal accepted the thanks with another bow, then turned and left with her guards. The doors to the library closed. A moment more passed, and then

Seraphina relaxed where they stood, chuckled as they brushed loose strands of hair from their eyes and turned to look at Holly. "Wow, so. Holly, is it? Strange, with your red hair you look so much like this other Wolf-Lord I met years ago. Had a really dumb name. Crotch yeast, or something like that."

Kanti snorted, a sudden, unwanted laugh, quickly stifled, its pain already inflicted. Holly glanced down at the raven-gryphon, sharp, snapped back to Seraphina, put on the false smile she would wear after shows with Shun, when members of the departing crowd came to them with story ideas, or business propositions, or romantic propositions. A smile to dispel annoyances. "Guru Veda, please. URGENT business. Life or death."

The red-furred Wolf-Lord, eyes wide at Holly's smile, Holly's tone, nodded wordlessly and motioned for them to follow as they started around the many towering aisles. Kanti and Holly followed, past the aisles and to another set of doors, smaller and humbler than those before. These doors led into a smaller study, more intimate. Walls and ceiling a polished red wood, stuffy chairs and pillows scattered. Tables laden with more books, older, almost crumbling. A tall fireplace burning in the left-hand wall, large enough for the average Wolf-Lord to step into without having to duck their head, casting the study in a warm, inviting glow.

"Guru Veda?" called out Seraphina to the room at large, remaining near the doorway as Holly and Kanti entered to look curiously around. "Guru Veda, you have visitors. They say it's important?"

"There's nobody here," growled Kanti, eyeing a narrow end table near the fire, covered in a multitude of colored crystals gently floating. "Not unless this alchemist knows an invisibility spe—"

The fire in the hearth billowed out, eye-searing, far enough to startle Holly off Kanti's back. The fires drew into the fireplace, burning almost white now, and then out of the fire strode a Wolf-Lord, short and black-furred, dressed in loose-fitting plain white trousers and a collar-less shirt. Around their neck and across their shoulders lay a white shawl, tasseled at the ends with cords of black.

More attention-grabbing were the clean white bandages wrapped tight around the Wolf-Lord's head, completely covering their eyes. In the relative dimness of the room, Holly felt sure she caught the ghost of a flickering light shining out from beneath the bandages.

"Guests," said the newcomer, voice low and curious. Holly struggled her way back to her feet, leaning against Kanti's side for support. Looked up and found herself the focus of the newcomer's attention, head tilted, one ear perked and the other down. A sensation of passing familiarity struck Holly, as if the two of them had met before in a dream.

"Guests," Seraphina echoed, squeezing past Holly to stand beside the new-come Wolf-Lord, head bowed and hands folded before them in submission. "Guru Veda, these are Holly and Kanti. They come seeking your help."

The stranger, Veda, nodded and stepped forward. Kept forward, a hand raised, slipping like a dagger into Holly's personal space to caress and probe at the mess of scars covering the taller Wolf-Lord's throat. Holly shuddered in horror at the touch and backed away from it, whispering as loudly as she could manage "Please do not do that."

"We insist," added Kanti, spreading a wing out to block between the pair.

"Holly, now," said Veda, wiping her fingers across the front of her shirt as if they'd been stained with something. She smiled up at Holly, utterly ignoring Kanti. "A pleasure to meet you, Holly. By your red hair and white fur, and that you have scarred, I guess you were once Princess Candida of Romulus? A new name is a good choice. Laura must have pointed you in my direction, that clever minotaur. Her research advances in the fields of fungus and soil alchemy are unmatched. And I love helping people. How can I help you?"

"With your mastery of Elementals and their lore," said Holly. She chose to ignore the earlier strangeness—creepiness, the voice of Shun said in the back of her head—and focus on the praise for her friend and eagerly-given offer of help. "We need to find our way to the House of Incarnation."

Silence. Utter, complete silence. For a moment, Veda stood as if frozen solid by Holly's plea for help. Her easy cheer drained away, leaving a small, slight, weary Wolf-Lord looking down, away, over to Seraphina. "My dear apprentice, would you kindly go to the kitchens for hot food and drink? Our visitors have come a long way, the hour is growing late, and I am sure they will need their refreshments."

Whatever Seraphina's unhappiness with the command, it remained unvoiced as they turned and left, slamming doors behind them.

Once done, Veda collapsed into the armchair nearest the fireplace. She dragged a hand down her muzzle, the hand balling into a fist upon reaching the scarf at her throat. "The House of Incarnation," she said, voice strong despite every other sign of her body. "That is a name I have not heard in a long time. A long time. You best tell me the whole story of why you come to be here, asking for things like that."

Holly nodded. "It began some weeks ago . . ."

Time passed unremarked as Holly recounted the journey so far, aided by Kanti when the strain on her throat grew too much. The happiness of life in Eishaven, tainted by the growing number of ill neighbors. Meeting Laura at the train station as she came home in time for the Elemental Migration. Being rejected by the Metal Elemental. Shun collapsing on the hilltop. The spell rot sweeping through Eishaven in the days which followed, Nessa falling sick. The meeting with the old unicorn knight, Nimue, and the hope she offered in the Waters of Life allegedly kept safe by the Elementals in their homeland, in the House of Incarnation. The stop in Quicken Bay to get the blockade runner from the Mechanist, and the close brush with death or capture at the hands of Holly's twin, General Regina.

"But what does it all mean?" asked Holly as she finished, looking to Veda in hope the Wolf-Lord had all the answers she needed. "Where House of Incarnation? WHAT is House of Incarnation? Never heard of it, trust me, know all stories."

"I do trust you," said Veda. Standing, Veda reached out a hand. A slim, leather-bound book floated from a far shelf and into her hand, startling both Holly and Kanti by the casual, almost brazen display of magic.

Flipping through the book, Veda stopped on a page midway through, dragged a finger down as she read silently to herself, nodded, closed the book and tossed it onto the chair behind her. "You would not know it from the stories, dear princess, because it was kept out of the stories, out of the histories, remembered now only by the Elementals and those who learn to hear them. And by Morgana le Fay, of course, but we can all agree there's no asking her for help."

Holly didn't care about Morgana le Fay. Right then, she didn't care about the stories or the histories, only about how time was running out.

"Please," she begged with a whisper, falling to her knees, pushing aside how the movement made the wound across her leg scream in agony. "Please, I beg of you. Tell me everything. Where is the House? WHAT is the House? The Elemental homeland—"

"Is all around us," said Veda, smiling. She sat again, another chair, farther from the light of the fireplace. "Any corner you turn, you might find it. They are Elementals, after all. Spiritual manifestations of the physical world's magic. Their realm, the spirit realm, sits parallel to ours, a sort of . . . mirror, or shadow. Dark Realm, Morgana le Fay called it, when she found her way there in the old histories. Not another level of existence, like Sheol or the Dreamlands, but certainly something similar enough. I have spent so much of my scholarly life trying to learn all that I can, and still, I fear that it can never be enough. No two accounts of Dark Realm are the same, you see."

"No two accounts?" asked Kanti. "So people other than Morgana le Fay have been there?"

"Yes, of course," said Veda. "The zakarians have surely been there more than anyone, this was their world long before we came here after all, but many have found their way to Dark Realm across the width of time. Scholars and spiritualists, famed gurus, masters of magic. Some say the 9-tailed kitsune who lead the Nameless Order, aged to be more magic than mere flesh, can come and go from there as easy as breathing. It is not a journey in the traditional sense. It is a matter of will, of knowing yourself fully and utterly, and in doing so, seeing through the lies of the world and to the truth. That is the path."

"Don't understand," said Holly. "Lies of the world? Need House of Incarnation! Need the Waters of Life! Lives at stake!"

To Holly's growing frustration, Veda nodded. "To be sure. Lives are always at stake. The world over, every hour, every minute, every bare second, is crammed to bursting with people suffering, dying. A storm, wiping a village off the map. A unicorn soldier, pressing his hoof down on a gryphon's throat until she stops breathing. A dragon, diving desperately for a clutch of eggs so carelessly dropped. A Wolf-Lord parent, listening to their child struggle for breath, silently begging for something, anything, to make it end. From a purely objective view, suffering and death are the natural state of this material world and its people. What makes you so desperate now?"

"MY people!" hissed Holly, gagging at the last word as she tasted blood at the back of her throat. "Please, help me!"

Veda's smile grew as wide as the sky and as bright as the sun. She knelt level before Holly, took Holly's hands in her own, and lifted her back up. "Stand tall, princess. I will help you find your way to the realm of the Elementals and the House of Incarnation. You will find the Waters of Life and save your loved ones from death. I promise."

"You promise?" Holly swallowed, tried to match the other woman's smile. "You promise. Thank you so—"

The doors opened again and Seraphina stepped back into the study, balancing multiple ornate trays laden with diverse food and drink in their arms. They paused, blinking as they took in the scene before them, frowned. "You two need any more privacy, or does the pirate make this a party?"

Kanti spluttered. Veda laughed. Holly, well aware of the implications in the other Wolf-Lord's comment, whispered "I like parties."

CHAPTER EIGHT

The bed was comfortable. More comfortable than any other bed Holly could remember ever sleeping in, long and wide enough for her limbs to roam without hitting the edges, covered with silken red sheets and pillows, and with a mattress to drown in.

Holly could not remember getting into the bed. She couldn't remember much of anything concerning the previous evening, not once dinner started. She remembered Guru Rathna joining them at some point. She remembered Kanti shapeshifting into a taller, male form. She remembered the spiciness of the meats, the sweetness of the mango and bael fruit, the scent of roses. She remembered laughter, a soft kiss . . .

As much as Holly liked to listen to her wife talk, she leaned forward and shut the kitsune up with a deep, loving kiss. Shun, surprised at first, quickly and eagerly returned it, a hand curling through Holly's thick red hair, a shiver racing down her spine to get her white fur standing on end.

Holly started at a strange ceiling, dark red stone finely carved with imagery from history and myths, heroes and villains and their respective conquests. So far south, having grown used to the cold north, she felt too warm under the blankets and threw them off to the side, where they gathered on Kanti's still-slumbering form. She rolled over and slowly stood from the bed, stretching away the kinks of an uncommonly good rest. She watched the progression of the sunlight through a doorway ahead of her, crawling swiftly across the stone floor.

A breeze carried through into the room with the sunlight. It felt good in Holly's unclad fur. She stretched again, more quickly, then strolled across the barren guest room and out onto the balcony, where the wind caught her hair and the sounds of an early morning greeted her. Birds singing from the nearest trees. The soft, indistinct voices of remaining faculty and students far down below, going about their morning business. Farther away, subtle but all-encompassing, the pull and push of the ocean.

Feeling strange, content to leave the terror for her loved ones in the past and in the future waiting, Holly didn't know how long she stood leaning on the wooden railing, bare in her thick fur, enjoying the endless moment. Eventually, she heard the creak of the bed behind her, the soft patter of approaching feet, the sudden weight as Kanti, his clawed hands feeling large and strong, draped Holly's black feather cloak over her. His voice, when he spoke, rang as deep now as it was light, almost squeaky, in his female form. "If you go around like that often, Shun is a very lucky kitsune."

Holly smiled. She reached up, grasped Kanti's hand still resting on her left shoulder. "Usually too cold in Eishaven. Fur . . . only grows so thick." The words did not hurt near as much as they had the day before, but still Holly could put no strength behind them.

"Come live with me, then, you and Shun and Nessa. I know you would love it."

"Mm. Maybe. I should get a move on, shouldn't I?"

"Hm," said Kanti, sounding genuinely thoughtful as he turned her around to face him, eyes roving her like she was the most beautiful of sunlit vistas. "I'd say you have a little time to spare."

Kanti whispered the last word. He leaned down, pressed Holly against the balcony railing. The kiss was not the eager, devoted sweetness of a kiss with Shun. The kiss was hot, burning, craven. Holly moaned into it, her lips parting before Kanti's tongue, greeting it as an old friend. His hands swept down her sides, nails dragging, teasing.

Loved and in love, Holly closed her eyes beneath the other Wolf-Lord's touch and gave praise to the joy of being alive for a little while longer.

***

Later, dressed in her plain black shirt and pants, Holly found Veda and Seraphina in the library, the former filling the time with stretches, the latter sitting on a table, nursing a cup of plum tea and rubbing their head in agony. "Hi, you two!" Holly whispered.

"Hi!" answered Veda, deafening, rising and readjusting her scarf. "Hi and good morning! Oh, you sound much better than you did yesterday."

"Oh God, not so loud," groaned Seraphina, eyes clenching shut. "God, I drank too much last night."

"You drink too much every night," remarked Veda, a gesture and flicker of magic levitating a teapot over to refill the suffering Wolf-Lord's cup. "The headache is merely karma. Luckily, I will not be requiring your services today, so you are free to return to bed or continue your own studies as you wish."

Seraphina's frown deepened. "If you don't need me today, why'd you even wake me up in the first place? And with an effing brass band spell?"

"Because I thought it would be funny," answered Veda, shrugging. "And I was right."

"I am ready to begin," said Holly, drawing attention back to herself. "Begin, please? The sooner I reach Elementals, the better."

"You speak the truth," said Veda. "Very good. But first, did you eat breakfast?"

Holly nodded. "I had a mango on the way here? Okay, two mangos . . . three. Never had mangos before. I might love them. Starting . . . to regret third mango. Fur near lips feels . . . really sticky. Not messy an eater, but—"

Seraphina hopped off their table and shoved their half-full teacup at Holly. "Please, I beg of you, drink this and stop rambling before you split my head open!"

Unsettled, Holly did as told. The tea lacked the copious cream she preferred, but it was sweet and did its apparent job of settling her nerves. She handed the cup back when she was done, cleared her throat, and looked to Veda again. "Ready, please."

The dark Wolf-Lord smiled. "Good girl. Follow me."

The pair of them returned to Veda's study. A flick of the dark Wolf-Lord's wrist and flames sprang to life in the fireplace. Holly glanced at it and then looked away, back to her new teacher. "Seen that trick before. Cult of the Burning King. I do not usually get along very well with those people. Usually, swords get drawn."

"If they have to be," sighed Veda, turning to look at Holly in the firelight despite the bandages wrapped over her eyes. "Thankfully for the both of us, that order is long behind me. They had wisdom, of a sort, and power, but I found the aims . . . lacking. Still, though, I've kept a trick or two since. That's the practicality of seeking knowledge from many sources.

"But enough about me. We are here for you. To teach you to see beyond the lies and delusions of this world, to know yourself as wholly and utterly as anyone can know you, so that you might journey into Dark Realm and retrieve the Waters of Life from the House of Incarnation. Does that about sum things up, dear princess?"

Holly nodded, though she still did not understand what all Veda meant about delusions and knowing herself. "But what is the House of Incarnation?"

"A fair question. Come, sit." Veda descended into a meditative lotus position, hands steepled in her lap. "My deepest apologies for not explaining this last night. There was so much ground covered already, I feared overburdening you so close to the start of your journey. Tell me, what do you know, or think, about death and the afterlife?"

"Not much," whispered Holly as she mirrored Veda's cross-legged position, struggling with it for the wound still healing across her leg. "Many believe dead descend into Sheol, dark and hungry underworld. Never learned much." She reached up, finding by long practice one of the strands of grey beginning to fill her red hair. A sign of age, of mortality compared to her perfect Wolf-Lord family. "Scares me," she finished, weakly.

"It is true," said Veda, capturing Holly's attention. "But it is not the whole picture. Life, in all aspects, is more complicated than that. We are each born a blank slate, a clean, beautiful spark of magic and life all bound up in flesh and bone. We grow up and we become a person. Experiences shape our personalities. We learn likes and dislikes, we love, we grieve, we RAGE. We form connections, friendships. We age. We die. All but the three Primes die. And that person we became, as you say, descends down into Sheol, to peace or numb torment, depending on the life they led. But that is not the end. The energy that went into them remains, returns to the universe, is born again. Another life, and the wheel turns again. Do you understand, princess?"

"I . . . think so," whispered Holly, chewing over the words. "So, the House of Incarnation is . . ."

"The spoke of the wheel," said Veda. "Or, put differently, the universe itself that the energy of life returns to for rebirth. The Elementals, incarnations of worldly energies rather than mortal energies, are its guardians from those who would misuse or corrupt those energies. If you want to get past the Elementals to where the Waters of Life are surely kept, you will have to approach the House with the purest intent, the most resolute certainty of who you are and what you are doing in your great chain of reincarnation."

"And you will teach me this," said Holly.

"Aye." Veda looked up to the ceiling, her smile content. After a moment, Holly followed her gaze and found herself looking at a strange mural. It was a large white circle, outlined in red. Within the circle, biting at each other's tails and turning in their own circle, were a unicorn, a dragon, and a gryphon. "Behold. The Three Poisons."

Holly beheld. Holly blinked. "That is a unicorn, a dragon, and a gryphon."

"It's metaphorical," said Veda, tone hinting at amusement. "They represent the three root evils of the world, the most basic causes of suffering. The gryphon represents confusion, uncertainty, delusion. The dragon represents greed and lust. The unicorn represents hate. To live a life, any life, is to be afflicted by the three of these to some degree, and it is by overcoming them that you may overcome the world and see the path to Dark Realm."

Holly swallowed, her knees aching from the unfamiliar sitting position. "How can I do this?"

Veda stood and gestured to the fireplace. "Through there. It is magic. The flames will not harm you if you are brave. Beyond, you will find yourself in the domain of the Magicahedron. It will tempt you with greed, with confusion, and with hate. Overcome them, and you will continue on your journey."

Holly stood more slowly. She moved to stand before the fire, watching the flames twist and move to the whims of their fuel. She felt the heat against her, seeping through her clothes and fur, and felt scared. She knew it natural and obvious to be scared. "Fire," she whispered. "Extreme cold. Silver. Wolf-Lords cannot heal from these. That we are all helpless against. If I step in there and am not brave, I will always be burned."

"Then for once," said Veda, "you stand on equal footing with all the rest of your kind. And I am certain you have been scared before and taken action anyway. That is greater bravery than acting without fear at all."

"For Shun," said Holly, reaching one trembling hand out toward the fire. The moment of contact, Holly almost recoiled, almost drew away and begged for another way, another path. But she stayed, and watched the flames pour over and around her hand, and did not burn.

"Go forth," said Veda behind her.

Holly let her hand drop back to her side and stepped forward, into the fire—

—and the fire was gone. Veda's study, with its books and lavish armchairs and ever-present scent of plum tea, was gone. Holly stumbled from the sensation of sudden, halted movement. She found herself in a long, dark tunnel. Black stone surrounded her, carved at blocky angles, wet with a glittering sheen of condensation. The air was cold, her breath billowing with each exhalation.

Holly looked behind her and saw nothing but smooth black wall. Ahead shone a distant light, far down the tunnel. With no other obvious options, Holly started for the light. The floor of the corridor was as wet as the walls, to her distress, soaking the fur of her feet, her steps a wet patter echoing away into the unseen distance. Her ears swiveled and strained, listening for the slightest hint of anything stirring in the dark. She heard nothing but her footfalls and the dink of dripping water. The whole place was as quiet as a—

"Tomb," Holly hissed, startled. She turned with a step to look more closely at the walls, saw at last the thin seams of hidden doors. Beyond rested the final remains of dead Wolf-Lords, returned to the quiet earth from which they'd risen.

Holly continued her turn, faced forward again, screamed as her next step found nothing but empty space. With a blink, the world had thrown her to the tunnel's end. She teetered on the edge, arms pinwheeling for balance she never found.

The fall was not far. Five feet, at most. She hit a bed of gold coins and rolled to the whims of the haphazard incline, coins and loose gemstones scattering before her. When at last she stopped, battered by the experience, she lay sprawled on her back, groaning, ears ringing with the deafening cacophony of the great heap of riches settling around her.

The riches of the dead.

Holly's breathing quickened. Still on her back, tail pinned awkwardly beneath her and a particularly large gem poking her right butt cheek, Holly clenched her hands, fingers dragging through the abandoned coins. Contemplating the sheer riches she had literally fallen into, a new, intimately familiar ache grew inside her.

Holly remembered. She remembered the hard, fraught months of living down in the ghettoes of Brillant with Shun. She remembered the nauseous hunger of living off food too cheap to be good for them. The pain of going to bed hungry and waking up starving. The fear of someday the crowds not showing up for their performances, their meager savings depleting, and the unyielding, armored fist of the city guard which would come next. No fare for the trains. She remembered whole days spent walking, hard stone roads beneath aching callused paws, walking from one performance to another, the full-body ache coming afterward, the looks of pity and contempt which came during. She remembered the odd jobs for scraps of coin, patching and re-patching clothes a dozen times over because nothing new could be afforded, the pricked fingers and strained eyes as she learned her trade by hand. Years later, and Holly remembered. She would always remember.

Clothing felt tight. Holly ignored this and rolled over into a kneeling position. She raked her hands through the gold coins, lifted handfuls of them up to watch the coins trickle from her grasp, giggled, lifted more up in cupped hands. Felt the weight and warmth of the gold and gems, soothing against the itch traveling slowly across her hands. Her muzzle split into a smile. Here was more wealth than she had seen since fleeing Cairn Romulus. With these riches, she could . . . she could never go hungry again. She could get FAT if she wanted. She'd never been fat before, not really, truly fat. She'd never had enough before, but now she could. She could have all she wanted. More than she wanted, and it could be others' turns to look at her with envy, her and her alone, laughing and ravenous with her gold, and her fine silks, and her beautiful scales—

Holly's hands opened with her shock, the gold coins clattering out of her trembling grasp. She watched, horrified as the raw red scales which had consumed her hands crawled up her arms, reaching the elbows as the skin tore and fur fell out in bloody, uneven patches. Gritting her teeth, she clawed at the advancing scales, then stopped as the most wretched pain struck from head to foot. She screamed, agony toppling her onto all fours, into the gold. She kept screaming, tears pouring from rolled-up eyes as her body tore itself apart. She felt it, every moment as muscles ripped and knitted back together, bigger, stronger. Bones stretched, broke, reassembled into a new, quadrupedal stance. A sick cracking resounded and Holly screamed anew, watching cross-eyed as her muzzle pushed out farther, thickened, new teeth sprouting jagged as her tongue lolled out of her mouth. She tasted the blood running from her lips and down her throat through the whole savage transformation.

"Help me!" she begged, or tried to, but all she heard come out as the scales reached her throat and her neck stretched to dragon-like proportions was a tremendous, ear-splitting roar.

Then, there was light. Blinding after the twilight gloom of the underground. Holly looked up, blinking away her sweat as she beheld the roof far above her open wide, and beyond it, the sweet, cloud-dotted blue of the sky.

God above them, to have wings.

The tattered remnants of Holly's clothes and fur fell away as another surge of muscle and size struck her. She barely noticed, breath coming in short, fire-tinged snorts from her nose as she stretched out, claws digging into the stone wall of the chamber like knives into butter, and began the long climb toward the surface. With each reach and pull upward, the dragon experienced a brief flare of exquisite pain as the final changes commenced. Scaled skin split, grew out past her rear legs into a sinuous, blade-tipped tail twice again as long as her body, smashing apart the stone around her with ease as it whipped about. The last scraps of Holly's face fell away, the dragon roaring in greater agony as twin horns grew outward, bloody and ram-like.

And then the surface, sweet, fresh air, the calls of frightened birds fleeing, and the greatest agony yet. The dragon gripped the edge where the torn mountaintop dipped down into the burial chamber, loosed a shriek as her back bulged for a moment, then BURST. Her tail thrashed, her body writhed, her agape jaws spewed a pillar of fire to the sky as the bare bones spread from her back, swiftly covered in sinews, muscle, flesh and skin, scales.

The pain faded. Freshly-born wings beat the air once, dragging the dragon from her death grip on the mountaintop. She laughed and beat her wings again, toppling trees with her gale force. The dragon rejoiced. She could fly anywhere. She could do anything. Whatever she wanted, she could take it, take it all, everything was hers, HERS, ALL OF IT, WHEREVER SHE WANTED—

"Holly!"

The dragon dropped back to all fours, twisted around to peer down into the chamber. The dragon blinked, shook her head, heard her name called again. Then Holly saw far down below, where she remembered the treasure had been only moments before—

"Shun," she growled. All thought of flight, domination, utter greed left her as swiftly as water from a sieve. She fell to her wife, becoming a small, tattered Wolf-Lord once more, the kitsune catching her from the air so the both of them spun. Holly kissed her, held desperately to her, the tears running fresh and warm down her cheeks as she closed her eyes—

—and opened them again to Veda's study, sitting cross-legged across from the other Wolf-Lord, mirroring her pose and watching her with the utmost intent.

"I," Holly began, voice cracking. She began trembling, realized she was still crying.

Veda reached into her right sleeve, drew out a small something wrapped tightly in white wax paper. Holly recognized it after a moment's blank staring as a piece of hard caramel candy, the sort the gryphons of Eishaven favored in their winter holidays. "Take this," said Veda. "You will feel better."

Holly took the candy in one trembling hand. Almost dropped it as she unwrapped it, hurriedly popped it into her mouth. The powerful caramel flavor exploding against her tongue did, somehow, make her feel somewhat better.

"It's alright," Veda continued. "It's alright. You're good. You've passed the test."

"It doesn't feel like I did," Holly managed, the candy slowly soothing her raw throat. She wondered at how much of the . . . dream, or the vision, had actualized in the real world. Her clothes lay torn around her. Her body ached, and her breath tasted still of smoke.

Veda sat back and smiled. "The lessons we learn, my friend, rarely feel how we expect them to. But you love so wholeheartedly, there is hardly room for greed of any sort. Go eat and rest. It has been a long day for all of us. You may not know this, but the long hours passed while you were gone. We will continue your learning tomorrow, when we are fresh."

Too weak to argue, Holly crawled to a chair and used it to haul herself up. Slipped and fell, forced herself onward. Wiping at her eyes with the back of a hand, she limped for the door, thoughts on food, and on finding Kanti to keep her company, and on far away Shun, slowly dying in their home, for whom Holly would give up the stars themselves.

***

It was early evening somehow, the time slipping away unnoticed. Holly told nobody of her experiences with Veda, only mentioning briefly when asked how things had "Gone well." Seraphina, already knowing what learning from Veda entailed, gave a look Holly recognized as pity and left to help with dinner. Kanti pressed the issue, pacing behind Holly as she put on her lone change of clothes. The other Wolf-Lord was transformed back into her more usual female form, the clearest sign of her distress Holly could imagine.

"When I first saw you, I thought you were on the verge of dying! You still look on the verge of dying! You should have brought me with you to Veda! Even if I couldn't help in your lesson, I could have . . . have . . . carried you afterward so you wouldn't have to walk half-dead on your feet, or something! God, Holly, I'm here for you, just—"

"Breathe," Holly remarked, the word muffled by the black shirt she was struggling to pull down over her head. Finally getting it on, she checked to make sure her trousers were buttoned and turned to her lover, hoping a smile was appropriate for the situation. "Just breathe."

Kanti stared for a long moment, one eye twitching worrisomely. Then she huffed and turned away, lashing her tail as she stomped toward the balcony and muttered to herself. "Stupid wolf . . . being smart like . . . stupid . . . worry for nothing . . . see how . . ."

Holly watched her go for a second, confused and worried, still tired, her hands clasping together as she struggled with the question she desperately wanted to ask. "Kanti?"

"What?" she snapped, stopping and turning to glare at Holly.

"May I . . ." Holly paused, swallowing as she dared a step forward. "May we . . . fly again? Just a bit? For the feel of it?"

Kanti's glare softened. Her eyes grew shiny and wet for reasons Holly didn't understand. She walked back over, dropping to all fours and shapeshifting into her gryphon form as she did, lightly nudging Holly's side in a gryphon sign of playfulness. "Of course we can. Any time you like. Just got to ask."

Smiling, heart lighter, Holly climbed onto the crow-gryphon as quickly as she could. Kanti waited with a saint's patience. Once she felt Holly was as settled and secure as she ever would be, she ran for the balcony, spread wings once through the doors, and LEAPT. The temple fell away behind them, the city soon far beneath them, the cool evening breeze streaming Holly's hair behind her.

"Hang on!" Kanti shouted, more out of habit then any genuine need. Holly kept her knees locked and her hands grasping the feathers and fur of the gryphon's back as she always did, lying down pressed against her, lost to the wind, to the change in momentum and pressure and speed of her twists and turns, her climbs and descents. Holly never felt in danger of falling off. She only urged Kanti on, faster, higher, more daring. Kanti always obliged.

At peace, Holly closed her eyes and tried to imagine herself as the one with the wings. The sweet burn of the muscles with every flap. The rush as the wind caressed over and across her every feather. The cold, the frost, the shock of wetness as she flew through a cloud or skimmed laughing over the ocean waves, turning to let each wing tip touch the waters and send them scattering behind her. She could almost feel it, almost . . .

The cares and worries had been left far behind when Kanti at last returned them to their balcony. Holly slipped off, giggling as she fought to keep her paws steady beneath her. Her heart felt like singing as she knelt before her lover, hugging her neck. "Thank you. Thank you."

"Any time," Kanti shifted beneath Holly's hold, was a Wolf-Lord once more, returning Holly's hug and kissing her gently on the cheek. "Any time."

"Oh, there you two are," said Seraphina from the door. "Come on, dinner's going to get cold if you take any longer. Didn't anyone ever tell you it was rude to keep your host waiting?"

Dinner, Holly decided, standing and taking one of Kanti's hands in her own, sounded grand.

CHAPTER NINE

It took Regina time to secure permission to enter the United Zakarian Confederacy with Butcher in their company to visit Eishaven. Others, primarily Queen Celeste and Butcher himself, urged Regina to ignore the official channels and go, in and out before they were noticed, but they refused. Something about the encounter with Candida had struck a nerve with them, in ways they found difficult to explain to others beyond a desire to prove their criminal twin wrong about as much as possible.

And so, they would abide by all possible rules, laws, and treaties in their conduct while visiting Eishaven, or they would not visit Eishaven at all.

"That's stupid!" shouted Butcher from atop his green-scaled wyvern, bellowing needlessly. "You're stupid!"

Riding atop Scattershot, Regina shrugged and said no more. It would have been pointless for them to bring up it had been entirely Butcher's fault everything had taken so long. The Confederacy's draconian laws against admitting any kitsune with four or more tails or who claimed membership in the Nameless Order were as legendary as they were thoroughly enforced. If the pair of them had been trying to go anywhere other than the refugee town in search of "murderous criminal elements", Regina knew they wouldn't have made any headway at all.

The ground swept by below them, transitioning from a deep, forested green into a harsh, snow-drowned white. Regina, hardened by years of military life, wondered how their soft, mild-hearted twin had ever managed to thrive in such cold, unforgiving climes. Not alone, they knew, feeling safe in their certainty.

"Am I allowed to kill?" asked Butcher, drawing Regina from their thoughts with his ridiculous accent. "My blade hungers for a bite of sweet, sweet flesh and bone."

"No," said Regina, refusing to look over or give the macabre question a moment's thought. "No murders, no killing. We are looking for answers. Nothing more."

"Pain, then," said Butcher, voice disturbingly light and cheerful. "I shall settle for pain, then."

Regina growled low, closed their eyes, counted until they no longer felt the urge to kill the Nameless Order assassin's wyvern out from under him and see how loud he screamed as he fell to his doom, opened their eyes again. Ahead, the snowfall began to clear. Through it, Regina saw the distant northern ocean, and nearer, a well-sized port town nestled between two competing forests.

Eishaven.

"We're there," Regina called, slowing their mount and angling downward for a landing in the east fields. Butcher followed close behind. Scattershot landed, the wyvern screeching at the cold as it kicked up plumes of snow. Regina unstrapped from their saddle and dropped to the ground, a hand on the wyvern's side as they looked around. They had landed halfway between the town proper and a large gryphon compound nearer the eastern woods, their arrival drawing less attention than they would have expected. In fact . . .

"Where is everyone?" huffed Butcher, sounding as if he was personally insulted by the quiet. "The town was bustling the last time."

Regina kept their quiet and kept an eye on the surveying kitsune. They were no fool. They did not believe for one moment Butcher was only an assassin of the Nameless Order, no matter how Queen Celeste had assured them. His knowledge of where Candida and Shun, a deserter from the Nameless Order, had been living for years was only one clue for her suspicions. This latest comment was another. And yet, for the moment they were only suspicions . . .

"How am I supposed to torture people for information if there's nobody around to torture?" continued Butcher, hacking at the snowfield for emphasis.

"You're a monster," said Regina, stepping a few more feet out from their wyvern, ears perked for anything. Movement caught their eye, drawing their attention to the gryphon compound. They watched, patient, as a red-haired minotaur struggled through the snow from one building to another, arms laden with items Regina could not quite identify from such distances. Folded blankets, perhaps. "Hmm."

"Hmm?" asked Butcher, coming over to stand beside them again. "What—ah. The minotaur."

Regina looked down at him, frowned. "You recognize her?"

"I do," said Butcher, smiling almost wistfully. "Laura, an alchemist of some achievement and a close, cherished friend of the bastard Candida. I would cherish another crack at her stinking hide."

Once more, Regina kept their peace and watched. The kitsune began to stride with full confidence toward the array of buildings, conjuring fire to clear his path of snow. Swearing under their breath, Regina signaled for the wyverns to stay before hurrying to catch up.

Nobody stirred at their approach. They reached the steps up to the log cabin the minotaur had disappeared into before even seeing a second sign of life, a crow-gryphon landing in a bad tumble in the center yard, coughing his lungs out as he staggered up and into another building, wings dragging behind him. He didn't even seem to notice the strangers near his home.

"I didn't know gryphons could catch cold," remarked Butcher.

"They can't," said Regina, suddenly nervous, suddenly wary. The sound of the coughing, the quality of it, sparked a shadow of a memory in them. They looked around again and considered anew how fully silent and motionless the moment was, more a graveyard than what should have been a diverse, thriving community.

Regina needed answers. They stomped up the steps to the door, banged a fist hard against the splintered wood. The sound traveled far around, loud and shocking as cannonfire.

Heavy, hooved steps approached from the other side of the door. It opened. The minotaur looked out at them, at first looking relieved, even joyous as her gaze focused on Regina's face. "Holl—"

But then she stopped, the rest of Regina perhaps registering with her, and her smile fell. She tried to slam the door closed and Regina bashed it back open with a shove. "None of that, now."

The minotaur backed away, hooves banging against the bottom step of a stairwell leading up to the second floor. She ducked to her right, toward a den well-lit by a burning hearth. Butcher danced past Regina in response, katana blinding-fast as he drew it and stabbed, through the minotaur's right shoulder and into the wood of the doorway behind her.

"AAUUGH!" The minotaur stopped moving, aside from her pained squirms, snorting and stomping a hoof against the floor in her struggle not to hurt herself worse in her pain. "Nnngh, damn it! You Wolf . . . Wolf-Lord bastard! Cult fanatic!"

"Hey now," said Butcher, drawing close to the minotaur to smile up at her, "that's no way to greet an old friend you haven't seen in years. The way your friends ruined everything for me and . . . well, you know, the least you could do is a friendly HELLO!"

The last word, screamed up into the minotaur's face, accompanied a twist of the katana blade. The minotaur screamed again, cutting off into a sob as the blood flowed down her shirt and something audibly snapped inside her. Butcher laughed and pushed his sword in deeper, the lust for murder bright in his eyes—

Stepping forward, Regina drew their sword and rested the blade on Butcher's shoulder. Though no pressure beyond the weapon's weight was applied, the act silenced him all the same. "That's enough. We didn't come here to kill anyone. Just ask questions."

"Bull!" screamed the minotaur, as she struggled to grip the katana piercing her shoulder. "I know who you are, wolf! I know you want Holly. You can't have her. I'll never help you!"

"I don't even know who this Holly you speak of is," said Regina. "I have come here for . . ." She paused, considering all she had heard so far, frowned. "You thought I was her at first. Candida changed her name?"

"To something that wasn't a mother's curse, imperialist scum!" The minotaur's left hand had pressed around her pierced shoulder as she'd talked, never daring to try pulling Butcher's sword free. Now the hand came away, blood-soaked but admirably steady as it dropped to a small belt case half-hidden beneath her white coat. Regina looked down to it in time to see her draw out a trio of shiny black pills, each of which began to sizzle purple as they became coated in her blood.

"What are," Regina began, getting no further before the minotaur tossed the pills at them. They hit dead-center on Regina's gilded cuirass and burst into clouds of an oily black smoke. Hissing, the smoke clung to the cuirass and surrounding patches of Regina's clothing, turned from black to red, Regina watching in shock and horror as wherever the smoke spread across their armor, a thick rust withered it away. After several seconds of frozen shock, they dropped their sword and started tearing their armor off. "What the fuck!?"

The Butcher started to laugh at Regina's predicament, lost his breath as the minotaur—Laura, Regina amended in respect—kneed him with the full of her strength in the crotch. He collapsed in on himself like a paper doll tossed onto the flames and fell away, allowing Laura to grab the katana pinning her shoulder to the wall by the weapon's hilt and pull herself free.

She ran.

Regina tore the last bit of metal off herself, wincing at the tingling pain of the corrosion glancing across the tips of their fingers. They snarled and jumped over the Butcher still whimpering on the floor, chasing after Laura into the den. Immediately they had to duck to avoid the Butcher's stolen katana thrown at their head. "Damn it, stop throwing things!"

"No!" snapped Laura from across the spacious room, before throwing a fist-sized tangle of thorny grey vines into the blazing hearth.

Regina clenched their fists, began to stomp across the den, began to growl "You do not say no to me!" They made it perhaps halfway through each of these actions before the first of the Ashen Vines curled creaking from the hearth and slapped at them. They batted it away, felt their legs yanked out from under them by another vine, sending them slamming down against the floor. They barely got their hands under them to push up when the first vine, rapidly joined by two more, bashed them back to the floor, each blow hitting with bone-creaking force, each blow piercing Regina with thorns, each blow timed to keep them from regaining their footing no matter how swiftly they healed.

"Stop—ow—freaking—OW—stop—DAMN—STOP IT!"

"No!" Laura snapped again. As all this went on, the minotaur retrieved a long-barreled steam rifle from a cabinet near the hearth, a beautiful weapon of brass and polished red wood which all gleamed in the firelight. Her eyes never left Regina as her hands, still steady with an alchemist's grace, slid a short cartridge of shining silver bullets into the chamber near the grip, then adjusted the rifle's sights for short-range firing. "I knew one of you would come for Holly, one of these days. She was content to believe all was well, but I knew. Too much bad blood for monsters like you to leave well enough alone. She was content, and for her sake Shun let herself be content. And for both their sakes, I started target practice."

From somewhere behind Regina, a thin stream of fire struck at the vines pummeling their back, their ears perking to the sounds of the Butcher screaming and charging onto the scene. Where the fire struck, the grey vines glowed red for a moment, then split, growing more thorny whips to now strike at the kitsune. He screamed once, Regina managing to turn their head enough to see him pierced through the gut by one of the vines, another wrapping itself around his neck and squeezing, thorns stabbing straight through, blood welling from his mouth, his nose, his eyes—

Then the kitsune illusion burst, leaving the vines grasping nothing. Regina perked their ears to the sound of unseen paws running across the hardwood floor. Laura caught them a moment later and raised her rifle to fire, the movement—well-practiced, the soldier in Regina had to admire—slowed by the injury to her shoulder. An invisible figure knocked the weapon from her hands, the act dispelling the invisibility spell over the Butcher. In the next moment the kitsune swung the sharp pommel of Regina's dropped sword into the minotaur's temple, the air ringing with a sharp crack chased by a groan. The minotaur fell boneless to the floor.

"The fire," wheezed Regina after a moment taken to be sure the minotaur was down for the count. "Butcher, the fire!"

The Butcher spun around, first to Regina, then to the fire in the hearth from which the Ashen Vines keeping Regina down grew. For a moment, a gleam they didn't like entered the kitsune's eyes. Then they threw open the nearest window, drawing snow from outside in with his magic and throwing it into the hearth to bank the flames. A terrible hissing filled the den, steam clouding the air. The vines drew back from Regina, flailing blindly at nothing for a moment more before crumbling away into piles of sodden ash.

Slowly, catching their breath, Regina clambered to their feet. They dusted themselves off, rolled the aches out of their shoulders, and then joined the Butcher in looking over the minotaur sprawled unconscious on the den floor. Along with the blood still leaking from her pierced-through shoulder, fresh red spread from a gash across her brow.

"More fight than I'd have expected," remarked the Butcher.

Regina nodded. "If not for that injured shoulder, she'd have had us both dead to rights. Perhaps Holly can pick her friends better than I thought."

The Butcher looked up at Regina with a friendly measure of disgust. "You're actually going to give a damn about that name change nonsense?"

Regina shrugged. "She is my sister. I can respect her that much. And it's true enough, Candida was a trashy insult of a name."

"Whatever," said the Butcher. He dropped Regina's sword at their feet, stalked away to retrieve his own sword where Laura had flung it on the other side of the den, returned giving the blade a slow twirl "So, now may I kill her? Before, I was bloodthirsty. Now, I'm pissed off."

"I don't care." Regina bent down to retrieve their sword, the fur on the back of their neck rising at the sensation of the Butcher contemplating a beheading. They stood and nodded to Laura. "Put her in one of the chairs and patch her up so she doesn't bleed out before we can get any questions out of her. Cauterize the wounds, if you need to."

"Oh, 'If I need to', of course," said the Butcher, grinning a monstrous smile as he squatted down and hauled the still-unconscious minotaur into the nearest chair at hand. Without preamble, he enveloped an index finger in bright orange flames and carelessly dragged it over the gash across her temple.

"Nnngh . . ." Laura groaned from the pain, squirmed where she sat in the chair, but did not wake.

"Watch this now," said the Butcher, still grinning. He tore the soaked-red coat from off the injured shoulder, the brown shirt beneath thankfully sleeveless. The Butcher pressed one hand over where his sword had entered through her shoulder, the other hand where it had exited, the soggy black fur squelching beneath the pressure he applied. Then he lit both hands aflame.

"AAAAUUGH!"

Her legs kicked and her back arched until Regina thought it must surely break. Her eyes shot open, rolling blind in their sockets as her fists beat upon the chair, a ragged breath in before another scream of utter burning agony. Her eye found the Butcher and stayed, the scream turning into a roar as a hand shot up to wrap around his throat. The glee left his face, the fire on his hands snuffed out as he took a rattling failure of a breath in—

Regina strode forward and lay the flat of their sword over the forearm currently involved in strangling the kitsune. "Let him go."

Laura continued to strangle the Butcher for several seconds more, an act of defiance Regina did not feel particularly interested in stopping, and then shoved him away and slumped back into her chair. Smoke rose from her burned shoulder, her body trembling with her weak, pained panting for breath, but her gaze remained defiant behind her glasses as she locked eyes with Regina. "You both should die."

"We want answers about my twin," said Regina, drawing their sword away and stabbing its point into the floor. "Where she's going and why. We almost had her in Quicken Bay, but . . . she slipped away."

"Good for her," hissed Laura. "I'll repeat myself. I'm not telling you anything. You both should die."

The Butcher snarled and feigned a bite at the minotaur's throat, causing her to cry out and jerk away. Frowning, Regina stepped closer, using their greater bulk to subtly push the Butcher away. To Laura, they said "If you know who I am, you know I was the only family to care for Can . . . for Holly as family. If I don't capture her—"

"What," spat the minotaur, "someone else will kill her? You're making me laugh, wolf. As if your tyrant parent won't just kill Holly on the spot the moment you drag her back home? Are you so deluded to really believe otherwise, or are you an even worse liar than your twin?"

Regina's frown deepened. They glanced around the cabin's main den, spotted a tray of tools on another lumpy chair where someone, at some point, had halfheartedly attempted to put a new shelf over the hearth. They stalked over to the tray, dug around until they found three long, smooth nails. They made a point of holding the nails and a hammer up for all to see as they turned back around. "Butcher. Hold her still. Hooves can be a tricky business."

The Butcher laughed, conjuring spell chains to wrap around and bind Laura to the chair. The minotaur's eyes widened. She snorted again as she struggled to free herself with strength renewed by panic. Butcher circled around the chair to hold his katana to her throat but still she struggled, kicking out at Regina as they approached and shouting. "No! Stay back!"

One kick hit Regina square in their gut, driving most of their breath from them. They caught the next, turned and trapped it between their arm and their side. Carefully, they aligned the first nail with the flat of the captured hoof. They had helped in the Cairn Romulus stables in their younger years, helping tend to wyverns, horses, and oxen. They knew how to shoe cloven hooves well . . . and how to do it badly.

"Please, God, no!"

"Where's Holly going?" asked Regina, looking over their shoulder at the minotaur. "Tell me now or you'll never walk right again."

The minotaur trembled, hair and fur plastered to her face by sweat as she met Regina's eyes. She swallowed, visibly steeled herself. "Go to Sheol."

Regina narrowed their eyes. Swung, hammering the first nail crooked into the hoof.

The minotaur jolted, eyes bulging, head banging against the chair as she barely restrained her scream. Her horns nearly caught the Butcher in the face, forcing him to swear and pull away. Regina nodded, impressed at the minotaur's strength of will . . . and readied the second nail. "You're going to remember this day. You're going to remember how we did this to you until the day you die. And from now on, every time you see my twin's face, you're going to see my face. And you'll hate her that little bit. So. I'll ask again. Where's Holly going?"

It took longer for the minotaur to answer this time. Regina could tell, reading the beast's features, how much she struggled with her answer, torn between loyalty, the pain she had suffered already, and the pain yet to come. Yet, again, through the tears in her eyes she steeled herself and glared at Regina. "Go to Sheol."

Regina tightened their grip on the hammer, hesitated for the barest moment, and then swung. The second nail went in.

Blood pattered across the floor. This time the minotaur screamed, a deep, agonized bellow which fell away into miserable sobs. The sound brought a vicious, shameful grin to Regina's muzzle. They let the moment play out, waited until the minotaur was spent and slumped panting in the chair, eyes rolling in her head, bestial face wet with tears. Then Regina readied the third nail, snarling to get her dazed victim's attention. "One! Last! Chance! I'm getting tired of asking, you stupid cow! Where's Holly!? WHERE!?"

From upstairs, a storm of dry coughing answered Regina's shout. They startled and looked up, then in the direction of the entrance hall where she remembered stairs to the second floor, silently berating themself for not checking the rest of the cabin for anyone else before setting to work on the minotaur.

"Oh, of course" said Butcher, leering. "The wife . . . and the CHILD . . ."

"Nooo," groaned the minotaur, seeming to rouse herself as she became less and less the center of attention. "You bastards. Leave them alone. I've got . . . a lot more hoof left to go."

Butcher laughed. "Bold of you to think my esteemed colleague attending to the poor souls upstairs would save you from me! Alone with a pretty little cow like you, I'd horrify even myself with the pains I could inflict. Heh. Heh. Heh."

More coughing from upstairs, making up Regina's mind for them. "No," they said, tossing the hammer aside and dropping the minotaur's leg. "We're done with her for now. We're BOTH done with her. Keep guard. I'm going upstairs."

"Aww, but Regina—"

Regina ignored the protest, striding away and up the stairs, chased by the minotaur's cries for them to stop. The second floor was darker than the first, the windows at each end of the hall heavily shuttered. Listening, Regina caught the faint sound of weak, rattling breathing.

Before they could act on this, a door at the far end of the hallway creaked open. A short, orange-furred kitsune in the slimmest of bed clothes stumbled out, three tails hanging limp behind her as she leaned against the doorway for support. A cough rattled her doll-thin body. Bleary eyes wandered the length of the hallway to Regina, stopped on them, brow furrowing. Her voice came out as a dead croak. "Holly?"

Regina stepped farther from the stairs, further into the cold light falling in through the circular window at the hallway's far end. The kitsune, who Regina guessed to be the deserter from the Nameless Order their twin allegedly paired up with, startled, nearly falling flat before retreating back into her darkened room and slamming the door with all the strength her obviously-sick body could muster.

For a moment, Regina stood indecisive. Then they walked down the hallway to the door, pushing it open after a quick test proved it to be unlocked. The revealed room was nearly shadow, illuminated only by the light coming in through the doorway where Regina stood and a dull, sputtering candle set on a desk beside a bed.

The kitsune, Shun, knelt on the bed, her breath harsh, her arm trembling as it held a katana toward Regina, her whole body crouched protectively over—of all things, in Regina's confused mind—a young filly unicorn in even worse health than the kitsune herself. Terribly young, coughing in her sleep, something nearly black staining the coat as it trickled from her mouth.

"Oh, of course" said the Butcher, leering. "The wife . . . and the CHILD . . ."

Fists growing slack at their sides, Regina struggled to put the pieces together. For the first time, they realized the enormity of the three years separating memory from reality. Holly, in defiance of every slight and slander Queen Celeste had leveled at her, in defiance of her own cruel slur of a name, had made a life out there beyond the walls of Cairn Romulus, away from all familial cruelty and contempt. And Regina had missed it.

The moment of silent confrontation lasted nearly a minute before Regina found their voice. "Where is Holly?"

If the kitsune was startled by the acknowledgment of the new name, she didn't show it. "Never . . . tell. Go away, General Regina. You're not . . . not wanted."

Regina dared a step closer. "I came here with an assassin of the Nameless Order. He is downstairs right now, keeping guard over your alchemist friend. He calls himself the Butcher and seems to bare you and my sister a terrible grudge."

The kitsune went rigid at this, eyes wide, darting briefly past Regina, chasing after the thoughts which must have been racing down the stairs to her friend in probable pain, certain danger. "Laura," she whispered, voice dry but eyes growing wet. Then, "You bastard. Probably think I'm a traitor, or Holly. You can't imagine the . . . the evils that kitsune—"

A coughing fit, brief but horribly wet, wracked the kitsune. The sword fell from her arm, the strength to hold it gone. When she was done, flecks of red glistened in the candlelight across her shirt. But still, she managed to gasp out "Servant of . . . Morgana . . ."

"What!?" snarled Regina, struck with horror and rage at the kitsune's words and all the implications they carried. But the moment was gone. Even as Regina stomped closer, the last of the kitsune's strength fled her, leaving them to fall back and away from the unicorn child, back hitting the wall behind her with a thud. Her eyes closed, the rise and fall of her chest barely discernible in the light from the candle.

Regina stood silent over the miserable scene, heart aching for their refusal to listen to their sister's reason for returning home when they had met in Quicken Bay, how much easier a moment's patience would have made everything. And now, knowing what duty and pity demanded of them, their hand trembled as they looked down at it, at the deadly claws gleaming in the dark.

***

Each step rang heavy as Regina returned downstairs. They found the Butcher and the minotaur still in the den, the minotaur's hands bound and ruined hoof bleeding feebly onto an old, worn rug, but no new wounds burdened them, so Regina could not complain. They looked to the Butcher, the kitsune gleefully tearing pages from a book and tossing them into the fire, and was struck by a memory. Gosse, young, late Gosse, laughing as they hurled Holly's practice sword off the castle wall and onto the train tracks far below, where it had been thoroughly destroyed long before Regina or Caelestis could retrieve it.

Snapping back to the present, Regina cleared their throat. "Spell Rot."

The Butcher startled, the mangled book slipping from his grip. But then he calmed, tails batting the air as he grinned. "Spell Rot!? Kahahahaha! You scared me there for a moment. Are the mongrel's loved ones upstairs, teetering on the brink of death? I love it! I couldn't have devised a better revenge! We don't even have to catch Candida, just busy her long enough for the plague to do the work for us! KAHAHAHAHA—"

"Go," said Regina, gesturing for the front door. "Go check on the wyverns."

The kitsune stopped laughing. His head remained thrown back for several seconds before he looked back at Regina, still grinning, his single eye loosing a baleful glare. "Why?"

"I want to talk to the minotaur," said Regina. "Alone."

The Butcher stood from where he'd been squatting, tails stilling behind him as he stalked toward Regina. His katana hung loose at his side, the extra-long blade dragging its tip along the ground, passing perilously close to the bound minotaur's tail. "You understand I don't work for you, right?" he growled, stopping a foot from Regina. His face barely came level with their chest. "You understand you have no authority but what I allow, right? That if I see it necessary, I am allowed, authorized, and actively ENCOURAGED to bring you to heel, right?"

Regina looked down at him, remembered the two they had left sprawled upstairs, and allowed a hint of their fangs to show. "I understand plenty. I still want to talk with the minotaur alone. You walk out that door, or I throw you out it, because unlike my parent, Queen Celeste, I'm not scared of getting on the Nameless Order's bad side."

"You're as stupid as your twin if you think the Nameless Order's the worst you have to fear from me." But the Butcher drew away, returning his sword to its scabbard as he edged around Regina. "But you know, checking on the wyverns might be a fun time. And after that, mayhaps I'll take a wee stroll through the town, seeing what I can eat or hurt or steal with all the folk too sick to stop me. If I get bored. So. Dinnae take too long, chum."

Regina watched the kitsune go, waiting until the door slammed shut before they relaxed. Tired, worn thin, they paced wearily over to the nearest chair, sat, and only then looked once more to their captive. The minotaur glared at them, fear and pain mingled in with the hate. It was a mixture grown long familiar to Regina over the course of their military career. "Would you like a piece of good news?"

"Bull," spat Laura again. "I have no reason to believe you."

Regina contemplated this for a moment, then drew their sword once more. The blade was clean, more so than it could have been from a hasty wiping while coming down the stairs.

The minotaur stared at the unused sword, swallowed, looked at the floor. "You didn't hurt them? Either of them?"

Regina nodded, then said "Tell me about my sister's life."

"Go to Sheol," said Laura. "That's all you're getting. So either kill me or leave."

Regina stared back, undaunted. From a pocket in their cloak, they retrieved a simple golden band, taken from the nightstand upstairs. "She married, and not even an attempted invitation to the wedding. She fell in love. She adopted, what, a unicorn filly of all things? There must be a story there. Cand—Holly, she loved her stories. Is she a good mother? Is she a good wife? Were they all happy? Before . . ."

"The Spell Rot?" finished Laura. "YES. Away from you, away from the rest of your evil, rotten family, she was happy! The lone happy, good, loving branch from your whole tree of evil! But what's it matter to you, anyway? General Regina! Hero of Romulus! Holly told us all about her life growing up, before she found us, and if you think I'm impressed by you, your ego truly marks you as the child of Queen Celeste and Morgana le Fay! You, who witnessed everything and said nothing! Who only comforted and defended when it would never come back to bite you! I label you a coward!"

"And I label you a fool!" Regina snarled, standing again, towering over Laura, blade smashed down upon a table near at hand. "A fool who speaks madness! My twin and I both were fathered by the late Amabilis, and I will not have their memory tarnished by—"

But the minotaur, Laura, threw her head back and laughed in the face of Regina's fury. A grand, heartless laugh, gut-shaking and tears-birthing, as if pain had never been struck upon her and the deadly sword Regina gripped trembling was a mere stick of varnished wood. It hobbled Regina, left her standing cowed and impotent before such furious mirth.

"My God" cried Laura, eventually gathering herself enough to open her eyes and look up at Regina, gaze tear-streaked and bright and vicious. "My God, all this time, Holly was terrified you knew and never told her, but you were kept as ignorant as she was! Hah! Go running home to Celeste if you really want to know why that might have been! Or better yet, ask your traveling companion peaking in through the window."

Regina startled and turned, in time to catch the barest hint of a red and blue figure ducking away from the ice-frosted glass in the far wall.

Rage, then. Regina spun back to Laura in her chair, growled, and raised their sword for a skull-splitting blow.

CHAPTER TEN

Holly woke with the dawn. Yawning, she rolled over in bed, her back to the balcony, and contemplated Kanti sprawled asleep beside her. The smuggler was "quite a catch", Holly recalled Shun calling the other Wolf-Lord on more than one occasion. Holly didn't know what fishing had to do with anything, but . . .

"I trust you," said Shun, the little spoon to Candida's big spoon as they lay in bed, still high on the excitement of their wedding night. It was a simple three words, innocuous to anyone else, yet for Candida they meant as much as "I love you."

"I just do not want you ever thinking you are not enough, or that I am bored, or—"

"Never!" laughed Shun, twisting around in Candida's arms to kiss her exposed throat. "You're not the sort to just 'get bored' of anything. Or anyone. We love each other, and we know we love each other, so we don't have to be greedy for each other's love. That's the Inari way, at least. And of course, like we talked about, we want to find someone to put a bun in one of our ovens eventually . . ."

Candida frowned. "We are looking for a baker?"

The memory brought a smile to Holly's muzzle. Life with Shun had been full of love, open and daring. It only seemed to grow year by year. Kanti had not been the first "new partner" she and Shun invited to share their bed for a night, but the pirate had been the first Shun invited back, and Holly, loving her wife, had obliged. She was glad she had, and not only for the practicalities of this second quest she found herself on.

"I am in love," Holly whispered to herself, marveling at the simple truth. All three of them were.

And once the quest was done and the day saved, as Holly believed it would be, she and Kanti would return to Eishaven, return to Shun. And the three of them would finally get to the baking Shun had promised.

Smiling, Holly leaned over to plant a light kiss on Kanti's forehead, then rolled over and stood to get ready for the day.

***

"My deepest apologies, my newest student. I have been called away for the day to attend to a nearby noblewolf's birth in my official alchemist capacities. I have served the family faithfully for many years, and would be sore to fail them in this hour. I have left for you special writings I have collected on the finer points of my philosophy, if you care to fill your time with reading that might prove beneficial in the long run. If you do not, the whole of the library and the temple beyond is yours to explore and appreciate. Do not bother the monks in their practices, and I am sure you will get along swimmingly.

"No, I do not mean that you will be swimming anywhere. Though, you may go swimming if you wish! Taking proper care of one's body is always vital, and for such purposes, the east sections of the university hold a sizable pool for those who'd rather not make the trip down to the beach. Enjoy, if such is your wish!

"With warmest regards,

"Guru Veda."

Holly frowned and set the letter back down on the hearth-side table she had found it on. Her gaze swept the old study, eyeing the various books laid out, the crystal instruments and half-full vials of strange and colorful liquids, and felt it peculiar to be in there without the elder Wolf-Lord to guide her.

Seraphina stood in the doorway connecting to the main of the library, arms crossed and a look promising impatience on their face. "I really appreciate you reading that whole thing out loud for the audience back home."

"Sorry. Does Guru Veda do this often?"

"Ugh, you have no idea. She's disappearing like this all the time. I think I've learned more from the books in this library than I have from her at this point. Sometimes I think she has a secret family nobody is supposed to know about, or something. It's annoying."

"Oh. I am sorry again."

"Whatever. So then, what will you be doing while she is gone, my . . . fellow student?"

"I do not know," answered Holly, truthfully. Her gaze settled on a number of carefully stacked books on the nearest armchair and she nodded toward them. "Are those the writings Guru Veda meant?"

"Probably. Let me see." Seraphina strolled over to the chair and picked up the top book. They flipped through the first few pages before pausing, a shocking blush rising in their cheeks before they swiftly slapped the book shut. "Ah, teachings, of course. Ahem. This first one is more to do with your . . . extracurricular activities with Captain Blackbird than with learning any meditation or . . . whatever. What a . . . what a prankster."

"Oh," said Holly, wandering closer. "Anything good in there?"

Seraphina chucked the book at Holly's head in answer, then reached down to pick up the next book.

Holly dodged the thrown object easily enough, turning to watch it tumble past her to land with a surprisingly heavy thud before the unlit hearth. Holly stared at the fallen book for a moment, and then her gaze rose to the hearth itself, tall enough for her to need to duck only a little to step inside, its inner walls dark at the moment, draped in shadow and the promise of future flames.

Flames . . .

"Oh, this is a good choice," said Seraphina from somewhere behind Holly, still sorting through the books left behind. "100 Poems on the Movements of the Heavens. A very good choice. It concerns the deep meditations of an ancient guru on the Dream Realm and how it connects to us and Sheol. You might want to start with this, if you prefer—"

"I have an idea," said Holly.

"I don't believe you," said Seraphina. The red-furred Wolf-Lord appeared on Holly's left, looking from her to the unlit hearth and back again. They frowned. "What are you thinking and how fast should I run to get your sex partner to stop you?"

"Guru Veda sends me into vision quests," said Holly, a smile growing on her muzzle as she stepped closer to the hearth, stooping down quickly to pick up the thrown book. "Magic lights the fire. I have magic. I could light the fire."

"Oh God," said Seraphina. "It's a worse idea than I could possibly have imagined."

"Not a bad idea!" said Holly, still grinning. "Good idea, I am certain! Whole temple at my disposal. Hearth, part of temple. No wasting time with books."

"You're sure happy to waste time in bed with Captain Blackbird," said Seraphina, eyes closing as they rubbed the bridge of their muzzle. "Oh, sweet cheese and crackers. There's probably no way I can stop you, is there? I've seen you deadlift before, girl."

Holly gave her arms a shake to loosen them up. She focused inward, as Shun had taught her to do in their scattered lessons on magic—the kitsune's own knowledge on the subject scattershot at best. She reached inward alongside a deep breath in, felt in the core of her chest a warm spark, like fire, white and stagnant in her mind's eye. The feel of it reminded Holly briefly of Laura's own lessons, the charts and diagrams of how the normal Wolf-Lord's magic pathways were supposed to course through their body. Of how her pathways were ill-formed, how they did not let the magic flow to heal and prolong her.

"But can do this," she told herself. Shaking her head and refocusing, she thought back to how Shun created illusions with a whip-snap of her tails, and how the day before Veda had lit the fire with a flick of her wrist, and to her own movements when she'd thrown her magic forth in a bid to escape Regina and their soldiers. She reached out with a hand as if to grasp her magic within it. Another deep breath in and out, and then she clenched the hand into a fist.

White flames roared to life within the hearth.

"Crap!" shouted Seraphina, staggering back and away from the sudden rush of heat. "Damn, wolf!"

Holly grinned, giddy with the rush of success as she stared at the swirling, roaring wall of flames, so bright as to be nearly blinding. This was a far bigger act of magic than merely lighting piles of sticks in the forest. This was an act of power, pure and simple.

"Okay, I know I've been mocking you this whole time," said Seraphina, from somewhere far behind Holly, "but you're not actually going into there, are you? You're not Guru Veda! You don't know if you actually did it right or if you'll start burning to death the moment you step into the flames!"

"There is only one way to find out!" Holly shouted back over her shoulder.

"NO, THERE ISN'T!" screamed Seraphina. "THERE'S PLENTY OF WAYS TO FIND OUT! LIKE JUST WAITING FOR GURU VEDA TO GET BACK AND ASKING!"

"I am not afraid," said Holly, this time more to herself than to the Wolf-Lord behind her. This had worked, she knew it. She felt the magic in the fire, not only her own but another magic coming from somewhere beyond the hearth. It had worked. And if it hadn't . . .

"No time for doubts," said Candida, and then she leapt forward into the hearth—

***

She fell into mud, deep and cold. Several seconds of startled and indignant squawking ensued as Holly struggled to claw her way up and out, the mud sucking her down into its grasping depths. Holly's body felt strange to her all the while, misshapen and heavy, too large for her and with too many limbs.

I transformed into a dragon in my last test, she thought to herself, slowly making progress up an incline studded with the exposed roots of rotting, moss-addled trees. *Have I started this journey already transformed?*

She found her answer as she at last pulled herself wholly free of the sucking mud, her body filthy as she lay collapsed upon the solid ground, panting for breath. Upon her back, she felt wings twitching, feathered, long and broad, burdened with mud. Rolling onto her side with a grunt, she stared at arms—no, legs, front legs— covered in strange scales halfway down, ending with sharp talons. Her muzzle felt hard, unresponsive, lips nonexistent. She still heard well enough, but not as well as she remembered, and her eyesight . . .

My word, my eyes!

She could see so much more, now . . . with a quick focus . . .

"Kora! Hold on down there, we're coming!"

Kora groaned and blinked, wincing as she forced herself to slowly stand back to all fours. She was a raven-gryphon, she remembered, unsure how she could ever have forgotten. A raven-gryphon, traveling through the southern swamps of . . . Schwarz Angebot, this was right. She was a knight of—

"Kora!"

At her name, Kora turned and ducked into a bow, wincing as the tip of her beak bounced against the sodden dirt. "My queen, forgive me."

The cardinal-gryphon sighed and shook her head. "There is nothing to forgive, except giving me a heart attack. I told you to stay back with the rest of the caravan. You are too far along to be chasing after suspected spies half-glimpsed in this infernal gloom all around us."

"Too far—" Kora began, confused before she sat and rested her talons upon her sizable belly. A flutter graced her heart upon remembering, having somehow forgotten, her children to be born. The physicians promised twins.

"You look like you've seen a ghost," remarked Sir Ida, the golden eagle-gryphon sitting to Queen Grimhilt's right and giving her wings a stretch. "At least, I think that's how you look, beneath all that mud and muck. You're sure you're alright? Do you need—"

"I'm alright," said Kora, struggling for a moment before getting her unfamiliar beak to curl its flexible corners into a grin. "Other than my pride, I mean. This still . . . takes some getting used to."

"But you will get used to it," said Sir Ida, giving Kora a warm gryphon smile while giving her own belly a pat. "Trust me on that. Though, how many times it'll take before you do . . ."

"Okay, enough girl talk," said Queen Grimhilt. "Kora, return to the caravan and get yourself cleaned up. Sir Ida and I will follow you shortly. It is dangerous to be stopped like this for so long. You never know what Avalon will try next."

"Yes, your majesty." Kora ducked her head into a bow, turned, and with a flap of her wings to dislodge some of the mud, she started the short but winding walk back to the caravan. As she walked, she let her thoughts dance and whirl. It was a supply caravan, meant to be in secret between the royal palace of Schwarz Angebot and one of the southern fortresses, where it was suspected the unicorn realm of Avalon had been secretly moving troops through the mountains for a surprise attack. Had it been only troops being delivered, Kora knew, they would fly rather than walk. But there was more, as there always seemed to be. Weapons and armor, food, medicines. Everything else a fortress would need to withstand a siege besides the bodies to man the walls. It made for a long, slow, wet trip.

She found the dozen wagons held up on a high road through the swamp, its sloped borders lined with newly-placed logs to guard against accidents. She found her husband, a bluejay-gryphon named Roberts, in the back of the lead wagon, making fretful conversation with the minotaur driver. At the sight of her coming up the slope toward the road, Roberts squeaked and leapt from the wagon, wings flaring before he flew to her, almost tackling her in his excitement thankfully restraining himself at the last moment. "My Kora! Where did you get off to!? My word, you look a mess!"

"Got in a fight with a puddle," said Kora, grinning despite her aching legs and the increasingly unpleasant feel of the drying mud in her feathers. "I guess the puddle won. You wanna help me up these last few . . ."

Roberts nodded and took to her side, a wing sliding under her to help take a portion of her weight. She sighed, satisfied, and made it the rest of the way up the slope without issue. With the ease of long practice, she ignored the looks she got from the other gryphons and minotaurs as she went to the water stores to wash away what she could of the mud.

"What really happened?" asked Roberts, standing close by and watching her as if she was a precious and fragile vase.

"I don't know," said Kora, the raven-gryphon frowning as she raked her talons through the feathers of her neck and tried to remember the moments before her intimate encounter with the mud. She remembered . . . wolves, and a fire, and quiet, heart-shattering desperation, but thinking back on it now, it all seemed a dream. "I think I merely . . . needed to stretch my legs and wings a little. It's been a long ride for all of us, and these little ones are starting to feel as restless as I am." She punctuated this last comment with a quick pat of her belly.

"But you can't just go wandering off on your own like that," said Roberts, the bluejay-gryphon drawing closer and giving her pregnant belly a rub. "What if the queen and her knight had returned before you and we were all left waiting for you to get back? Or worse, what if it was something more serious than a mud puddle you got in a fight with? I heard from the others, there have been sightings of unicorns in this swamp the last few weeks."

Kora rolled her eyes and began cleaning one of her wings, though quietly she enjoyed her husband's touch on her belly. It calmed the pair of beasties down. "I can't believe the queen would choose a route that was already rumored to be dangerous, my love. And besides, she and Sir Ida didn't seem too worried. Actually, I got the feeling when I ran into them that—no, not literally, my love—that they were annoyed by my sudden presence. As if I had interrupted something . . ."

"Now who's being paranoid?" asked Roberts, though he did so with the corners of his beak turned up in a smile. He leaned up to preen the feathers of Kora's cheek—

A wagon three down from them burst into flame and wood shrapnel, filling the air with screams and toppling gryphons. Kora staggered as a piece of burning wood as long as one of her primary feathers buried itself into her right rear leg. She crumpled to the ground, the pain too much for a scream, barely finding the presence of mind to put her wagon between herself and the direction of the explosion. She stared at the profusely bleeding wound and felt herself fill with the worst, most stomach-churning terror she had ever felt.

Oh God, what if that had hit my belly?

Beside her, Roberts was a fountain of obscenities as he struggled to load a bolt into his crossbow. All around them were screams, dying screams and screams of rage. The clop of hooves rang through the air, the sizzle of magic bolts flying, quick shots of light hitting the caravan from all directions out of the surrounding swamp. Gryphons counter-attacked with crossbows and flung fire-bombs. Minotaur drivers ducked for shelter with their weapons or else hurried about to set up defensive barriers of metal around the struggling caravan. Somewhere, distant but drawing closer, there echoed a terribly large and heavy stomp and crunch.

Kora curled into the tightest ball she could in her current state, wings wrapped tight around her, front legs gripping her belly as she kept her head ducked down. Breath hitting in bursts, tears streaming down her cheeks as all around her rang the sounds of gryphons, minotaurs, and unicorns dying. She felt the heat of magic bolts striking nearby, freezing her in place with fear even as Roberts began to pull on her to get her to move. "Come on! We can't stay here!"

"I-I can't!" Kora screamed back, breathless and blind in her terror, experiencing the world only through sound and heat.

Somewhere, Roberts swore and began pulling at her harder. "Kora, please! We've got to get with the rest! It's safer—"

But then he stopped, said another curse. Kora heard the twang of his crossbow once, twice, a third time. He cursed again, talons grabbing one of her front legs tight enough to draw blood—

Then, a flash of light and sudden, intense heat too close. A pained gasp, the talons jerking away from Kora as something heavy hit the ground beside her.

A moment, and then "Roberts?" Kora coughed, forced her eyes open and her wings down so she could see the world again. Ahead of them, three unicorns of Avalon lay dead, their white barding stained with the mud of the road and their blood from the crossbow bolts piercing their throats. Kora swallowed and slowly turned her head, a scream at last tearing from her beak as she beheld her husband slumped motionless against the wagon beside her, his glazed eyes turned up to the cloudy sky, a smoking hole in his chest from a unicorn's magic bolt.

Wordless in grief, Kora fell upon her husband's corpse and wept. Around her, the battle continued. Unnoticed, the tide turned as Queen Grimhilt and Sir Ida returned, catching the attackers unaware from behind. With them came new galloping hooves, a trio of Knights le Fay charging alongside the cardinal-gryphon queen. Within a minute, the attackers were dead or had fled, and what remained of the caravan was saved.

Kora knew none of this, not until later, when the grief loosened its grip enough for her to see, hear, and think once more. She felt a presence at her side and looked up, found Ida beside her, the golden eagle-gryphon's expression one of complete sympathy and sorrow.

"It's my fault," said Kora, barely able to whisper the words, bowing her head to loose another sob.

***

They reached the fortress Featherbound late the next morning, far lesser in number and worth than looked for. On the hills guarded behind the fortress, they burned the bodies of the dead in accordance with gryphon funeral rites, each burning accompanied by a song of lament or remembrance from whoever among the gathered mourners had been closest to the deceased.

Kora could not sing her song, retched at every attempt. Grimhilt, as Roberts' queen, assumed the duty in her stead, allowing Kora to remain behind and anonymous.

Afterward, Kora wandered aimless along the fortress walls and across its grounds, not knowing what to do with herself, now bereft of her most beloved. Ida watched her carefully, made sure she ate and slept and kept out of the way of the fortress' soldiers and engineers when she threatened to disturb them. Kora barely noticed, the world beyond her own body a vague and ever-shifting haze. She could not rest. She could not taste the food they made her eat. She could not feel her legs as she walked aimless from one side of the fortress to the next, nor her wings the few times she tried to fly. She did not feel the mud on her talons or the rain as it fell, or the growing chill in the air as winter approached.

She felt nothing but the weight of her belly, growing day by day.

They had been at Featherbound for two weeks when Queen Grimhilt, Sir Ida, and one of the Knights le Fay who had come to the caravan's rescue, Sir Lancelot, confronted Kora.

"I am deeply sorry for your loss," said Grimhilt, the cardinal-gryphon resting a wing across the unicorn stallion's back with intimate familiarity as she stared at Kora. "But I can't have you here disturbing the whole fortress. We have all lost loved ones. You are not alone except by your own choice. Right now, you are useless to me."

"I'm sorry," said Kora.

"What our queen is trying to say," said Ida, stepping forward to grip one of Kora's shoulder in her talons, "is that we think it would be best if you took leave from the north and its war for now. You are deep in mourning and it isn't safe for you or your children here. Is there anywhere you can go to birth them safely? Any other family you might have?"

At first, Kora stood there listlessly, the single word "Regina" echoing strangely in her head. But then she blinked and slowly nodded, talons moving to caress her belly. "I guess that I . . . have a cousin on the Floating Mountain. He invited me to refuge there before, when first my pregnancy became known . . ."

"A long trip," said Ida. "But well worth taking. Leave as soon as you can, while the skies here remain open and safe. Take the eastern route, through Gateway. Go as swiftly as you can and remain for as long as you and your children need. Please."

Kora swallowed, tears returning to her eyes, her first tears since the moment of her husband's death. "Schwarz Angebot is Roberts' home. I can't just . . . just leave . . ."

"Nevertheless, you must," said Grimhilt. The harshness had left her features, at least for the moment, and she looked with wholehearted sympathy at Kora. "For the sake of Roberts' memory, and what remains of him inside you, you must."

***

She left early the next morning, before the sun had fully risen. She left on her own, politely refusing Queen Grimhilt's offer of a small armed escort to the borders of the land.

"You need the soldiers more than I. And I need the quiet to think."

Kora did not fly the southeastern way as they had suggested, along the southern border of Gryphonbough and through Gateway to pass to the east of the Dragonback Mountains. Instead, she flew to the southwest, her thoughts on following the coast south and approaching the Floating Mountain from the west. She did not know what called to her about this way, be it fate or idleness or a daring for death, but so she flew.

The journey was slower going than she wanted. Her pregnancy made her stop frequently to rest, taking shelter in trees or against the rocky slopes of the encroaching mountains, ever on guard for Imperial spell drones or, worse, feral wyverns.

She spent the first night of her journey camped on the northern border of the Rotwald, torn between its sheltering boughs and the open plains between it and Featheren Valley. She kept her fire low and smokeless, cooking nothing but eating only of her dried food rations, every sense primed and straining for sign of danger. The talons of her right front leg idly caressed her belly, the life within feeling more fretful than Kora liked.

It was not the threat of the Empire which kept Kora on alert. The iron hoof of Avalon did not tread so far south, not yet. It was the forest which raised her hackles, the Rotwald. Rumor and myth abounded of the bloodthirsty horrors haunting beneath its signature red leaves. Spiders the size of houses. Wolves the size of bears. Ghosts and wights, trickster forest spirits. Wandering trees, ready to shift around a traveler at a moment's notice to hide the path back out. A hundred more Kora could not begin to recount, and more than a few which would find her, and those yet unborn within her, a meal well worth the risk of her fire and steel.

"Hello, trave—"

Kora screamed and spun, crossbow raised, talon barely restraining from pulling the trigger when she saw no beast of mimicry behind her, but a tall and handsome raven-gryphon like her, a red scarf wrapped around her neck and a long rapier strapped to her side. At the moment she stood blinking, her strange yellow eyes staring at the crossbow pointed squarely at her beak.

"Err . . . I can come back later?"

Kora loosed a nervous laugh and let her crossbow drop, turning to huddle with fretful talons before the campfire once more. "Sorry. Sorry. I am quite sorry. What little nerves I had are quite shot, you see, and I thought you might eat me."

"Not without your permission first," remarked the other raven-gryphon, the stranger walking around to sit across the campfire from Kora. "And just so you know, nothing in this forest is in the habit of asking for permission, so you'd do well to keep those nerves shot for the night. You must be a true stranger around these parts to not know to travel in groups in this forest."

Kora frowned as she watched the stranger stoke the fire, trying and failing to place the strange accent they spoke with. It reminded her vaguely of an Avalon accent, but not . . . "Where's your group?"

"Farther along the border, there," answered the stranger, nodding past Kora and in the direction the stranger had first appeared. "A little deeper inside the forest. As weapon smugglers, we are uniquely well-armed to deal with whatever might try at us, and feeling so secure, I thought I might invite the lone traveler I come upon into our relative safety."

"Weapon smugglers?" Kora's frown deepened. "Weapons for who?"

"For whoever needs them," answered the stranger, smiling. "Right now, that's mostly gryphons. Oh! I'm sorry, I've failed in my courtesies. Captain Blackbird, at your service."

Kora startled. A sharp pang of something, love or longing from another life, struck her heart. "Black . . . Blackbird? I've . . . heard of you."

"Most have." The raven-gryphon, Blackbird, stood and nodded again in the direction she had come. "Well then, you fair, mysterious traveler? Will you join me and my fellows at our camp to relax and make merry before our paths uncross?"

Kora began to stand, drawn inexplicably to the offer—and then stopped. She sat back down and stared into the low flames of her campfire, thinking she had seen a glimpse of a dead and burning bluejay-gryphon within them. "I'm sorry. My husband died the other day. I am on my way to Vogelstadt and the Floating Mountain to give birth to our children in safety."

"Oh." The cheer left Captain Blackbird's tone. After a moment she circled the campfire, placing a wing upon Kora's shoulder in commiseration. "I am very sorry for your loss. I have never known the particular love that you have, but I can appreciate the vastness of it, and of its loss. But knowing this, I cannot simply let you stay here, alone and vulnerable. I implore you to join me at my camp. It will be safer there."

"Safer . . ." Kora rolled the word carefully about in her beak, a kicking from her belly deciding for her. "Alright. Safety in numbers."

***

Five others comprised Captain Blackbird's party, a varied mix of gryphons who all welcomed Kora warmly. She kept to Blackbird's side among the group, listening to their raucous laughter and bawdy tales with a detached fascination, her curiosity rising as she noted none of them shared their leader's strange accent. They offered her roasted meat from their blazing campfire, and fruit and song, and made it easy for her to forget her grief for the night.

In the morning, she rose with the smugglers and with nary a word flew with them westward, merely another of their number. They flew for Port Oil, a grand city nestled within a crescent bay of high black cliffs, hired to deliver 12 bags of high-yield crystals to the local governor for use in long-term enchantments.

"The word is there have been attempted raids by Imperial privateers," explained Siegbert, the towering swan-gryphon tasked with carrying the majority of the bags. "None successful, but Queen Grimhilt's appointed governor is not one to take chances. Avalon gaining control of Port Oil would give them leverage over all shipping along the entire western coast of Heraldale."

Onward they flew. It was not a long flight from the Rotwald to Port Oil, and they only needed to stop for Kora to rest once. They flew, and Kora felt strengthened by the smell of the nearing ocean, the salt and spray, the call of birds and the scents of fish. Port Oil, upon their noon arrival, was a forest of ship masts, the bay crowded with ships, more than Kora would have thought safe. She saw the flags of many nations flying, from Schwarz Angebot and Vogelstadt, from Wedjet, from Gateway, even from the United Zakarian Confederacy far to the east.

"Something's wrong," said Blackbird, circling along the high cliffs surrounding the bay. "Kora, come with me. The rest of you, get those crystals to the governor."

Kora watched the others break away and fly for the large fortress at the thickest point of the crescent city, then turned and followed after her fellow raven-gryphon without a word. They flew down to the southernmost stretch of the port, where the line of buildings swept along the lower horn of the crescent. After a moment Blackbird landed before a tall and broad building, domed roof, red wood and grey marble. But for the lack of windows, Kora would have thought it a mansion. A sign over the front entrance proclaimed it the Cavernous Tavern.

Blackbird marched in without slowing. Kora followed after her, then paused to take in her new surroundings. Cavernous was the right descriptor. Beyond a short entrance hall, the building opened up into a central hall reaching through all three floors. Balconies and stairs led to surrounding rooms except for the far wall, dominated by the largest hearth Kora had ever seen outside the kitchens of Queen Grimhilt. Round tables decorated the main floor, enough to host a hundred or more, but aside from the pair of them and a drunken sphinx at the bar, no other customers could be seen.

"Oh no," said Blackbird, heading for the sphinx at the bar. "It is bad. Rosa! Attend to the pregnant bird!"

Somehow, Kora found the strength within herself to squawk in protest at this casual dismissal. Before she could do more, a petite snowy owl-gryphon appeared at her side from a higher floor, fussing over her as she half-led, half-forced Kora on toward the hearth.

"Oh my, just look at you! Quite ready to burst any day now, I'd say. Where that Blackbird finds gryphons like you, I'll never know. Come here, by the fire. Don't fret over anything, I'll have you taken care of, no argument. Are you a fish sort of gryphon? I'd wager my left wing you are, I've a beak for this sort of thing."

"I, I am," said Kora as the owl-gryphon sat her down before the hearth, all she could get out before the other woman began again.

"Right excellent, that is, and a good day you came here, the chef last night caught the biggest pike you'll ever see. It's been keeping nice and chilled ever since. I'll be right back with a serving of it, which I think should go nicely with pickles, yes, sliced pickles, and a steaming mug of . . . hmm, no, nothing too heavy with that load you're carrying."

"You're too kind," said Kora, but the owl-gryphon, Rosa, had already turned and started away, swiftly disappearing through a discreet set of swinging doors near the bar. She watched the doors swing squeaking on their ill-oiled hinges for a moment, then glanced to Captain Blackbird hunched over the bar in hushed conversation with the sphinx, and then finally looked back to the fire in the hearth. No escaping, she figured. Not unnoticed.

Time passed. At Rosa's insistence Kora ate two servings of the pike, alongside slices of pickle, fresh rolls drenched in honey and butter, and more bowls of sweetened goat milk than Kora had ever thought she could drink. Through it all, Rosa kept up the flow of conversation, somehow drawing Kora into it despite her every intent to keep to herself by the fire and wallow in grief. Rosa came from a large family. Three sisters, four brothers, two nieces, five nephews. Most still lived there in Port Oil. Two had moved east to Gateway. One had moved north to Schwarz Angebot, and Rosa had not heard from him in nearly a year.

"But of course, with large families such as these, you should always expect one or two who go quiet until they need some money or a roof over their head or someone to keep an eye on their baby for them, and of course with family you must oblige as well as you can. And to be honest I quite miss Paul, he had always been grand with parties, only I don't imagine there are many parties held up north in these days, are there, with the war going on. Men and women, young and old, flying off to fight for queen and country. Some might find it grand and exciting, but it's all frightening to me, and—o-oh dear, oh my sweet dear, you're crying!"

Kora ignored this last comment, thought it stupid as she stared blindly into the hearth, her cheeks wet, her breathing uncertain. She shook where she sat, a sob wracking her body, only one as she began futilely wiping at her eyes with the feathers of a wing. "Shut up, just shut up, you stupid old bird! I don't care to hear about your . . . your stupid family spread out to stupid places! Your stupid brother up north is probably dead! The stupid unicorns probably killed him and you'll never hear from him again, not for money, or for a roof over his head, or for, f-for ba . . . babies . . ."

The owl-gryphon muttered something, perhaps an apology, but Kora tucked in around herself, clutching her swollen belly, and happily did not hear it.

***

Kora awoke to distant screams and the growing smell of smoke, heavy and oily. Grunting, she hauled herself up and staggered from her bed of blankets and pillows, her body aching, her head still foggy. "What . . ."

Somewhere close, an explosion. More screams, the shattering of wood, a rising heat in the air. Kora shook off more of her sleep and cursed the Cavernous Tavern's lack of windows. She turned to circle her bed for her pack, wanting to be ready in case—

Her outer wall shattered, showering her in flames and stone. She screamed and fell, began to slide as the floor of her room—oh God, she thought, the floor for that whole side of the building—buckled and sagged beneath her. Broken wood and stone fell around her, dust choking, blinding, her talons chipping as she grabbed at the failing floor.

Then she got her wings raised, a solid flap gaining her air, away from the gaping wound where the wall had once been, out of her room into the central hall. In time for another blast to hit the building, sending it rocking around her, the ceiling falling, walls buckling, the fire spreading unchecked from the hearth. Tables burned. Bodies scattered about burned. Kora stared with horror at a snowy white wing poking out from beneath a fallen chandelier, flames creeping over the wood and wrought iron . . .

Talons grabbed the feathery scruff of her neck. Kora screamed and turned and there stood Blackbird, a dark shadow in the smoke and dust. "RUN!" the raven-gryphon screamed.

They ran. Once out of the ruin of a building, they spread their wings and flew. As fast as Kora could manage with her lungs choking and her limbs trembling and her whole lower body suddenly overcome with the steady, unmistakable pain of contractions. The whole harbor burned, the fleet which to Kora had seemed so impressive burning, sinking. Overhead, half-glimpsed beyond the rising smoke, the airborne warships of the Avalon Empire rained destruction down upon Port Oil.

Bodies lay in the streets. Blood cooked where it spilled, churned to mud in the dust by the stampeding feet of those who could not fly. The white flags of surrender had risen over the walls of the central fortress, unheeded.

Onward the pair of raven-gryphons flew, coughing through the smoke, wracked by terror and grief, and in Kora's case, pain bordering on agony as her whole body rebelled. Port Oil grew small behind them as they fled down into the Unclaimed Plains, skirting the coast, neither knowing where or when to stop to be safe, if there could ever be a moment of safety again.

Then a new contraction struck, stronger, unlike any Kora had felt before. Her body seized from the pain, wings paralyzed.

She fell.

The world spun around her, tumbling, grey land and grey sky, rocky, terror as she neared death—

Then Blackbird grabbing at her back, talons digging in deep enough to draw blood, the other raven-gryphon screeching as she pulled. The fall slowed in the last moment, turned from certain death into a sharp, bone-breaking roll.

Kora lay half-dead on her back across the dying autumn grass, rear legs twitching, a wing pinned broken beneath her, the taste of blood on her tongue. She stared up at the dark sky, the ash from distant burning Port Oil stinging her eyes, and found she could not gather a full breath.

Another contraction, worse than the previous. Kora's body seized, her scream choked and bloody. Vision blurred behind tears.

"Oh God." Blackbird appeared beside Kora looking no worse for wear, utter panic in her whole countenance as she took Kora in. "Oh God. I, I've never helped—"

The contractions struck again, again, almost continuous now. Beneath the pain Kora felt something gush from her. Knew the blood by the smell. She reached out blindly, talons grabbing Blackbird's red scarf, gripped it tight. She screamed again as she pushed.

Out there on the cold, abandoned field, the ashes falling like snow around them, Sir Kora of Schwarz Angebot gave birth. A near-stranger her only witness as she struggled and strove, bleeding, dying, feeling every second of the passing hours. And at the end of it, broken, empty, victorious, she could barely hold the pair of raven-gryphon fledglings, the edges of her beak barely forming into a smile as she remembered two of the names she and her late husband had thought of. "Carina . . . Bifrost . . ."

"I'm sorry," said Blackbird. The other raven-gryphon removed her scarf and gently took the pair of newborns from Kora, who tried and failed to keep hold of them. Blackbird wrapped the pair up snuggly. "I'm so sorry."

"The Floating Mountain," whispered Kora, talons twitching as her front legs dropped lifeless beside her. She breathed slow and shallow, everything seeming to relax inside her. "Get them to the . . . the Floating . . . . . ."

***

Holly opened her eyes and found herself sitting cross-legged in Guru Veda's study, the dark Wolf-Lord sitting opposite her, hands folded in her lap and expression expectant even with the blindfold. "Ah. You're back. I hope your solo efforts were . . . instructional."

Holly could not speak at first. She sniffed and rubbed her eyes, found tears were streaming down her cheeks. She thought she could still taste the blood and ash in her mouth. "Was any of that real? Was that another life I have lived, sometime in the past, or . . . or did the Magicahedron conjure it all from nothing?"

"I think you know who you need to ask for the answer to that question."

Holly blinked for a moment, and then stood and turned, running for the door and out of the study.

She found Kanti in their shared bedroom in his male form, her fellow Wolf-Lord sitting on the bed and reading a book. As Holly slammed the door closed behind her, Kanti startled and looked up, eyes growing wide as he saw something he didn't like. "Holly? What's wrong? What's happened?"

Holly stood there at the door, breathless and shaking, barely able to bring herself to ask "Carina and Bifrost. Did you get them to the Floating Mountain safely? Did they live?"

Kanti remained sitting for a long moment, staring slack-jawed at Holly. Then his mouth closed and he set his book down and stood, worry turning into wonder. "Kora?"

This was enough. Holly crossed the room to the bed and Kanti's embrace, crying once more, this time with joy.

CHAPTER ELEVEN

"I want to be sure there are no lingering misconceptions," said Guru Veda. It was a late evening dinner, Veda and Holly alone on the veranda to Veda's personal quarters at the Wolf-Lord's request. It was a simple meal of tandoori chicken and rice alongside cups of mango lassi, all of which Veda had—going by the dark Wolf-Lord's own word—prepared herself. It was a meal full of sweet and spice in perfect complement to the high and sweeping view of the temple and surrounding city, cast in warm tones by the slowly setting sun. Holly ate with relish.

"They are not your children," Veda continued.

"I can remember giving birth to them," said Holly.

"You remember giving birth to them as Kora," said Veda. "It was Kora who gave birth to them and died in the process. The Kora form went away to dwell in Sheol, and the energy of her was reborn a clean slate to eventually become you, Holly le Fay. A wholly different person in all practical matters. Someday, you will die, your form will go to dwell in Sheol, and your energy, your magic, will be reborn in another clean slate to eventually become . . . well, we just won't know."

Holly frowned as she looked away to the sunset, a dazzling display of orange and gold. She chose to accept the guru's wisdom and moved to something else from her recent experiences bothering her. "My friends from Heraldale, Laura and Kurt, they have told me much about the wars and histories there. The fall of the northern kingdom of Schwarz Angebot, its last ruler, Queen Grimhilt. If I understand my history right, I was already a young, young child when Kora died. How is that possible?"

Veda chuckled, sipping from her mango drink before answering. "That is simpler than you might expect. Our individual lives are links in great chains of reincarnation, but these chains are not bound by the same temporal causality we live by in our material lives. Your next life could be 100 years from now, or it could be 1,000 years in the past, before the Wolf-Lords were ever driven from Heraldale. That sometimes, though I don't think often, multiple incarnations of the same energy occur at roughly the same time is not overly strange."

"I suppose not," said Holly, though she still struggled to wrap her mind around it. She took a hurried bite of her rice to avoid needing to speak any more on the matter.

"What interests me," said Veda, the first to speak after several minutes of what Holly had hoped was companiable silence, "is that you used your own magic to activate the Magicahedron in the first place. I didn't know you were capable of that."

"All new to me," admitted Holly, putting on a smile. "Not . . . well-practiced. Beginner's luck"

Veda watched her closely, even though her eyes—if the dark Wolf-Lord had eyes at all—were hidden beneath her blindfold. "How long have you been using magic?"

Holly settled her hands in her lap. Her gaze found the sunset again, found much of the orange fading to dim red and dimmer purple, found the end of the day somehow sad. The question made her think on things she had tried not to. "After Morgana le Fay. No . . . after blocking Eternal Flames. Felt my own magic. The Burning King."

"Toqeph," said Veda. "The first unicorn created by God itself. Who created, in turn, the Wolf-Lords and our kin. Consumed in the Eternal Flames for all time . . ."

The dark Wolf-Lord's voice trailed away. There was heaved a heavy sigh. "I have not met or heard tell of another le Fay since the golden years when awesome Morgause, whom the unicorns and gryphons call Nero, ruled sublime in distant Gateway."

Holly startled and looked back to her host. Veda had herself looked away, not west to the setting sun—nearly gone now, the horizon a cooling purple—but to the east, where night had fallen and the stars rose twinkling and cold. The dark Wolf-Lord looked as old as the night itself in that moment, old and sad. And this was no wonder to Holly, though it filled her with wonder, for Veda spoke of an age more than 1,000 years in the past. "You lived the Golden Age?"

"Aye," said Veda, her voice gone soft and distant. "I hear you were a storyteller before your throat injury, and I trust you were a good one, but for me those days aren't stories, but . . . memory. God, to be there again. You can't begin to imagine, Holly. The light of the Sun turning the waters of the inland seas to gold. The majesty of the Dragonback Mountains rising to the distant south, wreathed in the shadows of their smoke. The gryphonsong, free on the wind. The sweet smell of Morgause's vineyards, laughter richer than any wine as the grapes were pressed in great parties. And Wolf-Lords at our forges, at our kilns, making our art for our beloved unicorns, for our beloved Heraldale, making it for the sheer joy of it."

Holly listened, bewitched. Veda gazed into the growing night, the stars caught in the tears running down the dark Wolf-Lord's cheeks. Her smile died and she looked first to her emptied plate, then to the west. The sun was all gone. The white houses decorating the cliffs and winding roadways from the university to the distant beach glimmered like ghosts in the dark. "All gone, now. All ash."

"I am sorry," said Holly.

"As am I," said Veda. The dark Wolf-Lord's shoulders heaved in a great sigh, and then she looked back at Holly, expression becoming a mask more inscrutable than the blindfold she wore alone could manage. "You have no sword."

Holly blinked, bewildered by this sudden swerve in the conversation. "No choice. Let it go to make it here."

"A noble sacrifice of something so precious to you, so vital," said Veda, nodding in what seemed to be approval. She stood and held her hand open and palm up over the table, Holly standing with her as she noticed the tingle of magic growing in the air. "And perhaps a sacrifice for the best. If your hopes do indeed all rest in the promise of magic, then I think this will serve you better."

There rang a high crack, like thunder near at hand, and then upon Veda's palm there rested a glimmering box of polished cherrywood, kept secured by a heavy gold lock. As Holly stood and watched, the lock clicked and the top third of the box swung up and open. Inside, nestled on red satin shot through with a gold thread, lay a foot-long rod of black Lunar Steel, the middle eight inches wrapped in black leather for a better grip.

"What is it?" asked Holly.

"A tool I made long ago for an heir I never got around to siring," said Veda, dropping her hand back to her side. The box remained floating where she had held it. "I give it now to you, if you will take it. No proper sorcerer would go without their staff."

Holly swallowed, reached out with her left hand and picked up the rod of Lunar Steel. Once she had, the box turned black and disappeared like smoke scattered by a sudden breeze. She hardly noticed as she turned her newfound weapon over in her hand to examine it in the light of the stars. "It is a good weight. Lighter than I would have expected. You said it is a sorcerer's staff—"

A pulse of magic, her magic, swept up Holly's arm and through the metal. She watched in surprise and awe as the rod lengthened, gained three feet, four, five, the spear-like end scraping against the stone of the balcony floor, the other end rising even with her eyes and twisting into a thick knob.

"Wow," was all she could think to say.

"Nicely done," said Veda, smile wide and bright. She waved a hand and disappeared the table and chairs between her and Holly. Another wave and the balcony they stood on grew out from the building with a cacophonous grinding of stone, doubling in width. The elder Wolf-Lord backed away, blindfolded gaze remaining locked on Holly. "In the Golden Age of the Wolf-Lords, Le Fay wolves used staffs, staves, or wands to aid their focus and quicken their spellcasting, in much the same way unicorns channel their magic through their alicorn horns. Now that you have begun to use it, you will need a solid feel for your magic if you want to find your way into the Dark Realm and the House of Incarnation."

Holly recognized an invitation to spar when she saw one. She widened her stance and bent her legs for balance, kept one hand on the leather grip near the middle of the staff and slid her other hand lower, nearer the stabbing end. The head of the staff lowered to aim at the guru, who Holly kept her eyes on the entire time. "How does this work?"

"Lunar Steel is conducive to magic," said Veda, taking on the warm but professional tone of voice Holly recognized when the other Wolf-Lord was assuming her duties as a guru. "You probably could have used your sword in the same manner, if you were trained. Call upon your inner magic as you have before, but focus it through the staff in your hands. Regard it as an extension of your body the way you would've regarded your sword. And focus, too, on what you want your magic to do. An errant thought at the wrong moment could turn a summoned bolt of lightning into a stream of bubbles. Not half as useful, unless you're entertaining at a birthday party."

"I have had to do that before," whispered Holly. "People celebrating birthdays suck."

Veda nodded. "This is known. When you are ready."

Holly was ready. The conversation had made her think of putting on plays, and this in turn had made her think of her beloved Shun and the kitsune's own powerful magic. Focusing, Holly felt for her magic, felt it come to her more readily than before, breathing and dancing like a fire inside her. She breathed in and breathed out, pushed the magic out and thrust the staff forward, thought of burning.

The fireball sped toward Veda like a firework, bursting harmlessly against the shield spell the dark Wolf-Lord cast with an outstretched hand. She laughed, grinning madly at Holly through the translucent white pane between them. "Hah! Excellent! Again! This time, focus not only on power, but form! These are the two vital components of any spell. Power and form!"

Holly nodded and tightened her grip on her staff. She thought of how her first fireball had reminded her of a firework and grinned, hurriedly slashing forward with her staff rather than thrusting.

The spinning discus of fire flew at Veda like a high-powered buzzsaw. She stepped aside moments before the fire wheel tore first through her shield spell, and then the stone of the balcony railing behind her, continuing another half-dozen feet into the open air before finally dissipating.

Two words came to Holly's mind to describe Veda as the elder Wolf-Lord turned to look at her again.

Manic glee.

"Alright," said Veda conjuring a fireball in each hand as she stepped even with Holly again. "Let's try you on the defensive now!"

For a moment, Holly struggled to think of how to conjure something like a shield. But then the fireballs were flying at her and she thrust her staff forward with a snap and burst of magic, shouting out as she did "Shield!"

The pane of magic which materialized in front of her was nearly identical to Veda's, shimmering white and translucent enough to see through, to watch as the orbs of fire splashed harmlessly against the other side of it. Holly had a moment to grin with satisfaction at her successful attempt, before the flames cleared enough for her to see a trio of Vedas stood opposing her now, each bouncing a fireball in both hands.

"Not too shabby," the three said in unison, taking a uniform step forward as they did. "But I won't be satisfied until you can do it without verbalization!"

Holly didn't know how long into the night they kept at it, exploring her burgeoning talent in magic down every avenue Guru Veda thought of. Hours, perhaps. Toward the end, it began to feel more like play than training. Veda threw all manner of spellcraft at Holly, trusting her to weather it as the stone turned to mud beneath her feet, as the draperies at the nearby windows came alive and grabbed at her, as lightning fell without thunder and blasts of aurora-like spells sent waves of crystal growing across where they struck. To weather the magic, to dispel it, to cast it at Veda in turn. Holly felt this trust, this strange affection, and at every chance fought to meet it.

At last, Veda dispelled a final shield spell and held a hand out to signal an end. Immediately, Holly collapsed against the nearest wall, panting for breath, her fur mussed up, her grip barely holding on her staff. But she grinned, too. Across the way from her, though still standing strong, Veda fought to catch her breath as well.

"Alright," said the dark Wolf-Lord, returning the balcony to its normal width with a wave of her hand, "I think that is enough for one night. You best get back to your beloved pirate before she begins to worry, and we'll get back to this in the morning."

Holly nodded, not having it in her yet to speak. She pushed off from the wall, leaned on her staff for support as she swayed for balance. She turned for the doorway back into Veda's quarters, paused, thought about it for a moment, and then after steeling herself for the act she turned and gave the other Wolf-Lord a full-hearted hug. "Thank you for this, Guru Veda. The time. The teaching. The staff. Thank you for everything."

For a withering second, Veda stood utterly motionless within Holly's embrace, as if petrified into stone by the act. Then she returned the hug with one of her own, body briefly shaking with a dry chuckle. "It is . . . my pleasure, young wolf. My pleasure."

Holly broke her hug and turned to go on her way, step lighter even though her tiredness still lingered. She crossed Veda's quarters to the door out into the rest of the university, humming something to herself. She did not notice Seraphina standing beside Veda's work desk away to the right until she had already grabbed the doorknob, the surprise of someone else there drawing a squeak and startled jump from her. "Oh, gosh! Sera!"

The red-furred Wolf-Lord said nothing, only stared at Holly, a hand idly digging the sharp end of a pen into the wood of Veda's desk. From the way that third of the room was raised an inch higher than the area Holly stood in, Seraphina stood nearly as tall as her, though with the hardness of the other's gaze, Holly felt somehow shorter. She swallowed and dropped her gaze to the pen currently marring the desk. "Should not do that. Guru Veda's desk. Probably prefers . . . undamaged."

Seraphina's arm jerked. The pen carved a ragged groove across the desk. One corner of the red Wolf-Lord's muzzle twitched upward, showing teeth. "Funny. I was getting the impression she preferred damaged goods. I'll ask her myself, if you think you can ever spare her."

"I hope so," said Holly. She swallowed, looked from Seraphina to her own hand on the doorknob. She turned it, pulled it open, hurried out into the corridor beyond, nearly slamming the door shut again behind her. And as she did, she felt as if someone somewhere had suddenly walked across her grave.

CHAPTER TWELVE

Regina stood alone on their bedroom's balcony and watched the last of the Sun fade away beyond the horizon. From a distance they might have appeared naked, dressed modestly in sleeveless shirt and trousers the same snowy white as their fur, as the billowing curtains caught in the night breeze around them, granting almost a ghostly air to the moment.

The castle of Cairn Romulus was almost quiet. On the wind, Regina heard the sounds of revelry rising from the banquet hall, where Queen Celeste, Caelestis, and Maurus indulged in the same extravagant feast as they usually did, this time joined by the cackling Butcher. Feasts, while the nation starved.

"Servant of . . . Morgana . . ."

Regina's grip tightened on the balcony railing at the memory of the renegade Shun's words.

"My God, all this time, Holly was terrified you knew and never told her, but you were kept as ignorant as she was! Hah! Go running home to Celeste if you really want to know why that might have been! Or better yet, ask your traveling companion peaking in through the window."

Even then, the minotaur still taunted Regina. Even then . . .

Regina let go of the railing, turned and went back inside. They looked at their sword on the silk bed for a moment, then ignored it and went to the fireplace sitting cold and dead across the bedroom. They knelt, threw in a half-dozen logs and a splash of kerosene for swift ignition. They took the flint and steel lighter sitting on the mantel above the hearth and struck a swift fire, letting the tool fall to the heavy carpet once done.

"The town was bustling, the last time."

Regina watched the fire grow. It was a large fireplace. They could have squeezed themself in at a crouch, if they wanted to. Plenty of room for the fire, plenty of room for what they wanted, if they only needed a moment to steel themself.

Quickly, with their voice raised loud and steady, Regina said into the fire "I request an audience with the Grand Council of the Nameless Order!"

Three seconds passed, one second long enough to make Regina begin to feel foolish. And then a voice burdened with a thick Inari accent spoke back at them from the flames. "Who makes this request?"

"General Regina of Romulus, seeking knowledge."

From here, a minute passed by in silence as Regina knelt before the fire, and then another. They imagine what was going on past the flames to wherever the stranger's voice came from. They imagined messengers running down echoing wood hallways to take the request to kitsune of higher and higher authority. Guards whispering to each other over what could bring a Wolf-Lord with so much blood on their hands to seek wisdom from the Holy Three. The long consideration to reject the request, and then—

"Your request is accepted," said the thickly accented voice. "You may have your audience. Step forth."

Regina wasted no words on giving thanks. They stood, and as they did the fireplace rose with them, grew tall enough for them to step through without even needing to fold their ears back, and the flames roared and thickened until the entirety of the fireplace's rear wall was obscured behind curling waves of bright yellow.

Hands clenched into fists at their sides, Regina stepped forward into those flames. There passed a moment of heat washing over them, heat enough to singe the tip of their tail curled tight against their left leg. Then they were through and found themselves in a new, disarmingly humble room of white wood panels and bright red lacquer, gleaming in the light of red paper lanterns hanging from a high ceiling.

Regina blinked at the change in location and looked behind them. Saw the wall dominated by a mirror image of their bedroom wall, their fireplace. They looked ahead again, startled at the sudden appearance of a red-furred kitsune in a dull blue kimono no more than a yard before them, four tails waving lazily behind him. He stared at Regina with a bright yet indifferent gaze. "General Regina. Welcome to Hidden Fire. Follow me."

A high doorway appeared in the wall behind the kitsune where there hadn't been one before. The kitsune turned and passed through the doorway without another word, steps soundless on the wood floor. Regina hurried to catch up after a last glance backward, the fall of their own steps seeming crude and deafening.

The kitsune led Regina down a short hallway and out into a wide garden lit by star-shaped lanterns floating high over the grounds. Sakura trees stood vigil at the garden's four corners, while red and pink Azaleas in defiant bloom wove along stone pathways in elegant patterns. At the garden's center rose a towering beech tree, 100 feet tall, grey bark and gold leaves. Beneath the branches of the tree, several more kitsune of various tail numbers sat in meditation.

Past the garden, down another, longer hallway, where the walls were sliding doors into unseen rooms. Following after their guide, Regina felt more than heard the footsteps of kitsune close behind them, hands ready on weapons not yet drawn.

They came to a new room, the closest the Nameless Order would come to a throne room. There was room enough for a hundred Wolf-Lords to sit comfortably, the walls were yet more of the red lacquered wood, mostly obscured behind thin and wavering flames lining three-fourths of the room. The fires along the far wall illuminated three kitsune in black ceremonial robes sitting in the lotus position. They were the oldest kitsune Regina had ever seen, the whole room heavy with the magnitude of their magical strength. Each was white-furred and red-eyed, each bearing nine tails standing tall behind them like the tails of peacocks.

The Holy Three. The leaders of the Nameless Order, who it was said had walked the lands even in the days of Toqeph the Prime Unicorn.

"General," spoke the middle of the three, her voice sounding impossibly young for a fox so old. "Long has it been since we allowed a wolf to walk these halls. Longer still for one as disgraced as a wolf of Romulus. Why have you come here?"

"If what you say is true and you allowed me here anyway," said Regina, voice tight as they forced down the anger at the slight to their nation's honor, "then you must have an idea of why I came already. I work alongside one of your own, a kitsune who goes by the title of the Butcher, to find and capture my renegade twin, but I do not trust him. He has made references to events I am unaware of, to unaccountable familiarity with my twin. I would be made aware of these things, if you can do so."

The 9-tailed kitsune to the right spoke next, his words almost incomprehensible beneath his Okami accent. "We are aware of the Butcher, and of your mission. He is a vicious but loyal monk of our order. He has met your twin before."

"How?" asked Regina. "When?"

"A year ago," answered the first kitsune elder. "In conflict through the Cult of the Burning King, led as it secretly was by the very Wolf-Lord who fathered you with Queen Celeste."

Regina's back stiffened. Their hands clenched at their sides. "The Wolf-Lord who fathered me is dead. Died long ago. I watched their remains pulled from the wreckage of a train."

"That," spoke the third elder for the first time, "is not the Wolf-Lord of whom we speak. The Butcher learned this truth from the source herself, and passed it on to us. And to many others. The rumors have long crept through the lands of Wolf-Lords, Jackals, and kitsune. Surely you have heard them yourself, somewhere."

General Regina! Hero of Romulus! Holly told us all about her life growing up, before she found us, and if you think I'm impressed by you, your ego truly marks you as the child of Queen Celeste and Morgana le Fay!

"Impossible," growled Regina, though her heart quailed and her guts curdled. "Impossible. Celeste . . . my parent would, would never . . . Morgana is the enemy of us all. A cursed traitor. Why would they have—"

"Power," answered the middle elder. "And for this, the story of the Wolf-Lords has been thrown into doubt. Chaos ravages your nation, and if it is not brought to heel soon, it threatens to drag all of us down with it. The madness of your Queen Celeste will make it so. Your blood marks you as cursed, Child of Morgana."

The strength fled Regina's legs and they fell to their knees. They found their hands and stared in mounting horror, suddenly sure they could feel the dirtied blood as it sped through their veins. For a bare-skinned moment, the monumentality of the lie their whole life had been turned the mortar of their mind into sand, dry and crumbling, utterly doomed.

Then anger rose sharp as a blade in their heart and steadied them, gave them something solid to grasp. Their parent, Queen Celeste, had mated with the Queen of Traitors, had in turn betrayed their family, their nation, their very people. And in return had gotten . . . gotten . . .

Regina and Candida. General Regina and Holly le Fay.

"Do not despair," spoke the right-hand elder. "History is not destiny. There is hope yet."

"Hope?" asked Regina, looking back up at the three kitsune. A part of them did not want the promise of hope, favoring the rage and the focus it gave. Another part scrabbled desperately for it, for anything to keep them from their own most treacherous thoughts. "What hope can there be for an heir of monsters?"

In answer, the middle elder gave a whip-crack of one of her tails. A white wood box appeared in the air before the elder and slowly drifted down to float before Regina. With another tail whip, the box opened. Inside, on a black velvet pillow, sat an old dagger, the blade long and thick, its silver-like shine dulled by the ages and stained red.

Regina frowned and reached for the dagger. Their hand closed around the hilt—

They knelt not before the Holy Three in the flame-walled room. They knelt instead upon black marble shot through with veins of white, the night sky open and perilous overhead, a wind full with the taste of salt washing over the wide balcony. From nearby came the sounds of music and laughter, the raised and jovial conversation Regina recognized from attending countless of Queen Celeste's royal banquets. Warm lights played across the balcony from behind them, and in the lights, the vague shadows of Wolf-Lords dancing.

Regina startled as a Wolf-Lord wrapped in black robes stormed past them, panting for breath as they made for the balcony railing with surprising speed for a form so wracked with age. Regina stared in wonder. The Wolf-Lord had been tall once, but now their shoulders slumped, their back crooked, their limbs horribly thin, clawed hands grasping the railing like spiders. Long hair hung limp down to the small of their back, hair which had been red once, now a dull and withered grey. All the horrors of old age, a malady nearly unknown to Wolf-Lords, seemed embodied in the figure.

"Sister!" cried a voice from behind Regina, a thunderous and queenly voice. Another Wolf-Lord came onto the balcony from the party, and in every way the first showed weakness and decay, this newcomer showed strength, broad-shouldered and unbent by the years, hair as white as their fur glimmering in its long ponytail, resplendent golden robes and a matching crown on their head.

Regina knew there could be no mistaking the pair. Any Wolf-Lord worth their schooling would have grasped the scene unfolding before them. The twins, Queen Morgause and Morgana le Fay, and the betrayal which signaled the slow end of the Golden Age.

"My sister, please, calm down! It was only a small thing. So, your glamour slipped. Nobody really cares."

"It was only a small thing . . . to you," hissed the dark Wolf-Lord clutching at the railing, head down. Regina could not see her face, but they could hear well enough the raw despair in her voice. "And everybody cares except you."

Morgause's step slowed, shoulders falling at this remark. "Morgy, please, you know I care—"

"Then stop this!" snarled Morgana. The sorceress whirled from the railing to glare up at Morgause behind her, causing both the wolf queen and Regina to flinch away from the sight. Morgana was not merely old, but ancient, her features withered and drawn, her body rake-thin beneath her robes, her fur falling in drifts to reveal skin gone grey and veiny.

"Stop summoning me out here," Morgana cried again, waving an arm to encompass the grand pyramidal palace the balcony was only a small part of. Her voice, even valiantly raised in anger, was hardly more than a dry whisper through a barrow. "I'm old, damn you. We're twins, but I'm old and you aren't, and everyone at your parties knows it. And they know it more year by year, no matter the glamour or trick. And they whisper among themselves, no matter how swiftly you turn a deaf ear to them, and where there once lived awe, there is now only pity. I hate it. Quite often, I hate you."

"You don't really mean that," said Morgause, head twitching briefly back the way the pair had come. "And don't act so wild. There are some who might be watching."

The Wolf-Lord crone snorted, a brief glimmer of a smile crossing her muzzle. It came and went, but her eyes remained shining, wet. A twitchy nervousness overtook her, spidery hands fidgeting with her left sleeve. "Wouldn't want to do anything to embarrass the reputation of Morgause the Golden. No. No, can't have that. But I can fix this. I am Morgana le Fay. I can make this all right again, if I only have the nerve."

"That's right," said Morgause, heedless of what Regina knew to be coming, reaching out to clap the dark

Wolf-Lord on the shoulder. "You're brilliant. I know you can—"

Morgana drew a short dagger from their left sleeve, the new and beautiful twin to the stained relic Regina still held. A moment passed in confusion and fear, Morgause stepping away. But the sorceress turned the weapon inward and stabbed, shudders of agony, her back hitting the balcony railing as she carved downward through her own chest, the bone breaking and the blood streaming thick and black.

There must indeed have been party guests spying on the sibling argument from the palace windows, for screams began to sound from behind Regina. None held a candle to Morgause's own scream, all veneers of propriety abandoned as she lunged toward her twin. "No! Oh God, Morgana, no—"

The angle was all wrong where Regina knelt. They could not see the moment Morgana pulled the dagger from her chest and plunged it hilt-deep into Morgause's, and they did not have the will to move. But they could hear the fated blow, and the fresh screams from the growing crowds in the nearby windows, screams of outrage and horror for this second moment of violence.

Morgause fell back, dragging Morgana down with her. This, Regina could see. The twins struggled a moment, Morgause heaving and vomiting red as

Morgana carved a ragged hole through her chest. The dagger was tossed aside. Morgana gripped Morgause's shoulders hard enough to tear through the gold fabric of her dress. And as Regina watched, blood and thin, twitching black tendrils poured from the ruin of Morgana's chest, seeping down and into Morgause's carved-open front.

Morgause threw her head back and screamed, eyes rolling, back arched. The wet sounds of tearing flesh and cracking bone echoed across the balcony. Her dress lay crumpled and blood-soaked around her. Her chest bulged upward, Regina certain it was ready to burst. Then the white Wolf-Lord fell limp, coughed out a wheezing breath. The black tendrils drew back up into Morgana's chest, bringing with them a fresh and glistening, still-beating heart. Morgause's heart.

Morgana pulled away to rest on her knees, arms at her sides, head thrown back, the wolf crone swaying where she knelt. A shudder struck her, another. She leaned to the side and heaved, a roiling mess of red and black pouring from her muzzle to splatter the floor, the stench of rotting flesh exploding across the balcony.

"I can't feel," wheezed Morgause. She lay limp of the floor, the wound in her chest healed away. "I can't feel . . . anything. Give me back my heart. Please. Give it back. I can't feel."

"No," said Morgana, giggling. She flew back up to her feet like a puppet yanked by its strings, another laugh escaping her, deeper and stronger. As Regina watched, all signs of age and frailty faded away from the wolf sorceress. Wrinkles disappeared and fur filled back in. Her back straightened with a sharp crack and the muscle filled back into her chest, her shoulders, her limbs. Her hair grew smooth and shiny again as it fell across her shoulders and down her back, not returning to the red of her true youth, but darkening to the ominous grey of storm clouds.

"God above," said Morgana, stepping over and away from her still-pleading twin, arms held wide to her sides as a new set of black robes materialized onto her with the quickest flex of magic. "God above! I didn't realize how much power I had lost until I suddenly have it ALL BACK!"

With this shout, the dark Wolf-Lord clapped her hands together. The burst of loosed magic reduced the glass of the windows across that whole side of the pyramidal palace to sand, cracked the stone and sent onlookers flying back. Regina fell away with a cry as the magic struck them. The dagger flew from their hand—

And suddenly they were back in the temple of the Nameless Order, sprawled on their back before the Holy Three. They remained lying there for a long several seconds, digesting the vision, the first-hand history they knew their twin would have paid handsomely to experience.

"If you saw what we suspect," said the middle elder at last, prompting Regina to prop themself up on their palms, "then there can be no doubt. Queen Celeste committed an unspeakable heresy in producing you and your twin. History is now poised to repeat itself, the destiny of the Wolf-Lords in the balance as twins once more come to betrayal and war. You know now what you must do to stop it all from happening again."

Regina did not answer at first. They grunted as they pushed themself up into a proper sitting position, and then from there to a respectful knee before the three ancient kitsune. They remained so with their thoughts even a mystery to themself, a terrible weight on their back, sharp and relentless.

"General?"

"Yes." Regina looked up, making no attempt to hide the tears in their eyes as they contemplated killing their twin, killing Holly. "I know what it is I need to do."

CHAPTER THIRTEEN

Another day and another night passed. Holly spent them alongside Guru Veda, learning how to feel and grasp her magic more swiftly, learning more of the intricacies of her magic, this newfound part of herself she was only beginning to understand. She learned how to describe it as like a fire, breathing and living, warming and enveloping.

"I remember Morgana having a similar feel to her magic, back in my short-lived tenure in her little cult. The raw strength was always so overwhelming. It could be hard to focus on much else. I think her ego would have liked that."

"I am more familiar with my wife's magic," said Holly. The pair of them stood again on Veda's balcony late in the evening, Holly going through old, familiar fencing forms as the elder Wolf-Lord looked on. Holly realized early in the morning the Lunar Steel of her staff was enchanted and malleable to her magic, able to do more than shift between rod and staff forms. She had spent the better part of an hour after breakfast turning it into every sort of melee weapon she could think of, and she had been able to think of many. Every sort of sword, from dao sabers to estoc. Axes, maces, war scythes, spears, kukri, war hammers, tridents, each form as capable of projecting spells as the traditional staff.

"Shun's magic is warm, too," Holly continued, staring down the slim blade of a rapier. "But exciting, invigorating. Does not smother. Makes you want to dance. I do not know if I . . . say right."

"You're doing fine," said Veda. A tone Holly identified after a moment of confused thought as sadness entered the dark Wolf-Lord's tone. "This Shun I have heard so much about, she is a good wife, I hope? She gives you a good life?"

Holly lowered the rapier, transformed it back into its staff form with a flick of her magic, went to lean against the balcony railing as she thought the questions over. "Yes. Best life could ever ask for. Love her much. Owe her . . . much." By then, the lingering pains of her scarred throat were all but gone, and though her voice could no longer rise above a whisper, it no longer felt like she was tearing the flesh to pieces to speak in more than stuttering fragments of meaning. "Without her . . .

would not be me. No plays. No Eishaven. No Laura or Kurt or Nessa. No kisses in the morning or paw rubs in the evening. No mugs of cider as we sit shoulder to shoulder, watching the auroras play overhead. Nobody to hold me tight and soothing when the monthly cramps hit, and nobody for me to hold when her cramps hit, or to celebrate the end of those cramps with too much of our favorite spicy calamari and udon. Shun is good. I love her very much."

"It sounds like it," said Veda. In the orange glow of the Sun nearing the horizon, Holly saw twin tracks of tears coming down the elder wolf's cheeks from beneath her blindfold. "A worthy wife . . . and as devoted to you as you are to her, with how she stormed into the very heart of Morgana's fortress to save you and your Nessa."

"I suppose that is true," said Holly, having never thought of it before, the truth too simple and obvious to need conscious consideration. But now, the love raw and in the open, the ache swelled in accordance. She took a sharp, pained breath, not crying but wanting to as she stood from the railing and turned to look west. To her naked eye, there was nothing beyond the sharp white slope of the town and beach than an ocean turned to gold by the setting sun.

To her mind's eye, though, she saw farther. She saw the harsh black coast of Romulus. She saw Eishaven.

She saw the cabin she called home with Shun and Nessa. She saw the forests of holly where she chose her second name, and the field where she made snow forts for Nessa and her friends, and the hill where she stood once upon a night, beneath the lights of a million Elementals, and felt like she could touch the world. The yearning rose like the ghost of a lost limb, wreathed in fears she would never see any of it again.

"Tomorrow. Do you think I will be able to enter Dark Realm tomorrow?"

"We shall see, my princess. We shall see."

***

Veda raised an eyebrow at the sight of Kanti following close on Holly's heels into the library study, nodding in greeting as she closed the door behind them with a kick of a heel. "Welcome, pirate. Any special occasion bringing you here?"

Kanti flashed a tooth-filled grin. "Just beginning to hear the ticking of the clock. Wanted to provide moral support."

The elder Wolf-Lord nodded again. "Always welcome. Now—"

"Where's Seraphina?" asked Kanti. And then, at Veda's blank expression, "your apprentice. Red fur, feels angry a lot."

"Ah, right, them." Veda fluttered a hand dismissively. "I told them they would not be needed today. Just as well. They told me they had business down in the village.

"And now, on to important matters. Good morning, my princess. Did you eat breakfast?"

"I did," answered Holly, assuming the increasingly familiar—and easier—cross-legged position. "A bowl of millet and milk, and some sliced mangos. I might have an addiction forming."

"There are worse things to get addicted to than a fruit," said Veda. She mirrored Holly on the floor, started to gesture to the fireplace before pausing, head tilting. "Do you have a question for me, my princess?"

"Yes," said Holly. "Why do you call me princess?"

"Are you not a princess of Romulus to the west? You don't have to worry about your secrets. Laura, our mutual minotaur friend, trusts me with hers."

"Am I a . . ." Holly frowned, working the question over in her mouth. "Perhaps. From the royal family, but do not feel a part of it. Surely cast out from even that distant claim to the throne by now."

"Surely," agreed Veda. "Very well. If you would prefer, I will cease. I never meant to make you uncomfortable. Just say the word."

Holly relaxed. "The word."

Veda loosed a quick chuckle, then gestured to the fireplace, a silvery, shimmering magic swirling around her hand. The fire leapt, burning white and pure. "It is time once more. Go forth."

Holly stood, shared a last look with Kanti, and then approached the fire. Despite her previous successful experiences, the old, instinctual fear returned to her as she felt the heat upon her body. This time she did not let the fear slow her, her gait steady as she strode into the flames with the whisper of "Shun, Nessa," beneath her breath—

—her breath swiftly stolen from her by the sudden, sharp cold. Holly staggered and stopped, struck momentarily blind. She stood on a field of snow, beautiful and dangerously familiar, a dark forest nearby, and nearer, an ice-choked river. Clouds consumed the sky, bleeding their snow upon the lands. From somewhere close came the push and pull of the northern ocean.

Holly, cold, ached with homesick yearning, her thoughts turning to the previous evening and her conversation with Veda. The idea the Magicahedron had granted her the chance to see her long-missed family again struck her and dug in until it could not be shaken. Her feet carried her up a rise in the land she knew by heart, her ears straining for the sounds her heart wanted. Laughter. The beauty of gryphon song. One of Kurt's aunts telling the children off for playing too rough—

Beyond the rise, the gryphon compound Holly and her family called home lay in burning ruin. Holly stood frozen, a ragged moan of horror escaping her. Her eyes raked the scene, beheld gryphons young and old scattered about, dead, burnt and hacked apart nearly beyond recognition.

"No. No no no . . ." Holly stumbled down the rise, fell, rose and ran for the scene of carnage. She shouted for survivors as she ran among the burning buildings, her eyes burning, the smoke acrid and the stench of meat and fat causing her to retch more than once. Yet onward she went, searching for something, any—

A minotaur horn, cracked and smoke-stained, barely glimpsed among the debris. Holly slid to a stop, splinters tearing her paws to shreds. She dug through the rubble, bleeding hands uncovering Laura's head, her shoulders and chest, her butchered arms and broken, mangled legs. Her eyes stared past Holly, vacant and blind in death, bloody foam still pooled in her slack-jawed mouth.

"Oh God, no," sobbed Holly. She staggered away, heart breaking, nearly fell as her feet hit something. She turned, her sobs turning to wails, shrieks of agony.

Shun lay pinned to the ground by a long katana driven through her belly, mouth open in a cry of pain which would never end. Beside her, throat slit and body burned, lay Nessa, the unicorn child a horror show of mutilations.

Holly fell to her knees, screaming. She beat her fists upon the ground, scattering the ashes, cinders flaring and scorching her. Heedless of the pain, she beat the earth, blind with tears and fury at the loss of everything, all she loved, all she cherished, torn away by . . . by . . .

Footsteps, heavy, drew near. Holly looked up, watched a Wolf-Lord in white armor step through the fire and smoke toward her, untouched by either, their features hidden beneath a full-faced helm.

Burning, nihilistic hate ignited in Holly's heart. She stood, drew her spell rod, let it become a black sword as she charged. The Wolf-Lord stranger caught her blade with their own, the skies resounding with the thunderclap.

Holly pulled away, swung again. Drove the foe back. She advanced, screaming with each swing.

Knocked the foe's sword from their hand.

Opened their belly.

A final swing, the foe's helmeted head flying off, their body falling into the mess of their guts.

Holly stood panting for a blood-splattered breath. She felt sick, tired, empty, dread spreading through her like frost as she stared down at her foe's head. Before her, the metal of the helmet sagged, wax under a candle flame.

Regina's face lay revealed, wide-eyed and frightened.

Slowly, Holly fell to her knees, her eyes trapped uncomprehendingly by the sight of her twin. Her mouth opened to scream—

—but the sudden loss of the vision, the return to Veda's study, silenced her. She slumped over, out of her meditative pose and onto her side, trembling with the shock of all she had witnessed. Somewhere nearby, she felt Kanti worrying over her, the smoke and ash and blood still caked across her body. She heard her lover's voice pleading with her to say something, to say anything, to at least breathe steady for her.

Eventually, Holly stirred, got a hand pressed against the floor, pushed herself back up into something close to a sitting position. Kanti knelt beside her, wiping away at her with a wet cloth to clean away the grime from her vision. Holly, too weak to resist, allowed herself to be maneuvered around, her eyes only for Veda watching her, Holly silently begging for the slightest word of affirmation.

"I'm sorry," said Veda. "You failed."

CHAPTER FOURTEEN

"Holly, wait! Stop!"

Holly did not stop at Kanti's voice, but she did slow down from a harried sprint across the temple grounds to more of a quick march. Slow enough for her fellow Wolf-Lord to catch up. "I cannot stay here any longer after what I just saw."

"What you just saw was an illusion!" Kanti was nearer, her shadow looming up beside Holly's across the sun-bleached stone beneath their feet. Her hand grabbed at Holly's shoulder, threatened to pull her black feather cloak off before Holly shrugged the hand away. "Just, please stop for a moment and think about this!"

They reached the courtyard where Kanti's stealth airship had remained since the day of their arrival. Holly hurried up the rear ramp into the craft and to the front, hitting the levers for the power-up sequence as she went. As she heard Kanti come aboard behind her she at last turned to address her fellow Wolf-Lord in the loudest, most commanding whisper she could manage. "I need you to fly us. I do not know how and time means everything right now."

"Holly . . ." Kanti stepped toward her, slowly, expression a peculiar sort of anguish which Holly didn't think she had seen before. The black Wolf-Lord reached her, reached out, hesitated a moment before resting her hands on Holly's shoulders, not quite gripping them as she seemed to want to. "Holly, I'm scared too, but it was only—"

"Kora was real," said Holly, the words at once shutting Kanti up. "Kora, and Port Oil, and the twins left behind. All was real. I cannot sit idle and hope, warning unheeded. Something terrible has happened to my home. I have to see, I have to help."

"If you're wrong," said Kanti, "then I don't know if we'll have enough time to get back here and resume your learning to reach the Waters of Life. We're risking the lives of all our loved ones on . . . on fear and confusion."

Holly wanted to scream, to beat herself upon the other Wolf-Lord, to make her understand the words Holly couldn't find as her brain ground away. She felt a child again, Celeste beside her with a knife, pricking her childhood stutter out of her. "Kanti! I am scared. But.

But always. But always go to the rescue. Against all sense. Help."

For a moment, the pair stood at an impasse. Holly knew the other Wolf-Lord was right about the risk being taken. But she also knew the blood and soot covering her when she came out of the vision had been all too real. She knew, and yet . . . yet . . .

The impasse ended as Holly's ears perked to the nearing sound of running, across stone, then up metal. She seized Kanti by the shoulders and threw her aside. A moment later a katana appeared from thin air mid-thrust, burying an inch of Lunar Steel into the top of Holly's right breast.

"AAUGH!"

Holly slid back a step before regaining her balance, grabbing at the unseen hands holding the sword. The invisibility illusion faded, revealing the Butcher's one-eyed leer, his rancid breath across Holly's muzzle as his grin spread wider. "Hello, my most hated foe. You miss me?"

Holly did not miss him, landing a kick dead-center up into his groin. The kitsune wheezed and drew in. Holly snarled and pushed forward, forcing him back more as she hissed to Kanti "Go!"

Not another word of protest separated the pirate from the pilot seat. The airship creaked, rose, swung westward as Kanti worked the levers and control crystals.

"You can't escape," growled the Butcher, voice full of bravado even as Holly forced him backward, onto the still-lowered boarding ramp. "We're coming for you, Princess Candida, and I will have my revenge for you making my beloved Morgana discard me like a grown-boring lover!"

"The name is Holly, now!" Blood pattered the metal floor of the airship as Holly drew the tip of the sword from her chest, forced it upward into the grated ceiling. "And I would gladly give Morgana back to you! She is just the worst!"

"Take that back, you bitch!" The Butcher cracked his tails behind him like whips. Streamers of fire leapt from the tips of the tails, three striking the inner walls of the airship and setting the cargo nets aflame, two more splashing against Holly's arms.

"Gah!" She dropped him, backed away as she batted out the flames creeping up her sleeves. On instinct she ducked, felt the Butcher's katana brush the furthest tip of her lone whole ear. Then the kitsune laughed as he loosed more fire from the palm of his free hand, a thick stream of flames sweeping left and right across the insides of the airship, scorching metal and cracking the glass of the forward cockpit, setting alight the pilot's seat and all else which was flammable.

"Oh God!" screamed Kanti. She was barely heard over the shriek of stressed metal and roar of winds as the airship careened out of control, sending all three inside it stumbling and grabbing for whatever hold they could. All around, crystal shattered and sparks shot from the craft's jeopardized inner workings. "Oh God, oh God!"

They dropped like a drunken stone. Holly barely managed to lunge up and double the Butcher over with a swing of her spell rod to his gut when the airship crashed across the first of the many white square houses making up the seaside town, skipped off it with a moment of desperate upward motion, the lowered ramp glancing the roof of the next square building down and tearing off with the shriek of metal and crash of shattering stone. The airship flipped end over end. Holly first felt herself strangely weightless, then felt herself thrown, black feather cloak tearing on a jagged piece of metal left by the lost boarding ramp. Pain erupted through her as she hit stone and rolled, not stopping until she struck the raised eaves.

Holly lay crumpled there for a moment, dazed, not sure which way was up or down, or which was her left hand and which was her right. Then she managed to get a hand flat underneath her and pushed herself up, aching everywhere but marveling over how nothing seemed broken, or not broken enough to slow her down at any rate.

From all around, there came shouts and screams, the continued crumbling of stone and splintering wood. Holly pushed herself up and onto one knee, looked down to find the crippled airship had barreled down the hillside and across the rooftops of two more buildings before managing to come to a stop against a small grove of banyan trees. It was a twisted ruin now, leaking smoke from several punctures through its outer armor, its open rear tilted up and toward Holly, the innards dark and smoking.

A small crowd had begun to gather around the fallen craft when black-furred hands grabbed at the outer edges of the open rear. Something inside Holly relaxed as Kanti half-dragged, half-hauled herself out of the crashed craft, the black Wolf-Lord flipping over with an unheard grunt to hit the ground back-first.

"Kanti!" shouted Holly, forcing herself to her feet before dropping over onto the next roof and stumbling to its railing. "Kanti—"

"HOLLY!"

Holly's heart fell at the old voice. She turned. Three buildings along her row, Regina stood upon another rooftop, a steam rifle readied at their shoulder, barrel trained straight on at Holly.

"Come quietly!" Regina yelled, chambering a round. "Please!"

Holly's fists tightened. She turned back to Kanti down at the wrecked troop carrier. She looked back up at Holly, tried to force herself to stand despite a leg twisted the wrong way by the crash. Her tears matched Holly's, who for once did not struggle to read another's face. They both understood.

With a sob, Holly turned away and ran for another roof edge, leaping over the parapet even as a CRACK rang through the air and the white stone exploded beneath her. She landed on the next roof over, rolled, kept running, counted the seconds until Regina could fire again, ducked through a row of potted trees as the next shot rang. The trees toppled with a hail of shrapnel bark.

Holly fell again, bounced against the side of the next building, hit the white cobblestone street. A Wolf-Lord in a doorway stared aghast at her, smoking pipe falling from their slack muzzle. Holly ignored them and ran, dodging around market stalls rapidly clearing at the sounds of violence. At her passing, some called out to her, or for the town guard.

Holly ran without aim or plan, taking streets at random, thinking only vaguely of putting as much space as possible between her and her twin. Twice more, CRACKS split the air. Twice more Holly felt the heat and speed tear past her, a nearby wall or stretch of cobblestone shattering.

Kanti was injured, as badly as Holly had seen anyone injured. But she was safe, out of the fight and below Regina's notice. All was on Holly. If she could reach an open area to take off in flight from, some back part of her brain told her, she could . . . she could . . .

Holly, unable to think any more steps ahead, turned down another street. Ahead, two blocks down, she saw the beginnings of a park. She ran faster, fought back against the stitch in her side and the ragged pain of her lungs, flinched away as a shop window shattered to her right. Past the glass, another intersection—

A blast of fire poured across the road in front of Holly, rising high and bright enough to blind all sight of the park and hope of escape. Holly skid to a stop, stumbled away from the heat of the fire, one arm raised to shield her eyes, the other moving down at instinct to where her sword once was. She watched, on-guard as the Butcher strolled out of the fire blocking off the street, five tails twining lazily behind him, long katana and sheath draped across his shoulders. He smiled at her, a warm, familiar, mocking smile. "Hello again? So soon? My lucky day."

Holly growled, flexing her magic and sending a mental command for her staff to transform into a black-bladed longsword. "Butcher!" she hissed, her weakened voice trembling with rage and hate. "You really should have died in the crash!"

"Hah! As if you'd ever be so lucky." Butcher drew his katana, sheath clattering to the cobblestone road, blade dragging at his side. The harsh scratch of steel on stone irritated Holly's ears. "Never so lucky, but certainly alone. Alone and in need of butchering!"

Holly backed away two steps, three, stopping as she noticed movement in her blade's dim reflections. She looked behind her and there stood Regina at the other end of the street, closing Holly in, the steam rifle slung on a loop across their back and their white sword drawn.

"Crap," said Holly, turning aside to better keep both foes in sight. Her chest burned from the blessedly shallow stab at the start of the chase, her front stained and sticky with her blood.

"Don't try to run," said Regina, stepping closer. "You were lucky last time, and saved by friends. That won't happen again, Holly."

"For God's sake, don't humor the mongrel with that silly name game," said the Butcher, swiping his katana through the air in front of him and giggling. "Now stand still and scream when I hit ye. Only one eye, so depth perception's not worth a bloody tosser."

Holly swallowed, changing her stance to rest her sword on her shoulder, her eyes scanning for anything she could use for a distraction, anywhere she could run for an escape. "Dumb accent. How did you find us? We have been among friends!"

"Not all your friends," promised the Butcher with another giggle, raising the fur on the back of Holly's neck. At the same time, Regina drew something from the folds of their white cloak, something long, slender, and black. They tossed it, Holly dancing back as it clattered at her feet. Her heart stopped.

The long, slender black horn of a minotaur, the bottom jagged and broken, dulled with a sheen of dried blood.

"Laura."

"She kept her silence well," said Regina. "In the end, she earned my respect."

"What was left of her," giggled Butcher. "After what I saw in the cute little cabin, I'm not the only butcher running around! Kahahahahaha!"

Holly stood and stared at the broken, bloodied horn. The world tilted beneath her feet, the sky blinking out, the air twisting in her lungs. Hot poison surged electric in her veins, magic pooling in her hands as her heart curdled in her chest. Holly couldn't breathe. Holly couldn't see. Holly couldn't think.

Holly screamed. She reached out with her free hand, wrenched Butcher's sword from him with her magic, grabbed it from the air. She spun, leapt, hammering both swords down upon Regina. The other Wolf-Lord barely raised their sword in time to block, the force driving them to their knees.

Holly kicked. Regina fell to their back, muzzle red-splattered and twisted aside, broken. Holly stomped them once in the throat, then stabbed down at them with the stolen katana—

Fire burst against Holly's back, staggering her. She bit against the pain and spun out of the fire's path, reaching out with her magic again. The bars in a nearby hardware shop's windows tore loose and smashed Butcher into the opposite wall. With another flick of her magic, the bars turned into a half-dozen yellow-eyed snakes and began biting the shrieking kitsune.

Completing her spin, Holly swung the katana down, but Regina had already rolled out of reach and regained their feet. They stared unsteady at Holly, sword raised in their long-favored defensive posture. "Sister—"

Holly SHOVED with her magic. Regina flew backward, into and through the wall of the building behind them.

"Even Regina pitied you like a retarded pet."

"No." Candida's arm ached. She ignored it, wiping furiously at her eyes, hating the tears she felt there. "No, you're lying. Regina l-loved me, always."

Holly ran to the broken wall, swords raised for an overhead slash. She reached the rubble—

CRACK rang the air, Holly thrown on her back, a scream torn from her, right side splattered across the ground.

"It was pity," said Gosse again, more firmly, stepping closer. "Pity and embarrassment that they had to share a face with you. There was no love, no pride, no joy, only contempt.

Regina staggered back out onto the street, armor ruined, cape torn, eyes wide and bloodshot as they raised their steam rifle for another shot.

Fighting through the pain, Holly thrust a hand out, a burst of magic turning the rifle into a rain of holly leaves. Regina gaped a moment, then dove for their dropped sword. Holly used her own spell-sword to leverage herself back to her feet, then swung. Regina yelped, fell bereft the fingers and thumb of their right hand. Holly followed after, a stomp of her foot once more pinning the other Wolf-Lord to the street.

Silence but for their shared struggles for breath and the crackle of the Butcher's flames and the patter of Holly's blood to the brick street. Holly's right hand clamped over the gunshot wound, trying to stem the loss. Her sword trembled in her left hand as she held it pointed to Regina's throat. Their eyes met, twin eyes, wide and frightened. The idea came to Holly to press in, tear Regina's throat as they had torn hers, render them full twins once more.

"Go on, then," said Regina, trembling. "Go on. Do it. Kill another sibling. You have no choice. I won't stop. If you want the Waters of Life, if you want to save your wife and child, you're going to have to KILL ME, DAMN IT!"

Holly growled, baring her fangs. With titanic effort she raised her sword, trying to think of every hurt, every slight. She hated her twin . . . hated . . .

As Regina lay catching their breath on the ground, Candida kicked the sword from her sibling's slackened grip, giving her own a playful twirl before bringing its tip to the other Wolf-Lord's exposed throat. "I win."

"So you did."

"You went easy on me."

Panting, Regina still somehow managed a grin. "You've been working hard all day and I've been standing around doing nothing more strenuous than glaring at guests asking too many questions. You'd be surprised how uneasy I took it on you."

In utter misery, all strength failed. Holly's arm fell and her sword slipped from slack fingers, returning to its base rod form. Holly swayed where she stood for a moment longer, managed to bite out "Regina . . . family . . ." and saw the other Wolf-Lord's soften with a measure of Holly's misery before her legs gave out, sending her toppling to the ground beside her twin. The pair lay on the street in a growing pool of their shared blood. The last Holly felt as darkness stole over her, the trembling grip of Regina's hand taking hers.

CHAPTER FIFTEEN

The cold came first, bitter and bone-deep, driven through Holly's body by a wind like the spikes of a train track. The frost lay heavy in her fur.

Sound returned next. The crackle of the frost in every movement. The howl of the wind through the tall space, echoing mountain-high. The crunch of feet on snow and ice, unseen figures moving around Holly, private words passing among them. Once, in the endless stretch of time encompassing her trackless thoughts, Holly thought she heard the hyena laughter of the Butcher.

Pain seeped through the cold's numbing weight. Pain from her bones, from her organs, from her skin. Something was wrong. She felt eaten away, diminished in ways she couldn't grasp. If only she could . . .

At last came sight. Holly found herself in a large glass room. Beyond the glass, windows thrown wide open, the tall black peaks of the mountains of Cairn Romulus.

Old prison home.

Holly hung by her wrists in shackles in the middle of the room, bare down to her fur. Through the fur, she saw scars. Long and thin scars, clean, surgical. Ragged scars, the work of madwolves hacking away. Scars like star bursts, burn scars, half-moon scars. Yet, where Holly would expect the worst of all, her right side where Regina had shot her, there was nothing. Holly saw smooth skin, the beginning fuzz of fur already growing back, and nothing more.

"God," she whispered, the lone word torturous to speak, the scars marring her throat remaining. "How long . . ."

The floor a few yards ahead of her opened with the grinding of gears and stone. A lift rose into the room. On the lift were four Wolf-Lord soldiers in the black and red armor of Romulus, accompanied by—

"Caelestis," whispered Holly.

The black-furred Wolf-Lord, slight of build and dressed sharply in red, glared at Holly as they stepped off the platform. Clawed hands clenched around nothing at their sides, their narrow muzzle working but saying nothing as they paced before Holly, tail twitching.

"Caelestis," whispered Holly again, watching her older sibling nervously as the shorter Wolf-Lord continued their pacing. Caelestis' ear twitched but they said nothing, only turned to one of the accompanying soldiers and gestured. The soldier stepped forward and held out a heavy box of cherry wood. Caelestis stood between Holly and the box as they opened it and began sorting through it.

"Where am I?" asked Holly. She looked away from her sibling, glancing nervously at the soldiers standing witness to her bared imprisonment. "How long have I been here? Where's Regina? Butcher—"

"Our nation of Romulus, beset from all sides by the craven resentment of other lands, stands tall upon firm, unflagging laws," said Caelestis, closing the box with a hard snap. "Without our laws, our order, we are nothing. Above love, above mercy, above blood, we must have our law and order."

"Unjust laws," hissed Holly. "Unjust order."

"Against our just nation," Caelestis continued, ignoring Holly's words as they turned and walked behind the bound Wolf-Lord, the black, knotted whip in their hands clear for all to see, "Crime is treason, and must be dealt with by the harshest measures. Justice allows for no sentiment."

"Not asking for sentiment!" Holly begged, twisting her neck as far as she could to keep her sibling in sight. "Just a deferred sentence, please! Lives at stake! Let me save them, please! And then I will return, I promise, and I will stay, and you can—"

Two paces behind Holly, Caelestis stopped, drew back, and then swung.

CRACK.

Holly's head snapped forward, body jerking and a sharp gasp of pain escaping her. The right side of her muzzle bled from the whip's blow.

CRACK.

Holly jerked again, pain searing across the back of her right shoulder. Only then did she notice her red hair had been crudely cut away, down to nearly nothing, the premature grey surely shining through all the more clearly.

"You are a criminal," snarled Caelestis, at last allowing some emotion to show through. "Criminals are animals! It is nobody's fault but your own that I must speak to you in the only language you can understand!"

CRACK.

CRACK.

CRACK!

Holly shuddered and writhed beneath her sibling's blood-spilling whip, her struggles to remain stoic against the torture failing as the minutes carried on, grunts and gasps of lost breath devolving to screams, groans.

CRACK!

CRACK!

Beneath the snap and crack of the whip, beneath Holly's screams, there was the wet patter of blood streaming through white fur to drip and pool upon the stone. Somewhere above, hidden from Holly's bowed head, the sun rolled uncaring across the white sky, burning at Holly's torn and bleeding back through the glass roof.

CRACK!

CRACK!

CRACK!

Caelestis' whip struck wherever it could reach. Holly's back. Her shoulders and upper arms. Her ass, her outer thighs. Once upon the back of Holly's head, sending her for a moment crashing into all-consuming, pain-muffling black. Caelestis kept their pace steady, almost leisurely, going for the long haul. Where the whip struck, skin split and pain sprouted, again and again. Time passed, minutes became meaningless, Holly remembering only the stretch as Caelestis drew back, the hiss as they swung, the CRACK, and then the next moment's stretch. She reeled drunk in her chains, screams dying away, the taste of blood in her mouth, breathless begging for Caelestis to stop—

And then Caelestis relented. Their steps were soft and their breathing harsh as they circled back around to stand in front of Holly. They stared down at her, lips of their muzzle twitching, eyes wide, the whip clutched reverently in their hands. The red of their officer's unicorn was darker now, wet with blood.

Holly hung boneless, her chains not quite long enough for her knees to reach the floor for a proper kneel, trembling as the seconds passed and no more blows came, allowing her minimal Wolf-Lord healing abilities to do as they could.

"Do not mistake this respite for mercy," said Caelestis as one of the watching soldiers stepped forward to take the whip from them. "I merely find myself hungry and in need of a long bath with my favored maid. Do trust me when I say that the days ahead will be filled with many more sessions like this one. Stuffed to the brim with them, you might say."

Holly heard these words and, though she lacked the strength then to speak, her heart quailed. Not only for the future of pain facing her, but for her family. Shun, Nessa, so many others in Eishaven, waiting for her to return with the Waters of Life. Waiting for her to save them.

"Please," she managed, voice hardly a whisper as her eyes remained dry.

"This is the Light Room," said Caelestis, gesturing all around. "A gift from Lord Beauty of the distant Avalon Empire. Enchanted against the wind and cold outside, almost impervious to physical harm. Even your freakish strength and your apparent development of magic. Of more interest to the two of us right now are the special time dilation enchantments, the last master work of Morgana le Fay. You might be thinking you are running out of time, but trust me, within this box of glass and magic, you still have all the time in the world. Every hour here is only a minute out there, or so I've been told. I am curious to step outside and see if it lives up to the hype. I hope it does, because I have so much more in store for you."

"Please," Holly begged again. "My family needs me."

"Then they really should have picked better, then," said Caelestis, tail waving as they returned to the lift with their soldiers.

The lift lowered into the floor.

Holly remained, bound and alone. Through the glass, the sunlight cooked.

CHAPTER SIXTEEN

Regina stood in their room, enclosed in rich tapestries and draperies of gold and burgundy. Lunar Steel armor and shields mounted along the walls, swords and spears, axes and war hammers. Deep carpet beneath their paws, bottles of the good wine cluttering the tables. The Butcher, naked and well-used in the previous hours, slumbered in the bed. Somewhere a clock ticked the seconds away, into minutes, into hours, into days.

Regina stood bare before a mirror, their snow-white fur thick and pristine, unblemished by scar or discoloration. Their muscles were solid, honed to perfection in training and war. Their proportions, female in that hour . . . alluring and robust. All of them perfect but for the maimed right hand, short two fingers by Holly's blade.

"Your vanity befits your accomplishments, my prized general."

Regina's lips tightened, their back straightening as Queen Celeste strode into view behind them in the mirror. The gowned Wolf-Lord glanced at the kitsune in the bed for a moment, looked at Regina with one raised brow. "Your taste in lovers is . . . of little concern, if kept discreet. Well done."

"Thank you, your grace." Regina kept their gaze forward, even as the queen drew close behind them and gripped their upper arms tight, claws digging into the flesh. "How may I serve?"

"As you already have, my prized heir. With loyalty and ferocity."

Regina frowned. "Your grace, Maurus is your eldest, it is they who—"

"Stayed in the castle and did nothing," snarled Queen Celeste. "While Caelestis is a thoughtless sadist with no imagination for greater glories. No. I have decided. It is you who has overcome all obstacles and all . . . sentimentalities. You shall sit on the throne when I am gone, High Princess Regina."

"May that day not come for many years," said Regina.

"Such goes without saying," said Celeste. They kept their grip on Regina's arms a moment more, body pressed close against Regina's back. Then they let go, turning for the door with a last remark over their shoulder. "Do be ready for dinner soon. And leave your lover for the bed."

Regina nodded, though this could not be seen by the departing queen. They waited until they were alone, then looked to the kitsune in their bed, a pleasant warmth developing in their core and traveling to wetter climes as they reflected on the two nights of passion which had so far been shared. It had started as a passing desire, a curiosity. Their twin, after all, had taken a kitsune to bed. And the Butcher, to Regina's unspoken relief, proved himself both willing and . . . capable.

"Hmm . . ."

But no time then for further dalliances. As Celeste had said, dinner was soon and they were expected.

***

Regina dressed to dinner as plainly as they could get away with in their newfound position of prestige and authority. Their white and gold military dress uniform was cleaned and pressed, enchanted against stains of every sort. That evening it was accentuated, at Maurus's insistence, by a gold-clasped white cape reaching down past their knees.

"You are a Wolf-Lord born to strike an imposing figure, my fine sibling. No imposing figure can achieve the fullness of its potential without a cape!"

Maurus would never, could never, strike an imposing figure. They slouched decadent in their seat at the long table, gobbling up meat pies and caviar-laden oysters as if each morsel were the first and last bite. They washed the food down with long, messy quaffs of plum wine, their lips and the grey fur of their muzzle stained black as they laughed and told ribald tales about other times of revelry and excess.

Caelestis alone laughed at the bald nonsense Maurus spoke. They did it in quick, hissing giggles, always grinning, even as they gnawed on the bones of their food to the last scrap of edible tissue, then tossed them aside for the scurrying servants to collect. The fur of the cheeks and their hands was stained red, bloody red, but they showed no signs of caring.

"—quickly had one of my guards shove him over the wall and down into the moat! Bwahahahaha!"

"Did he scream?" asked Caelestis, bouncing in their seat as they asked. "Oh, please tell me he screamed, dear sibling."

"All the way down," promised Maurus, their words somewhat muffled by the sudden bite of pudding clogging up their muzzle. "Until he broke his neck on the side of the moat, anyway. Quite a mess."

"Gah!" Caelestis snarled and banged a half-eaten rib against the feasting table. "Broken necks are no good!

So quick. He wouldn't have even been alive and aware when the crocodiles began to eat him."

"I've told you already, there are no crocodiles in our moat." Queen Celeste kept their voice low, demanding all force themselves to listen harder. They ate quickly, knife and fork cleaving through steaks and chops like a soldier on the march, the blood and the grease dripping from their muzzle the lone crack in their civilized shell. "The beasts do not do well in our colder waters. You will need to go farther south for them."

"More food!" shouted Maurus, raising their glass. "More wine!"

"There is a fort on the southern coast," said Regina. They tapped their fork against their plate. "An old castle. We can renovate it, bring it up to modern standards, make it a place fit for a princess of Romulus as they oversee our southern lands."

Caelestis rolled their eyes and waved a hand dismissively. "Blech. Leave the overseeing of things to the soldiers. That's the sort of thing you brutes are good for, isn't it?"

"No, no, plum wine, you fool! Plum! This is cherry wine!"

"There's more to ruling than marching in and burning a few buildings when people stop obeying you," said Regina. "They grow our food, make our money, shape our lands. If all you offer in return is an armored fist, before long you won't have any of them left."

"Oh, there'll always be more of the common rabble for us," said Celeste. They brushed long bangs of white from their eyes with greasy fingers, then raised their glass. "Come, I will have that cherry wine."

"You worry too much," said Maurus, voice once more muffled behind a thick mouthful of pudding. "Stop worrying! Your evil twin is locked away and soon to die, so please, try some of this pickled eel! It is quite succulent!"

Regina looked down at the offered platter, and then at the expectant faces ranged around the table, both those of their family and of the servants. They frowned and stood, wiping their hands clean with a napkin. "Apologies. I just don't seem to have much of an appetite today."

"Oh, screw you, you self-righteous cur!" said Caelestis. The words had started in a laughing tone, finished as a snarl of genuine anger as they too stood from their seat. "You've been sitting there all evening, staring at us and judging! You've no right to be so judging of us, cur! Family! Don't you give a damn about your family anymore!?"

"You're drunk and not worth talking to," said Regina. They stepped aside and pushed their chair in, turning to nod farewell to Celeste and Maurus. They began to turn for the door, before a glass of wine struck them, splattering much of their left side in purple.

"You're sober as fuck and not worth talking to!" screamed Caelestis, grabbing for another glass to throw. "You used to be great to know! You used to be awesome! Now you're sullen and depressed all the time! Go have some more fun with your new fox toy if you hate being around us that much! Or better yet, break your stupid twin free or something, go live with your real family! Cur!"

Regina caught the next thrown glass before it could hit them, passed it over to Maurus as the grey-furred Wolf-Lord hurried to their side. "Siblings, please—"

"No," said Regina and Caelestis together. It almost made Regina want to smile, but such times of easy reconciliations were long behind them. "If you have any . . . newly-learned reasons to object to me," Regina continued, pointing to Celeste still sitting at the table's head, "there's the Wolf-Lord you should take it up with. Otherwise, good night. Try again in the morning, when you're sober."

"Screw you, I'll drink in the morning now!" Caelestis hissed, but Regina had already turned away.

It was a long walk to Regina's quarters from the dining hall. They heard Maurus' following paws the whole way and kept their pace slow enough the heftier Wolf-Lord could keep up without too much issue. They did not turn to face their pursuer until they were at their door, drawing themself to their full imperious height. "What do you want?"

Maurus, though clearly winded, held no hesitation. "You must understand how hard this all is for Caelestis, please, dearest sibling. They and I both knew I am . . . unsuited, to the throne. It ever seemed a hideous burden to me. We all thought you the obvious choice. But these, these rumors of you, and Candida, and your . . . parentage . . ."

"What do you want?" repeated Regina.

"What do YOU want?" mirrored Maurus.

Regina bared their fangs. "Wordplay suits you no better than the throne."

Maurus stepped closer. "You want to free Candida."

Breath hitched. Muscles tensed. Regina dropped a hand to the Lunar Steel dagger kept ever at their side, a casual move as they looked aside at their bedroom door. There came to their mind's eye the image of the Butcher crouched against the wood, ears spying, teeth gleaming. "If I wanted that, I'd never have brought her in."

"Bringing her in," remarked Maurus, "bought you the throne. Celeste has no heart for granting pardons. Other hearts in that chair . . . might differ."

With comprehending slowness, ears remaining turned to the door, Regina looked back at Maurus with a raised brow. "You speak dangerously."

Maurus shrugged and smiled, closed the distance further to rest a heavy hand on Regina's right shoulder. "Nay, nay. I speak so only in hope that when the time comes, you find your heart in . . . the right place. One sibling to another. Good night, Regina."

"Good night, Maurus." And for the first time in a long while, Regina meant it.

CHAPTER SEVENTEEN

For Holly, three days passed before she saw another visitor. People came and went in her hours of crumbling half-sleep, leaving bowls of water with her old name on them, retrieving the emptied bowls, cleaning her waste, the little of it there was. No food, only water. In the endless waking hours she stood or hung as the chains on her arms permitted, the growing agony of her arms keeping her ever from a true, restoring rest.

Hunger curled at home in her empty belly.

For endless waking hours, she watched her unchanging surroundings. The tall black peaks of the mountains, snow-capped where the ceaseless howling wind did not scour them bare. Storms rolled in, cast all in shadow as the sleet and hail fell, or rarer times when the thunder rumbled and the cold winter rain battered the all-encompassing glass, frightening and fragile to Holly despite the declared enchantments. At other times there would be no storms to hide Holly, leaving her alone and breaking, baking beneath the slow crawl of the hateful sun, blasting away all darkness and shadow, blasting away all hope of secrecy and focused thought, of sleep and escape.

Some hours, she passed the time with recounting stories of better days to herself. Stories of adventures, war, heroes. Villains. Increasingly as the days wore on and wore her down, she screamed to fill the glass, as loud and for as long as her scarred throat allowed, until the red stained her fur and dripped to the floor.

At the end of the three days of loneliness and hunger, the soldiers returned in the lift, four of them, and Holly knew they were soldiers even without their arms or armor.

"Prince Maurus sends their warmest regards to the prodigal sister," said the lead soldier, moments before their fist smashed across Holly's face.

After the soldiers left, hours later, Holly hung by her chains and stared at the floor, not seeing it. She focused on her breathing, a painful struggle beneath the bruises, and allowed herself, at least until sleep took her, to hate.

CHAPTER EIGHTEEN

Three more days passed from Holly's perspective. Days of loneliness and water. On the third day there were scraps of ill-cooked meat left with her water. Holly ate the meat, struggled to keep it down after so long with nothing. Sick, her belly gurgling protest, shivers racing the length of her body.

When she woke, muzzle caked with drool and blood, she found Regina waiting for her on a three-legged stool. Gone was the fanciful gold and red armor, the flowing cape. They dressed plainly in white shirt, trousers, and a high-collared leather jerkin. From one hip hung their white Lunar Steel sword. On their other hip was holstered Holly's black Lunar Steel staff, formed at the moment into a wand. A large sack sat beside them.

"Would you be insulted," Holly whispered, each word a croak, blood-tinged to her weathered ears, "If I said I had expected Celeste to visit before you?"

"The queen will be next," said Regina, their voice low and controlled as they stood and stepped closer. "Very soon, now, you will be visiting them. The others, Caelestis and Maurus, have gotten their fill. I have been allowed a last minute alone with you before the soldiers come."

Holly, her back numb from the scars of Caelestis' three whipping sessions, nodded in understanding and the barest relief. She hurt and she was tired, and she saw no more hope. "It is nearly over then?"

A long parade of emotions crossed Regina's face. They stepped closer and reached out to caress Holly's cheek and through her hair with a hand bound within a black, steel-edged glove. The same hand, Holly recognized, as the hand she had chopped a few fingers from in their last fight.

"It is almost over," Regina answered. "I'm going to unshackle you, for a moment. I will help you get dressed. And then, my soldiers and I will escort you down to the throne room. Queen Celeste and our siblings, Maurus and Caelestis, are waiting for us there. There, you will be declared guilty of your crimes against Romulus and the Nameless Order. Murder. Treason. Terrorism. To restore our nation's honor and good standing with the Nameless Order, our honor before the other Wolf-Lord nations, you will then be executed. Do you understand?"

Holly did not want to answer this. She looked past her twin, through the glass, out onto the mountains wandering northward. It was late in the day, by the sun. Clouds ranged across the sky but did not wholly consume it. In the distance, if Holly squinted, she could make out La Tour Gelée, the Frozen Tower, the tallest waterfall in all the nations of the Wolf-Lords. It fell from the highest peaks of the Black Mountains to the ground and beyond, down into caverns deep beneath the mountains where swam the strangest fish, eyeless and cold as the ice which fed them.

"Candi . . . Holly, are you listening to me?"

Holly looked to her twin. She pulled against her shackles for a second, then allowed herself to fall slack again. "Regina, please do not let this happen. Let me go back to my family. I beg you. Let me see them again before the end. Then . . . then I will come back to my death. Gladly. Just let me see then again, please . . ."

"You know I can't do that," said Regina. Her voice remained as much a whisper as Holly's. "I wish I could. I'm sorry."

Holly shuddered with a tearless sob. She hung limp by her arms, the strain on her shoulders and wrists agony. But still, it was better than to remain standing for one more minute. In the dark of her thoughts, the darkest question rose, slipped from her cracked muzzle. "Did you know about Morgana?"

"Hm?"

Holly looked up at Regina, tried to make her voice clear and strong as it had once been. "I met her. The Wolf-Lord who truly fathered us with Celeste. Morgana le Fay. It is how I found my second lover, Kanti, and my daughter, Nessa. No time for that story. Did you know? Did you ever know the truth when I did not?"

Regina, for once, did not try to meet Holly's gaze, their eyes turning down to their gloved hand. "I suspected . . . something. Something which set the two of us apart from Maurus, and Caelestis, and Gosse. We were children of an affair, I eventually settled on, though I never imagined who . . ."

"We were different," Holly agreed. It was a small thing, utterly unimportant against everything else, but Holly was relieved to learn her twin had not been in on the secret. "And all those years, my only friend. Only family, seeing past my disabilities. Loved you. Cherished you. Wished desperately to be you. Is that why? The only reason why? Because I was your only full sibling in all this mess?"

And then, the question coming to Holly with a stab of pain in her heart, "Is that the only reason why you are sad right now?"

Regina frowned and clenched their fist, looked up and past Holly for several seconds, prosthetic hand dropping to rest on the white sword's hilt. "Yes," they said at last. "I wanted you at my side. My sister. My twin. All that is mine, the war, the victory, it could have been ours. I wanted it to be ours. But you were born wrong, and when the moment came you failed and you ran. Now you've failed again and are right here where you started. Love never stood a chance."

"No," said Holly, looking down. "I guess it did not."

The distant sounds of an approaching lift told them both their conversation was done. Holly's manacles clicked open and she shuddered to be rid of them as she stood. Quickly, wordlessly, she dressed in the clothes Regina provided, the tattered black shirt and pants of the soon-to-be-executed.

The soldiers arrived and herded Holly onto the lift. Regina stayed at her side, a hand resting on Holly's left shoulder. Though her own hands had been left unbound, Holly could not bring herself to reciprocate this last, aching familial touch.

The lift slowed to a stop on the castle's main floor. The doors rolled aside, the soldiers stepped out, and together, they walked. The tall halls and portrait-filled corridors were empty aside from them. No servants. No other guards. Not a sound but their relentless march. Cairn Romulus stood lifeless in ways Holly had never imagined in her life spent living there, a servant and slave.

"Queen Celeste has ordered the castle cleared for the evening, but for our Nameless Order guests and our most elite soldiers," said Regina, answering the unspoken question. "She wants to take no chances with infiltrators or sympathizers."

"Sympathizers?" asked Holly. "For me?"

Regina said nothing else in response, and Holly made no further attempt to break the silence.

They walked. The corridors were as Holly remembered them. Blue marble cast a hundred shades by stained-glass windows revealing a late evening sun. Heading toward her death, she did not remember or reminisce on her life there, full of work and sweat and miserable hopes. She remembered evenings in Eishaven, curled in front of the fire with Shun and Nessa, Kurt and Laura, drinking warm cider, their laughter and gasps and cheers like song as she told them stories. She remembered the warmth of kisses shared between her and Shun and Kanti, their growing love and familiarity. She remembered joining the gryphon song and walking the streets of Eishaven, snowflakes cold on her twitching ears. She remembered . . .

Another lift, hidden behind a false wall. Holly's stomach dropped with the lift as it descended, away from the light and into the darkness of the black mountain's heart. Regina's hand squeezed Holly's shoulder once, then fell away.

The lift doors opened, the room beyond drenched with the macabre dance of shadows and flames in shallow braziers. Holly hesitated as the soldiers in front of her stepped out, could not help it, fear, utter fear locking her limbs and clenching her heart. Die. They all wanted her to die. She was going to die. She didn't want to die. She wanted her family, her home, to hold them and tell them everything was going to be okay. This wasn't fair. None of this was—

Someone shoved Holly forward. She stumbled, almost fell, caught herself on a pillar. Swallowing, she walked forward, away from the lift and the only chance of escape.

"At last, the prodigal child returns."

Queen Celeste sat imperious upon their tall throne, draped in a black dress swiftly descending into blood red. They watched with bright, bloodshot eyes, hateful and hungry as Holly approached. Below them, at the left and right of the foot of the throne, stood Maurus and Caelestis, each in a stark, minimalist robe of black and crimson respectively. Maurus looked fatter than Holly remembered. Caelestis clutched their whip as if in hope of one more chance to use it.

Near them, leaning against a brazier and dragging an oiled rag along his blade, the Butcher of the Cult of the Burning King, the Butcher of the Nameless Order, watched Holly's approach with an air of eagerness, as if this were all a mere show and he couldn't wait for the juicy bits.

Regina stopped walking and Holly stopped walking with them. Their guards retreated into the shadows hiding the full size of the throne room, where Holly got the impression of more kitsune watching the ongoing tragedy. More warriors of the Nameless Order, circling for her blood.

"My queen," began Regina, voice containing only the slimmest of tremors, "I present the killer and traitor, the renegade Princess . . ." Regina paused, glanced over at their twin for a moment. "Er, she goes by Holly now—"

"I don't care," said Celeste. They stood to their full height, stared down at Holly with utter hatred and poisonous satisfaction. "Look at you, Candida. A filthy, rotten mongrel. At last, everything I expected of you and nothing more."

"My parent," Holly began, hoping against all hope to plead her case to this last, ultimate authority, to find even the smallest shred of familial love which might allow her to, if not save her family, at least be with them in their final hours.

Celeste reached out, long claws black and gleaming in the firelight. The power of their Lightning Elemental surged forth and struck Holly, bolts of lightning arcing across her body. She screamed, twitching and jerking in place as every muscle failed her, every thought was swept from her mind, her nose filling with the stench of crisping fur and her weathered ears full of screams and the crackle of power. Time fell away, meaningless beyond the pain.

Eventually, the lightning stopped. Holly collapsed to her hands and knees, gasping for air, smoke rising off her.

Laughter from high above, Celeste clapping once, twice, sighing in satisfaction. "At last, this pathetic tale comes to an end. You always liked your tales, didn't you, Candida? You always liked your stories? Now here's your story. The oldest story. All Wolf-Lords know it. There were two siblings, twins. One was strong, and whole, and Good, and the other was weak, and dark, and Evil. The weak, evil twin betrayed her sibling and spread ruin across the land, but eventually, the strong, good twin brought the evil to heel. The day was saved, and everyone who deserved it lived happily ever after. And so, the wheel turns, the cycle repeats, and the story is told again."

Heart thundering in her ears, Holly forced herself back up, growling until her scarred throat burned as she glared past her parent's head. "I am not Morgana le Fay. Regina is not Queen Morgause. We are your children! I'm begging you, parent, please, just listen! Just a moment of mercy—"

More lightning. Holly fell again to her knees, the tears steaming as they streaked down her cheeks. Breathless, unable to scream now, she heard Celeste say "There is no mercy."

The fire-lit braziers paled before the onslaught. The shadows of the throne room burned away, revealing for a brief moment the Nameless Order kitsune lurking within, arms raised to shield their eyes.

"Enough!" cried out Maurus. "You're going to kill her!"

The lightning again cut off. Holly sagged where she knelt, a hand gripping at the pain in her chest, terror striking her that her heart would give out long before whatever execution method Celeste had planned.

"I knew you wouldn't have the stomach for this the moment you sent soldiers to beat her in your stead," snarled Celeste. "Begone with you! Caelestis, you too!"

"What!? But I tore her to shreds with glee—"

"I SAID OUT!"

A long, silent moment, and then Holly caught the rush of feet past her, toward the lift, Maurus' heavier tread slowing for the barest moment as they passed where Regina stood. Struggling to look up, she saw Maurus and Caelestis gone from their places beside the throne. She didn't know what to make of this.

"Now then," said Celeste, voice dripping with the mockery Holly had grown up knowing. "Candida. I strip from you your title and any claim to the throne. I expel you from this family, from this nation you betrayed in your weakness. And for your weakness, you must die."

The Butcher stood from where he'd been leaning against the brazier, grin wide as he gave his katana a twirl. As quickly, Celeste raised a hand to stall him. "No. I want my prized heir to do it."

"But I'm the Butcher!" snapped the kitsune, tails whipping the air in agitation as he looked up to the throne. "I butcher as I please! Yer daft if ye think I'm here for any other reason!"

"You can butcher her body as you please afterward," growled Celeste, the lightning sparking among their claws brooking no argument. "But death by twin will HURT more. I want this to hurt. NOW, Regina."

The command rang through the dark throne room like a thunderclap. Regina stepped forward and away from Holly, their movements stiff as they accepted a steam rifle from a nearby guard. Holly watched, numb and hopeless as her twin turned to her and raised the weapon to their shoulder. The barrel lifted, then lowered, well-polished iron and wood aimed down at Holly still kneeling. Holly stared into the black hole at barrel's center, and then past it, for the first time in her life fully meeting her twin's eyes. Regina, stone-faced but for the tears streaking down their cheeks and wetting their fur, did not blink as their thumb drew the hammer back.

Then, with an almost lazy ease, Regina turned from Holly, lifted the barrel, and fired.

Queen Celeste slammed against the tall back of their throne, a choked cry driven from them by the silver bullet punching through their chest, unheard beneath the greater outcry from the surrounding kitsune and royal guards. For a last second their eyes lit up with horror at what had happened, quickly dulling to death as their body burnt away outward from the silver wound, top half toppling from the throne to the floor, followed seconds later by their bottom half.

Screams of horror and outrage spread through the throne room, washing unnoticed over the twins as Regina dropped the steam rifle and turned to stare down at Holly. Still meeting their gaze, Holly slowly stood, her pain forgotten beyond the fresh-bound hope, the hope birthing new strength.

"KILL THEM!" the Butcher shrieked.

Holly grabbed the black hilt at Regina's side. Regina gripped the white. They spun apart to stand back-to-back, weapons drawn against the black-armored guards and grey-robed Nameless monks charging from the shadows of the throne room.

Holly turned wand into sword and knocked aside a spear thrust, grabbed another below the blade, pulled, sliced. The kitsune toppled back, headless.

Instinct flared and Holly stepped and turned, stabbing a guard coming in at Regina's blind side. Her twin grabbed the guard's dropped axe, spun and tossed, axe head burying into another guard's chest and slamming them into one of the braziers. It toppled over, its fires a spreading flood across the throne room's tapestries and carpets.

Pain, a three-tailed kitsune slashing Holly's cheek with a flame-threaded whip. Holly caught the next swipe with her sword, twining the whip around her blade and yanking. The kitsune stumbled forward, into a guard's spear thrust.

Before Holly could dispatch the guard, the flash of a katana nearly taking off her muzzle forced her to stumble back. The Butcher snarled and advanced with katana and his own fire whip. Holly continued to backpedal away from him, dodging and blocking the blows she could, turning with the glancing blows she couldn't. His reach was longer than hers, faster than hers—

Regina fell past between them, kicking a guard over them and into the spilled fires. The Butcher pinned them to the floor with a foot and raised his katana for a killing blow. Holly lunged forward, transforming her sword back into its staff form and sinking three inches of the sharp end into his exposed side.

"GLRK!"

The Butcher jerked back, off of Regina, off Holly's staff with a wet, sickening squelch. His one visible eye wide with pain and panic, he clamped a hand over the wound, free hand grabbing for the nearest weapon he could find, a fallen spear.

Three guards and one Nameless monk left aside from the Butcher, charging Holly with diverse array of spears and swords. She blocked two thrusts with a shield spell, trapped the Butcher's spear between her arm and her side, stepped back and swung the kitsune into the path of the last two assailants. They stumbled to avoid him, in time for Regina to step in and take both their heads off.

Two guards and the Butcher remained. The kitsune dropped his captured spear and punched at Holly's legs with a burst of fireballs. Holly danced back and away from them, catching a glimpse of Regina engaging the last two guards as the Butcher followed after her. The air cooked, thick with smoke and the stench of burning.

Holly's back hit a pillar. The Butcher dove at her, teeth bared, open palms thrust forward to loose a wild stream of flames. Bracing for the coming strain, Holly cast another shield spell from her staff, larger than the first. The fires washed blinding over the translucent white shell of magic for a second. Then the attack died out and the fires faded, allowing Holly to see the Butcher was nowhere in sight.

"Coward," she said, dropping her shield.

Three yards off, Regina kicked the last guard into the burning remnants of a fallen tapestry, his slit-throat cries weak and brief.

They alone, Holly and Regina, stood among the flames and cracked stone of the throne room. They watched each other for the longest moment, catching their breath as the enormity of what they had done for each other, the rest of the world be damned, settled over them.

Coming to herself, Holly turned for the lift and ran, staff returning to its rod form as she went. "Regina, hurry, before anyone comes down! We can escape on Scattershot, go back to Akela—"

She heard no footsteps following her. Holly reached the lift, threw the grated door open, stopped. She looked behind her and saw Regina still among the carnage, their back to Holly as they stared up at the throne of Romulus. An empty throne awaiting a new claimant. "Regina?"

Their shoulders squared. Their fists tightened at their sides, their sword trembling. "Celeste. Morgana. Our parents were old fools. But now we decide our places."

"Reg, please," said Holly, stepping closer still. "We're running out of time. I'm running out of time. We need to go."

Regina ignored her at first, striding up the first two steps to the throne, past the ashes which were all that remained of Celeste. Then they turned back to Holly, muzzle spreading in a hopeful, loving smile, the equal of any Holly had received from Shun or Kanti. "No. We don't need to go anywhere. Don't you see? This is all ours now."

Holly looked around at the dead bodies and dying fires, and then back to Regina with a heart slowly dropping. She saw, in her head, where this was all going. She knew it as well as she knew any of her favorite stories of history, as inevitable and tragic as any of them. "I don't want any of this. I just want to go and save my family—"

"I AM YOUR FAMILY!" Regina screamed, startling Holly back a step. They stood panting on the steps to the throne, their eyes shining with tears as they reached a hand out, palm up, inviting. "Forget everything else. Celeste. Morgana. The Nameless Order. Eishaven, forget it all. None of it matters. WE matter. Together, the twin queens we always could have been, we can remake Romulus under our image. A new and better Romulus. We can be free. We ARE free. Free of our pasts. Free of our failures. Free of the story! We are not enemies! You are not Morgana le Fay! I am not Queen Morgause! History ends here. The story ends here."

"Your homeland of Romulus is dying," said Laura, drawing Holly from her thoughts. "Dying like a rabid beast that KNOWS it's dying. Would be a mercy, I think, if it were put down rather than forced into this slow, pitiable death spiral. Thank God and anyone else listening you got out of there when you could."

"Let Romulus die. Let THAT story end," said Holly, more to herself than to her twin. She let her staff drop from her hand to clatter on the floor, then held her hand up and out to Regina, mentally begging the other Wolf-Lord to take it. "I need to save my family. Come with me. Please."

Regina stared down at her, aghast and awed. The hand not holding their sword rose, then faltered, drew in, a moment's doubt striking them, reluctance to abandon the throne, the nation, all which had been promised to them. The hand wavered, began to reach out again, Regina taking their first step down the stairs from the throne—

Pain erupted through Holly's heart and out her chest. She seized up, a breathless, blood-frothed cry fleeing her, Regina startling and nearly falling. Holly gagged on a rush of blood up her throat and looked down, groping hands finding the red-smeared katana blade jutting out of her, hot to the touch, burning to the touch. "G-God . . ."

The whisper of flickering flames behind her as the Butcher dropped his invisibility illusion and leaned into her, his breath tickling the side of her neck as he gave the sword buried in her back a twist, forcing another scream of pain from her. "I told you . . . revenge . . . you little bi—"

Holly's white sword sailed past Holly's neck, impaling itself through the Butcher's head with a solid THUNK. The kitsune fell away, dragging his sword out with him, carving another few inches through Holly's chest as he went. She staggered, choking on blood, able to feel the frantic, slowing beat of her sundered heart as she fell.

Regina caught her, sank down to their knees as they cradled her, face a blurry wash of tears and voice a sob. "No! No, no. It's going to be alright, Holly, it's going to be . . . it's . . ."

The wound wasn't healing. Holly heaved, drenched herself in red, unable to focus on words spoken, unable to breathe, unable to stop the shudders beginning to wrack her body. But even as her vision dimmed, as her heart ever slowed and the cold of fear was supplanted by the more total coldness of death, she saw uncomprehending as Regina drew from their belt a dagger, an old dagger, old and stained.

The hand trembled. Regina drew in their last deep breath, looked down at their dying twin to steady themself, forced a last smile. Then they buried the blade into their chest and began to carve through the bone and through the pain.

"N-no," Holly managed, a hand blindly grabbing at Regina's shoulder and slipping away without strength.

Bone cracked. Regina shuddered and coughed out their own mouthful of blood. The dagger fell from their hand, crooked and spent. The beating of their heart rang thunderous in their ears as they grabbed Holly back up, the feel of heavy magic building in the air Regina's only hope this would work as they dragged their frighteningly limp, frighteningly cold twin up into a hug, the ruins of their chests pressing together, blood and fluids and flesh mingling.

"Please," begged Regina, eyes clenched shut and tears streaming, feeling the pressure growing in their chest. "Please take it, please—AAAUUGH!"

Time lost meaning. The Wolf-Lord twins clung to each other, tearing at each other's backs in the throes of their shared agony. The world around them twisted, turned askew, shattered until all was dark.

Then Regina fell away with a hard thud to the floor, eyes wide and sightless, chest a craggy, sodden ravine. No breath stirred past their lips.

Holly remained half-leaned against their twin's legs for a moment, mind trying to piece itself back together after falling so perilously close to the end, only to be snatched from death so violently. She managed to get her hands beneath her and slowly pushed herself up into a sitting position. Hands reached up to feel between the mounds of her breasts, found the skin scarred but whole beneath the sheen of blood from the Butcher's last, nearly fatal attack. She shook, turned aside, vomited up the torn remains of her old heart. The new heart beat strong and steady in her chest. Her twin's heart . . .

"On a moonless night, when Wolf-Lords are at our weakest, Morgana visited Nero's castle with claims of family love, and then took a knife, and then carved out her sister's heart to put inside herself!"

Holly got to her feet and looked around at the devastated throne room. The air stank. The fires still dimly burned. More bodies than she cared to count ranged dead across the floor, Wolf-Lords and kitsune. The ashes of the late Queen Celeste lay scattered across the throne and the steps leading up to it.

Regina lay dead at her feet. Holly knelt, unable to cry even as the grief struck her in one endless moment of torment. With shaky hands, she closed her twin's eyes, then folded their hands over their chest. An old piece of gryphon mourning song came to her from one of too-many funerals she had attended in Eishaven, the words slipping from her without thought and with too much care.

"I had a dream last night,

It was such a worrisome dream,

There was growing in my garden,

A holly tree

"A graveyard was the garden,

A flowerbed the grave

And from the green tree

The crown and flower fell.

"The blossoms I gathered

in a golden jar,

It fell out of my hands,

And smashed to pieces.

"Out of it I saw pearls trickling

And droplets rose-red

What could the dream mean?

Oh, my love, are you dead?"

The words became a spell. Holly felt the magic coalescing in the room and looked up. A yard away, at the very foot of the stairs to the throne, a fissure appeared in the air, a tall and cragged black fissure, and from it leaked wisps of purple and pink light.

"God, why now," asked Holly, not truly expecting any answer. She stood, summoned her staff to her hand with a flex of magic, stepped over Regina to stand before the magical fissure in the air. The air hummed around it, no music, only noise, accompanied by a shimmer like a mirage in the desert.

Her stance widened, her sorcerer's staff gripped in both hands and aimed toward the fissure in the air,

Holly breathed deep in and out, pulling in her magic as Veda had shown her and then pushing out, out, into the fissure. It opened at her touch like a door which had never known a lock, became a sheer plane of swirling purple and pink magic, crackling at the edges with bolts of blackness. Holly swallowed, lowered her staff and stepped forward, hand out to touch the dark portal—

CHAPTER NINETEEN

Holly woke up. She lay on her back on the sand, though it did not feel like any sand she had walked on before. She felt warm waves lap against her right side.

A beach.

The air carried no taste. Heavy air, charged, the air before a tremendous storm. If Holly lay there and listened, she could hear the slow, gentle push and pull of the waves upon the beach, and the rumble of thunder near and far, and a low, insistent whistle of wind tearing across the great, open expanse.

Holly sat up, rolled until she knelt in the sand, and opened her eyes. The world was dark. Incomprehensible. No light fell upon the world. No sun, no moon, no stars. Yet, Holly could see. She dipped her fingers into the beach and lifted up the sand in the bowl of her hands. Each piece of sand was a marble of black crystal the size of a pin's head. With each movement of her hands through the sand, the marbles shimmered with a stark white light. As the sand ran in thin cascades from her hands back to the beach, the shimmers spread away from her like ripples in disturbed water. The light kept going, on and on across the beach and across dark fields of black, crystalline stone, disappearing into the distance.

Lightning crashed across the black sky, revealing dark mountains shrouded in further darkness. Every few seconds, the lightning came, bolts of the purest white dancing across the expanse of the sky.

Holly stood, breathing in and looking around with the same eyes she had used to see Nessa's magic, Shun's magic, Veda's magic. Seen this way, rather than dark, the world she found herself in was blinding in its brilliance. It was all magic.

Closing her eyes to it, Holly noticed what seemed a shooting star rocketing briefly across the dark ocean before flying up, up, up. Holly's gaze follow it, a gasp driven from her as she beheld the vast and numberless flight of the Elemental Migration. High, high above her, higher than the mountains, crossing through the darkness like endless stars.

She had made it after all, then, she understood. Dark Realm. The spirit world. Homeland of the Elementals. And somewhere ahead of her, the House of Incarnation and the Waters of Life waiting inside.

Holly followed the Elementals. Away from the ocean and off the beach, onto the broken black stone of the lands beyond. She walked in weariness and grief. Her every step sent light rippling through the dark world. Never banishing the darkness, never lingering, merely glimpsing, complimentary. Here and there, a spire of glittering crystal rose from the ground. Here and there, a streak of Elemental magic, as fluid as water, as sparkling as polished gemstones, fell like a star to streak around her, beside her, through her, rising again to encourage her on.

The world turned around her. The lightning poured and the mountains passed her by. Beyond, Elementals stood sentinel, crystal stars in the dark shining every color and hue. She found the ground perfectly smooth and reflective, mirroring the world with utter perfection. Holly walked among the Elementals across the mirror plain, her steps gaining speed.

Far ahead, at the deep center of the Elementals, a dome wreathed in shadows untouched by the light of the Elementals.

Within the dome, facing Holly, a narrow triangle opening, through which shone light a rainbow-tinged blue.

Dark Realm turned once more upon its gyre. Holly was there now before the door to the House of

Incarnation. She slowed and raised an arm to shield her eyes against the harsh light of Magic Incarnate, her clothes rippling beneath the breeze, her hair long and red again, streaming behind her. Beyond the light, Holly heard voices. A rising chorus to meet her, welcome her to quest's end. Voices she knew, KNEW, should have been familiar, as if from another life . . .

"You've made it, then."

Startled, Holly stopped and looked to the shadows beside the opening. Guru Veda stepped out of them, the dark Wolf-Lord a splinter of shadow thrust into light, bereft there of all the gentle calm Holly knew, replaced with resentment and grief.

"It is you," said Holly, not understanding what she meant by this until she said it. "You never left the Cult of the Burning King at all, did you?"

Veda's expression, even hindered as it was by the blindfold, became recognizably mocking. "No, that was a lie. One of many you were happy NOT to see through. It would be very peculiar, I think, to leave an order you yourself founded."

Holly stepped back, realizing only then her staff was gone, had not made the journey to Dark Realm with her. "It cannot be, you . . ."

"Everything I've done, I've done for you . . ." Veda reached up and slipped the blindfold up and off. Purple star sapphire eyes stared out at Holly, eyes she had known only briefly but which she would remember forever. "My daughter."

"Morgana," said Holly. Word became reality and there stood the imperious sorceress, white-furred and black-robed, her grey hair sweeping down to the small of her back. Holly backed away another step, her new heart already breaking as she remembered the days spent together with the other Wolf-Lord, sharing meals and learning. "No, no, no . . . How many lives do you live?"

"Enough," said Morgana, drawing no closer. "If it makes you feel any better, our mutual friend Laura has no idea of my truth. She sent you to me in nothing but good faith."

"I never doubted," said Holly. "But was it all a lie, then? Were you ever helping me? Or was it all another try to make me your heir?"

"Can't it be both?"

Holly remained silent, looked from the Wolf-Lord who had fathered her to the opening into the House of Incarnation, trying to gauge if she could make it.

"But I was always trying to help you," Morgana continued, drawing Holly's eye back to her. "Everything I taught you, every lesson, was to get you here to save your family and your town. Even if I truly didn't want to."

"Why? Why help me? Last time we saw each other, I had just ruined your life's work and you threatened me with ruin."

"It was a bad day all around. Emotions were high. I also told you I was impressed. I still am. Even more so, now, with everything that has happened since."

Holly frowned. "Then why wouldn't you want to help me?"

"Because if you fulfil your quest, you will die."

"Liar," said Holly, immediately and without a moment of hesitation or pause. "Liar and witch. How could I die? The Waters of Life—"

"Will destroy you utterly." Morgana looked to the doorway into the House of Incarnation, Holly alarmed to see her star sapphire eyes shining not only with their own luster, but with tears. "I knew it the moment you came to my Guru Veda persona for help, the moment you explained how you needed the Waters and I felt the magic which had been awakened within you by your encounter with the Eternal Flames some 16 months ago. And so, I took my time preparing you for this journey, stalled what could have taken only a few hours so that I could find some way for you to survive . . ."

Holly turned away as her mother spoke, stumbling, hands pressed against the smooth stone of the House of Incarnation as she understood at last what the dark Wolf-Lord was talking about and why.

Candida screamed voiceless as the Eternal Flames ate up her hands gripping the sword, ate up her arms, shoulders into and through her, blasting away time and space, thought and reason. The Flames pushed through her sockets and into her brain, into her mind, burning.

Beyond the white pain. Mortal pain was fire and she was ash, crumbling, skin and muscle and bone eaten by the Fire and blown away by errant winds.

"When I saved Nessa and the rest, I was destroyed by the Eternal Flames in their place . . . and then I was remade by the Flames."

And so it was. Ash turned to fire. The Fire turned to bones, and into muscle upon the bones, and into flesh and fur upon the muscle. Candida le Fay opened her fire-born eyes, and breathed deep with her fire-born lungs, and watched the remainders of the Eternal Flames flow away, back down the black sword, the cables, back to the orb, which itself sank back down to the depths of the volcano's heart.

"If you go in there," said Morgana, "you might save your wife and daughter, but the Waters of Life will put out the Eternal Flames which make you. A fate worse than death. You will become like stone, unliving, unknowing, never to see the peace and rest of Sheol."

For a minute, Holly leaned against the black stone of the dome, leaned and stared, able to see a ghost of her reflection. Then her hands curled into fists. She beat against the stone and whispered "It is not fair." And then again, louder, a snarl as she hammered her fists against her reflection. "It's not fair!"

Morgana stood in the shadows, silent. Holly whirled on her, the taste of blood in her mouth. "Regina died for me to stand here! My twin! Their heart beats in my chest so I could save my family! You are telling me they died there so that I can die here!? No more magic, no more stories, no more family! Just this moment, waiting for me here all my life. Years of being the disgraced daughter, of being the criminal and outcast, of being the villain, when all I wanted to do was save the people I love. This is my reward, and IT'S NOT FAIR!"

"No," said Morgana. "It's not fair."

Holly didn't know how long she stood there, looking at her family and catching her breath from all the screaming. Eventually, she swallowed and straightened her back, squared her shoulders. A steadying breath and then she turned to the doorway, head high as she readied herself for the end.

"You can come with me," said Morgana, voice the closest to weak and trembling Holly had ever heard it. "Please. You don't need to go in there."

"Of course I do," said Holly, putting on her favorite smile, the one she saved special for Shun. "My family needs me."

Three steps, and Holly stood inside the House of Incarnation. For a moment she was blinded, an arm raised against the brilliant shine. At first, the magic of the House spun and shoved at her, tried to trip her up, pulled at her hair and buffeted her like a bullying wind. Then, it settled. Holly let her arm fall and pushed forward, the ferocity of the power in the air drawing her onward. Magic-soaked eyes beheld the grandest of halls, mirrored in black stone. In the reflections stood the shades of a vast host, diverse in form and age. Holly saw other Wolf-Lords. She saw kitsune and Jackals. She saw dragons, unicorns, gryphons. Even a zakarian. But most of all, she saw at the center of the House of Incarnation a white pillar, like the spoke of a wheel. It came to chest height, and atop the pedestal sat a broad bowl of star-scattered stone, a dazzling rainbow light shining from its depths.

"Come back to me, Holly," spoke Morgana back at the doorway. "Come back!"

Beside the pedestal stood another of Holly's incarnations, from another place and another time. A cardinal-hippogryph. Holly knew her at once by her red feathers and white fur, her horn long, her eyes blue and sad and wise. Rising on her wings, her talons beckoned toward the bowl atop the pedestal.

"That was the best haul I've made in weeks. The name's Shun, by the way." They held out a hand. "You a they, a she, a he?"

"Er, she, I guess." She took their hand after a moment of eyeing it and they shook. "You?"

The kitsune hesitated a half-moment before answering with a "He, obviously. Name?"

"Oh, right, sorry. Sorry. My name is Candida. Those illusions were amazing."

Holly stepped forward. As she did, a fresh burst of magic swept out from the bowl. Holly raised her left arm to shield her face, grunted as she was struck, stumbled and fell to a knee as all sensation left the suddenly-heavy limb. She beheld then how it had turned to a white, marble-like stone, smooth to the touch from the claws of her fingers nearly to her shoulder.

"Am I safe now, Princess Candida?"

"But I promise you, on my life, that you are safe now, and I am going to keep you safe. I promise."

Gritting her teeth, Holly stood. Somewhere behind her, Morgana screamed for her.

Kanti landed hard on her feet, stumbled into Candida, slammed them both into the train carriage door. A breathless second, Candida listening, ears perked to the sound of approaching footsteps on the other side of the door.

"Crap," whispered Kanti. Her arms slid around Candida, hands finding the small of the other Wolf-Lord's back. She looked at Candida, their muzzles almost brushing. "Permission?"

"Granted."

Holly continued the march to the bowl. The magic rose as a song all around her, readying to strike her once more even as her remaining hand grasped the lip of the Waters of Life.

***

The storm rolled over Eishaven from the north and against the wind. The people of the town watched it come from their windows, or heard the boom of its thunder as they lay coughing in their beds, glimpsed the sharp crash of its lightning. Those able went to watch its coming from their open doorways, breaths held in anticipation. The storm spread across the width and breadth of Eishaven and even farther beyond, to the farthest satellite homesteads along the southern rail and in the forests to the east and west. It was a dark storm, the deepest dark any living in Eishaven had ever seen or heard tale of, and for the briefest time, day turned to night.

The rain started slowly at first, scattered drops falling heavier as the seconds bled into minutes. Yet even from the start, the rain was a breath-stealing wonder. It fell as dark as the storm, but each strike upon the earth, the buildings, the people, burst with light like a firework, rainbow light scattering. For those who felt the touch of the rain, disease fled and strength returned. Wounds which had not yet scarred were undone. Breathing steadied. Fevers faded. Pain became memory, cast aside by joy.

The Waters of Life fell, and before even 10 minutes had passed all those who had been suffering from the Spell Rot, even those upon the very steps of Death's door, were healed and out on the streets, singing and laughing in the rain, dancing heedless of the splash of mud. Friends embraced and lovers kissed, fearless. All was well.

Beneath the heavy rain, the waves crashed against the black shore to the north, drew back, crashed again with a spray of water and ice and salt on the tongues of the crowds gathering through the town. Holly passed them all by, at last alighting in the snow field between

Eishaven-proper and the collection of cabins she had called home now for over three years. She stood tall, gathering her breath as she took in the figures standing almost sentinel in front of the porch of her own cabin, soaking in the healing rain. Shun. Nessa. Laura. Kanti. Her most precious people. At her arrival, they ran for her, calling her name. Holly stood and watched them come, putting all her furious, aching love into her smile.

And then the last of her magic bled away into white marble, and Holly le Fay, once known as Princess Candida, knew no more.

EPILOGUE

Two weeks later . . .

The snow fell heavy over Eishaven. Bitter winds from the north sent it scouring across wood and stone, the cold seeping with little grasping fingers through windows and under doorways, stealing into the cloaks of those few walking the frozen streets. Overhead, the sky loomed white and gigantic, the sort of sky which, if stared up into long enough, might get the innocent forgetting all sense of up and down.

Kanti, transformed into her raven-gryphon form to better stand against the cold, found Shun exactly where she had expected to find her. The kitsune stood wrapped in scarves and cloaks in front of the statue which had once been their mutual love, arms wrapped around herself as she looked up into eyes which in life had been full of more love than the world could endure. Beside Shun sat Nessa, the unicorn curled in on herself as she worked a puzzle cube over in her magic.

Without a word, at least at first, Kanti stood on Shun's other side from Nessa, following the other woman's gaze to Holly's smiling face. For a few minutes the small, fractured family stood there, all the tears shed for the moment, all the grief turned old and bitter.

"I guess I'll be leaving, then."

"If you want to."

"Laura decided to come with, after all. Wants to track down scattered family if she can, and . . . well, she'll know better what to look for."

"Yeah. I guess she will."

Kanti looked down from Holly's visage, to Nessa at first, then to Shun. Her heart ached, so many things she wanted to say then, so many apologies and promises, but none of them came to her. The best she could do was "There has to be a little hope, my darling. Just a little. I won't give up, I promise. If there is anywhere in the world where I can find a way to bring Holly back to us, it's in Heraldale. No matter what it takes, even to world's end—"

"For her," said Shun. She nodded, reached out to stroke a hand down the feathers of Kanti's neck. "For her, whatever it takes."

Kanti nodded, tried at a smile as she pat Shun on the back with a wing, then turned to walk back into town where Laura and the ship were waiting. Shun's voice made her pause. "Kanti? A last promise, please."

"Yes?"

"If you can't find a way to save our Holly . . ." At last, the kitsune looked to Kanti, her eyes the eyes of a dead woman walking. "Find a way to avenge her. And if you can't do that, don't bother coming back at all."

Kanti said nothing, nodding again before turning and taking wing. Her red scarf flapped in the breeze of her flight. To the west, the warring lands of Heraldale waited.

***

In another place . . . another time . . .

Fire and magic lit the winter night of the Second Expansion War's last bloody battle. A thundering death cry wracked the forested land as the last of the northern dragons plummeted from the sky. The body hit the King's Canyon bridge and erupted into a fireball of blue flame, the heat and force cracking the white stone beneath.

For a moment, night turned to day, illuminating the two clashing forces. Through the woods to the canyon's west massed the unicorns of the Avalon Empire, hooves beating the earth and snow as they galloped among the trees. From their horns streaked bolts of red magic at the many-towered fortress across the canyon, blasting chunks of stone from the high walls and tearing through the gryphon defenders.

From the fortress walls and towers the gryphons rained down flocks of arrows and crossbow bolts in return, each weapon striking true. Yet, with each exchange the balance grew more and more in the unicorns' favor, their numbers greater, their morale boosted by the death of the dragon.

As the night-shattering blaze died down, a dozen unicorns in heavy steel armor jumped the burning carcass and charged the fortress gates, the first to touch hoof to the bridge since the battle's start. Three gryphons in gold-edged leather and mail flew from the gates to meet them. There flew a swan-gryphon, a spear as slender as his neck clenched in his talons; a golden eagle-gryphon, her battle-axe as broad as many of the opposing unicorns stood tall; and at the lead a cardinal-gryphon, half the size of the others, her wings sheathed in feather-styled blades, a helm-like crown upon her brow.

The foes met. The cardinal-gryphon swept low, dragging her wing-blades across the unarmored bellies of two unicorns and spilling their guts. She flew over another unicorn, letting the swan-gryphon's spear skewer the mare. Landing on all fours she spun with wings spread, taking another unicorn's front legs out from under him and letting the stallion topple over the side of the bridge.

"Flee, you hooved devils! Go back to your lying master!"

A chorus of enraged neighs answered the cardinal-gryphon's declaration. At the sound of hooves approaching she turned, but the golden eagle-gryphon was already there, bisecting the stallion with a single swing of her axe. Another stallion paused at the sight, eyes wide in terror, allowing the swan-gryphon to fly over his larger companion and skewer the unicorn through the chest. A laugh left his beak. "Ahah! We might rally yet, if these are the best soldiers left to face us!"

"Hush, Kurt!" The golden eagle-gryphon blocked a charging mare's horn with the flat of her axe, before reaching out and tearing the unicorn's throat loose with her bare talons. "You always jinx us with such talk!"

"And you always overreact to such—"

With husband and wife distracted by battle and banter, the cardinal-gryphon alone saw the skewered unicorn halfway stand with the last of his strength, horn glowing. She shouted and dove between him and the swan-gryphon taking the barrage of magic bolts to her gut, chest, right wing, and a final bolt searing an inch off her feathered neck.

PAIN. World-tinting pain as she fell, all thought turned now to the agonizing task of simply breathing.

"Grimhilt, no! Ida, get her out of here! I'll hold them back!"

"But Kurt—"

"GO!"

More pain then, the world tilting as the golden eagle-gryphon picked her up in her front legs and flew for the fortress gates. Grimhilt clenched her talons tight against her neck and gut, her pain-hazed vision remaining locked on the swan-gryphon staying behind to slow pursuit. His spear flashed red and blinding in the light of the nearby dragon fire, untold numbers of unicorns now charging his position. "K-Kurt, no . . ."

The closing fortress doors hid the end of that fatal stand as Ida continued to carry her to relative safety, past barricades and cowering guards to the once-grand hall at the center of the fortress, its pillars crowded by the bodies of the dead and dying, its tapestries torn up for bandages, its tables upended and braced against entry points. Those defenders able to stand gathered around them as they passed, gryphons tearing out their feathers and the few friendly unicorns stamping their hooves.

Before Ida could shout for a healer Grimhilt rolled out from her hold, barely managing to land on all fours and having to lean on the far larger gryphon for support all the same. "Call the rest in, secure the gate . . . retreat to the inner sanctum . . . we must hold them off until help arrives . . ."

"The scouts have returned," shouted a raven-gryphon Grimhilt did not know, her gold eyes alight with terror. "King Erentil and his people are nowhere to be found throughout the Elderpine. All the south is heavily defended against aid from Lady Quetzal. The city of Gateway is still under siege to the southeast, the sphinx-folk were routed at the forest's edge, and the King of the Elkbough Woods to the northeast will not arrive for many more days!"

Panic began spreading at these words, some gryphons shouting for a final charge to death, others hurling hate at the unicorns among them. Grimhilt swept her gaze through the ruined hall, her ruined people. Hope drained from her as surely as the blood seeped from between her talons. She struggled just to stand. "We should . . . should have been able to rally . . ." Even as she said this it sounded foolish. They'd lost the war against the unicorns long before whatever betrayal had led the Empire to their last hidden fortress.

"All that remains now is survival," she said to the hall at large. Panic stilled as eyes and ears turned to her once more. "Above all, you must survive. Flee.

Surrender. Swear whatever oaths you must to escape to your families. Endure the tyranny of the unicorns however you can . . . and trust to fight . . . fight another day."

What protests sprung up at this doom she ignored as she looked at Ida supporting her. "Take me to her, old friend . . ."

"What? No, we need to get you to a heal—"

"Ida, please, I'm tired . . . so tired it will be a blessing to . . . just please let me see my hope again."

Another day, a day when her husband stood there with her, Ida might have argued more. Through a doorway in the back the pair left the grand hall and those soldiers marshalling under Grimhilt's final command. They supported each other as they traveled through passageways and down stairwells to a chamber deep within the earth, their path lit by staggered torches weak within the cold. With every step the journey grew harder, every breath more ragged, pace faltering with every minute of lost blood trailing behind them. By the end of that serpentine tunnel Grimhilt could only slump against the wall beside the oaken door as Ida opened and rushed through it.

"I'm cold . . . Death himself creeps the halls for me, led on by the blood . . ." She couldn't help the laugh that shook her body and sent blood dribbling from her beak.

"My people think me dead already by a year and a half... now it happens here, forgotten, unknown . . ."

"Please don't say such things!" Ida hurried back into the corridor, wings beating in a hover, a tightly wrapped and softly mewling bundle cradled in her front legs. She sat beside the cardinal-gryphon and passed the bundle into her weak but groping grasp. "Your daughter, my queen."

Trembling talons pulled away the silk blankets so that she could see the gift to the world with fresh eyes, like it was the first time all over again. The child was hardly three weeks old, her front half like a gryphon, her back half like a unicorn, a straight horn the color of polished ivory sprouting from her forehead. The child possessed her father's shocking blue eyes, bringing Grimhilt to tears, and in time would grow up to have her mother's vibrant red plumage. "A hippogryph . . . so blessed . . ."

She turned away so that her sudden fit of coughing wouldn't tarnish the child with her blood. Hurriedly she handed the bundle back to Ida, slumping further down the wall as she did. Sight had begun to lose its color, sound its vibrancy, smell its potency. "Soon . . . go, Ida. Escape while you can."

"No! My queen, please, you mustn't—"

Another cough, more blood down her front. Grimhilt affixed the golden eagle-gryphon with a stare, pleading with her eyes to be understood. "Can't you see that I'll only slow you down now!? Go! Go now while you can . . . a hidden exit from that room will take you far out of here. Return north . . . return h-home . . . return to your fa-family . . ."

A sob escaped Ida then, the full weight of all that had happened perhaps now hitting her. She held the bundle and the child within closer. "My queen . . . Grimhilt . . . of course."

Grimhilt nodded, struggling now to keep her eyes open. She felt so tired, so eager to see departed friends and family again in the peace of Sheol. "Featheren Valley . . . live in peace . . . promise to love her..."

"Of course," said Ida, her voice now thick with tears, finally accepting. "Of course, yes—"

"Swear it," said Grimhilt, anxious to get this last promise. "Swear that my daughter, my Galaxy, will be loved. She needs . . . she'll need all the love possible for the coming hardships . . ."

"I swear it," Ida said, and finally Grimhilt could smile. She reached out with the last of her strength to caress the bundle her oldest friend carried, before closing her eyes. With a sigh she relaxed into the peace of Sheol.

Ida remained beside the body of her fallen queen for another moment, the golden eagle-gryphon watching for something, anything to hint at life. But then the bundled-up hippogryph she held began to squirm and cry, soft sounds of confused distress. Then, Ida looked down at the babe balanced in the crook of her arm as she stood, rocked her gently until she quieted again. "It's alright, little princess. It's alright. Let's get you home."

Holly's story will be concluded within the series

Legends of Heraldale

Brian McNatt lives in humble and comfy Chickasha, Oklahoma, his life kept magical by many rambunctious Corgis. He has self-published one stand-alone Western/Samurai/Fantasy novella, *Estranged*, as well as his Fantasy Heraldale Universe series, all available on Amazon. He has also had short works published in multiple magazines.

You can find him on Facebook and Twitter, where he is always happy to discuss the finer points of Fantasy and Sci-Fi with fellow fans.